THE PATHLESS SKY

Chaitali Sen

THE PATHLESS SKY

Europa
editions

Europa Editions
214 West 29th Street
New York, N.Y. 10001
www.europaeditions.com
info@europaeditions.com

Copyright © 2014 by Chaitali Sen
First Publication 2015 by Europa Editions

Library of Congress Cataloging in Publication Data is available
ISBN 978-1-60945-291-9

Sen, Chaitali
The Pathless Sky

Book design by Emanuele Ragnisco
www.mekkanografici.com
Cover photo © Alan Lagadu/iStock

Prepress by Grafica Punto Print – Rome

Printed in the USA

On the seashore of endless worlds children meet.
Tempest roams in the pathless sky,
ships are wrecked in the trackless water,
death is abroad and children play.
On the seashore of endless worlds is the great meeting of children.
—RABINDRANATH TAGORE, Gitanjali

CONTENTS

THE PATHLESS SKY

MORNING

I t mattered to him that he woke up alone. After stumbling around the apartment in the angled morning light he found his wife Mariam asleep on the floor of the nursery. Instead of carrying her to bed he shook her awake, telling her it was time to get ready for work. Only when she picked herself up off the floor, looking as ragged as a cloth doll, did he begin to soften his approach. He asked her if she needed to stay home. She shook her head and dragged her feet to the bathroom.

They were both sullen during the short drive to the university, unable to talk about anything but their plans to meet back at the car at six, at the end of their workday. He watched her walk into the library, aware that at a certain point over the past twenty-four hours something had shifted, something that had led her to sneak out of their bed and lie in that empty room on the hard floor. He wondered if she'd felt an urge to nurse in the middle of the night, at an hour when their daughter might have cried from hunger. She might have responded to such a cry in a semiconscious state, so that her departure from their bedroom was not deliberate at all but an involuntary maternal response. But it had been months since she last complained about pain in her breasts. After the labor it was all she could talk about, the mysteries of her body. She leaked milk. She stuffed cabbage leaves under her bra to stop the leaking, and she seemed to carry this scent, a revolting, lingering odor of blood, milk and cabbage. But her body was healed now, the swelling of her breasts shed with the weight through weeks of mourning.

He went to his office feeling unsettled. Looking out the window as he always did before sitting at his desk, he realized how angry it made him to find her on the floor of the nursery. He was angry at her for grieving again. He felt betrayed by it, and because he was distracted by these feelings he did not pay close attention to what was happening outside. There were a few students, a dozen or so gathered on the lawn outside the library. He couldn't figure out if they were waiting to get in or if they had just come out. It surprised him to see so many students at once. For most of the year, the campus had been pulsing with activity, the lawn filled with students shouting and making speeches, but since the riots, they were outnumbered by the militia, enforcing laws against political gatherings by breaking up groups of three or more students. The students who decided to return after the riots moved about the campus cautiously now, avoiding each other. Many of the students had not returned, to honor the ones who had been killed, or defy the military regime that was claiming to restore order. His colleagues were waiting to hear if the college would remain open after the end of the spring term, if their positions and salaries were secure, but John was waiting for something else. Both he and Mariam were waiting for something else.

It looked as if the students had been expelled from the library. Two militia guards stood at either end of the crowd. A few students argued with them, but most wanted to avoid a confrontation and walked away.

The phone rang. He stepped back, without moving his eyes from the window, and picked up the receiver. The woman didn't wait for him to say hello. It was Misha, Mariam's supervisor. Her friend. "Something's happening. You have to come here."

Of course something was happening. He had been watching it, but hadn't seen it. All he saw was Mariam on the floor of the nursery.

"You won't be able to get through the front entrance," Misha said. "Come around to the east wing."

He left his office, slipped past his colleagues gathered at another window and ran down the hall, down the stairwell of the science building and out across the lawn. He reached the secluded east wing of the library and heard a tap on a window. Misha pointed toward the wall and then disappeared. A moment later a cellar door opened. "Come down here," she said.

He went down a ladder, into the cellar of the library. There was a faint, salty smell, a smell not unlike sea air—the smell of limestone. She led him to a stairwell. "Take these all the way up to the fourth floor."

"Why is the militia here?" he asked.

Misha didn't answer. "I think Mariam is in shock. She wouldn't even tell them her name. I tried to get them to let her go home. I explained everything to them, what she'd been through."

Clearly Misha would give him no answers. He started up the stairs. By the time he reached the fourth floor his lungs burned and he stayed hidden on the landing while he caught his breath. When he opened the door a young woman stepped back, startled. He walked past her toward the reference desk and she followed him, her heels brushing the carpet. Straight ahead, a round-faced militia guard blocked the door of Mariam's office.

The guard stopped him. "Who are you?"

"That's my wife in there. I'd like to speak to her."

"How did you get in here?"

"Through the front door," he said, lying, and the young guard looked appropriately confused. He stepped aside and let John look through the narrow glass panel of the door to the storage room where Mariam had a desk—a makeshift office. The room was dark except for a ray of gray sunlight shining down like a spotlight from a high window. Mariam sat motionless in a chair in front of her desk, her profile exaggerated against the light, her eyelashes longer, her cheekbones higher, her jaw line sharper, her dark hair parted around a jutting ear. When he tapped on the door she turned to him, perfectly calm.

A man in a well-tailored suit came into view, a man who was alone with Mariam, standing behind her. He came to the door and opened it. John recognized in him the weighted confidence, the lack of humor and self-doubt required of men in their thirties, years off from middle age, yet no longer youthful. At the moment, Mariam was his captive, and John saw him as nothing less than a rival.

"That's my wife," John announced. "What do you want with her?"

The suited man questioned the guard. "Where did he come from?"

"I don't know, sir. He said someone let him in."

"Who let you in?" he asked John.

"One of the guards at the front."

"The front entrance?"

"Yes," John said with conviction. It was a gamble, since he had not taken a good look at the front entrance. He had only seen the guards outside, dealing with the crowd of students. He assumed there had to be guards inside, and with the militia there was always the possibility of some kind of communication breakdown, of someone not following orders. The militia guards were young and inexperienced, living out their ten months of mandatory service with varying degrees of enthusiasm. John had been one of them, many years ago, and since then the system that bred them had not changed.

"I'd like a moment alone with my wife," John said.

The man thought, and conceded. Perhaps he wanted to check the front entrance to corroborate John's story. It didn't matter. A few minutes with Mariam was all he needed. After he saw her he would have a better idea of what to do.

The guard held the door open for him. John stepped over the threshold and waited for the door to close, but the door remained open with the guard standing there, watching them. Mariam held her hand out and he knelt in front of her, forgetting for a moment the guard at the door and the man in the suit, regretting only his foul mood that morning. She had been so unreachable and he had panicked. Her fingers were cold. He put his forehead against hers.

"How did you get in?" she whispered.

He spoke into her ear. "Misha called me. What do they want?"

She said she didn't know.

It might have looked like they were plotting something, but they were only undoing some of their silent parting that morning. John pulled back and looked at her eyes. He couldn't read them. "Are they interviewing everyone?"

"Yes, I think so."

He shook his head. "I don't understand what this is all about." He wanted to ask her why the morning had started so strangely. "Did you know they were coming?"

"I didn't know," she insisted.

He brought her ear close to his lips again. "Mariam, just answer their questions. Misha said you refused to answer them."

"I don't want to talk to them."

"But you have to. Just answer their questions so they'll move on."

It was possible Misha was right, that Mariam was in shock. She seemed listless and unafraid.

"You have to go, John."

"I'll wait for you by the car. Answer their questions and get out of here. Leave the building and come to the car. Get it over with."

"I will," she promised, and he kissed her dry lips. She sank into him, giving him some comfort before the guard told him to get up. The man in the suit was in the room again, standing next to them. John stood up and faced him. "Who are you?" he asked.

"I'm from the Inspector's Office," the man said.

"But who are you?" John wanted to know if he was police or military. He had never heard of an Inspector's Office.

"We're just finishing up here. The guards will see you out."

"Can I speak to you alone for a minute?" John had decided to tell him that Mariam was in a delicate state, that if her behavior seemed odd it was because she was grieving. It was for no other reason than her grief.

"The guards will see you out."

There were two guards by the door now. He looked at Mariam once more. She nodded, and he was confident she would be more cooperative now, that she would be out soon, but as the door slammed behind him he wondered if he'd made a mistake. Mariam was alone again, locked inside.

"I'll wait here," he said.

"We have to take you outside, sir." They were polite enough as they pulled him along to the elevator. When he was let out of a back door he could see that he'd been expunged. He made his way slowly to the car, reeling, shaking, disturbed by the unnatural quiet outside. He went to the car and sat on the hood, waiting. He watched a black car drive up to the library exit.

A fear that had been gathering in John's mind finally took form; he and that car were waiting for the same thing. He headed toward the car when the exit door flew open and four militia guards came tumbling out, off balance, ill-postured, struggling with a load. In their midst there was a patch of blue fabric, the blue of Mariam's dress. He ran and shouted at them, ordering them to hand her over as if the chain of command ended with him. Her hands and legs were shackled but it took three of them to hold her while the other opened the back door. The one who held her legs entered the car first. He pulled her in as she cried out, the same wailing cry he'd heard when she was in labor. She cried in a way that would make them want to shut her up. John ran fast but she was sealed up before he could reach her. He heard her crying still, though it might only have been an echo.

He ran back to his car and followed the black car out to the road. Within a few minutes it covered a considerable distance, weaving expertly in and out of traffic. John struggled to keep it in view. He caught up with it near Government Square, where the road was congested with military jeeps and police cars. As the car wove through the gridlock John almost lost them again, but once they were clear of the Governor's Palace, the car slowed and stopped beside a tall iron gate in front of the courthouse plaza.

John stopped behind it and got out of the car. He ran forward in a rage, ready to pound on the black car and make a scene here in Government Square. At least Mariam would know he hadn't left her.

They waited until John was close enough. One of the guards came out of the car and stood ready with his baton. John stopped too late. He caught it in the head, the swing of the baton, and fell back into a black, bottomless well.

He was kicked awake by a police officer in a crowded jail cell. When he tried to sit up a splintering pain radiated from his left ear, shooting across his eyes, his jaw, and over the top of his head. John couldn't get past the pain and the high-pitched ringing in his ear in order to get a good look at any of his companions. He only had some shadowy sense of their movements and their smell. He touched his ear and felt the swelling around it, and the thickened texture of his blood-soaked hair. The officer kicked him again. "Get up," he said. He got halfway up before the officer grabbed his elbow and pulled him out of the cell, down a labyrinth of corridors to a large populated room lit with flickering fluorescent lamps. There were many rows of desks and lines of people down the aisles. The room reeked of cigarette smoke and perspiration, of fear and stress and exhaustion. John was taken to a desk in the corner and pushed into a seat. Under the ringing in his ear the sounds of the room were a low, constant hum, punctuated every now and then by someone shouting.

"Is my wife here?" John asked. The man behind the desk ignored him, his fat fingers laboriously writing tiny words into the tiny rectangles of a long form. The man looked weary, the skin under his eyes swollen high with fatigue.

"Sign this," the man said, sliding a form across the desk. "Someone is here for you." His voice was faint and warbled.

"What is this?" John asked.

"It's a report of your arrest, for trespassing."

"I'm not signing this. I wasn't aware that I was arrested. I was attacked with a baton." He looked around for the man in the tailored suit, or the guard that hit him, but the room was too full to see anyone.

"You can't leave unless you sign it," he said. He made a show of picking up the telephone. "Someone is waiting for you. We can tell him to go."

John grabbed the pen and signed. "What about my wife?"

"Your wife isn't here."

"How do you know that?"

"Your name is John Merchant. No woman named Merchant was brought in today. Unless your wife is one of those modern ladies who refuse to take their husbands' names."

"Maybe they didn't record her name. I followed her here."

"And then what?"

"And then I was hit with a baton in the head."

The man shrugged. "We need to make some room. Take this to the window on your way out." He handed John the form and called over an old man whose son was missing. The old man gripped the back of John's seat, waiting for him to vacate it.

John gave the release form to someone at the window and was handed a paper bag containing his wallet and car keys. "We did you the courtesy of parking your car. If you hurry you can get it out of the courthouse lot before the gate closes."

John had to make his way through a long waiting room before he could get to the exit. Somewhere in the middle of the room he heard his name. He looked up and saw the top of Vic's head, his curly hair and his sharp black eyes and his hand up in the air, waving him forward. John reached him and Vic pulled him toward the door.

When he got outside he gasped and coughed.

Vic waited for him to recover. "My car is on the street," he said.

"My car is in the courthouse lot," John said.

"We'll go in my car. We'll get your car tomorrow."

He was too tired to argue. It was dark already and it occurred to him Mariam might be at home, waiting for him. How else would Vic have known to find him here?

"We should take you to a hospital. Your head looks bad."

"No," John said.

"We should take a picture at least."

"How did you know I was here?"

"It was the first place we looked. You should have told someone where you were going."

They reached Vic's car, but John looked back at the courthouse, wondering if he should return and wait like all the others. There must have been some reason to wait, he thought. Vic opened the passenger door and nudged John into the seat. Vic got in the car and drove out cautiously through the vacant streets.

"There were a lot of people in there," John said.

"It's been that way since the rebellion," Vic said. He never called them riots, which suggested nihilism, anarchy, not an organized upsurge, and he would never use the same term the military used to justify their arbitrary actions. It was all the same to John. No matter what they called it, the consequences were dire.

"What about Mariam?" John asked.

"She isn't here, John, but we'll find her."

"They took her from the library."

"I know. I went there to look for you."

Vic parked along a row of brick townhouses across from the canal. This was the street on which they lived, in the same townhouse, in identical apartments down the hall from each other.

John went ahead of Vic. They entered the shabby vestibule of their building, where the fleur-de-lis pattern of the wallpaper, barely visible under layers of dust and smoke stains, suggested a more stylish past. He pulled his keys out of the paper bag before he reached the top of the stairs. At his door, he fumbled around the keyhole until Vic took hold of the keys and let him in. John turned to him. "Thank you," he said. He was grateful Vic had come to get him, but he couldn't talk to him now. "I'll come and find you later." He let the door slam shut and locked it behind him.

He stood still in the foyer, listening. He didn't hear a sound beyond the blood rushing in his ears. He switched on a light and walked carefully through the apartment. The bedroom door was ajar. They always left it that way, but he stopped before reaching it, called out to Mariam, and waited for the silence to settle. He looked inside and saw the bed exactly as they had left it that morning. During the riots they had locked themselves in this room, grieving the loss they'd suffered together, their grief seeping into the sheets, the mattress, the floor. When they came out of it, the air was still thick with smoke and the canal wall was shattered. They were under martial law, but the only thing he cared about was Mariam.

He closed the door and went to the kitchen, switching the light on, finding a glass, filling it with water, drinking. Then he took the glass to the liquor cabinet and filled it with whiskey. He drank it in a long swallow that burned his throat and made his body feel like it was overheating from its core. He put an ice pack on his head and wandered into the dining room. It was still cluttered from a small gathering they'd had only a few days earlier, just the two of them and their neighbors, to celebrate the arrival of a book he was going to publish in England. He only had one review copy, sent by parcel post, and Mariam had swooned over it. She kept repeating how proud she was, how proud she was. "Let's celebrate," she insisted. It only occurred to him now how strange that was, how it must have appeared to their neighbors as a kind of mental breakdown when she showed up at their door asking them to come and toast a book they didn't even know had been written. What was there to celebrate when their world was falling apart, and why didn't Mariam share their dread?

On Saturday she made hors d'oeuvres and opened a bottle of cheap champagne. She displayed the book on the table, and eight people stood around it choking their champagne flutes and staring at the book, waiting for it to do something extraordinary. John was afraid to look at anyone. He felt foolish, presenting people with a book that was going to be published overseas and read by no one. And the arrival of the book had shaken him, as if contained within it was not a geological history but a chronicle of his mistakes, layers of them, page upon page.

Not when it was in pieces, when it was nothing but a mess of papers and notebooks filled with scribbles and drafts and ideas he had endless chances to articulate in the isolation of their cabin, not when work and sex were of the same continuum, when their whole existence was a perfect darkness, filled with a profound connection to each other and everything around them, but in this bound form, which came about after, after he brought her here. A confluence of factors made it necessary for them to leave that life behind. That was what he told himself but a small part of him had wanted a reprieve, some possibility for escape. Sometimes the escape was all he could think of. He imagined it so fully that when he finally did get away, all of the things he'd imagined simply happened, as if they'd been pre-arranged. At the International Geological Congress his confidence was infallible, his future suddenly opening up before him. On his last evening, he spoke to an American woman at the hotel bar, and he spent the rest of the night fucking her in her room. To plunge into her unfamiliar body seemed like a fitting end to his trip, the only thing left to do, but on the flight home he wished he could die, that every strange grinding noise could be the last breath of the engines. He came home late, exhausted, feeling ashamed and transparent. He saw Mariam at the top of the stairs, saw her take in and shake off the look of him. By the time he met her on the stairs and took her into his arms she had recovered, remembering her news. She was pregnant again. She'd been afraid to say anything before he left, but she was already at fifteen weeks, and there was a heartbeat and a fetus that was the right size. "Did you suspect anything?" she asked. He must have, but he couldn't remember. He could not remember anything about her body before he left, but he was grateful, so grateful for the distraction.

At her strange party someone commented on the cover. It featured a stark black-and-white aerial photograph of the Belet River Valley, all of its gorges obscured by a thick cover of foliage except for the largest one, the one that cut through the campus of Mount Belet College. That great earthly gash was pictured at the bottom right corner, just below his name. Mariam had found the photograph in the college archives. They had met on a bridge above that gorge.

There was no question of authorship. It was a book about the geology of their country, written by a geologist, but he knew it was more than that, more than what it would have been if he had tried it alone. The book needed something other than land features and rock records. It needed something to connect the geography and the geology of the country, to populate and inhabit the land and give the account some warmth. Because it wasn't his area of study Mariam was the one who provided all that research. They discussed it often, struggling together to understand the link between geology and humanity. It was miraculous to her that these mechanistic forces inside the earth had created civilizations that bound people for generations to one place, those generations consuming elements of the land, putting the land in their blood, and returning their blood to the land. It was beautiful to her in a way he couldn't quite understand, and sometimes he felt he lacked something when he saw her moved so deeply. She was obsessed with earth as a place, but place only has meaning for people, for humans and their consciousness. For him it was an interesting puzzle for the earth and all its compulsions and humanity and all of its compulsions to exist together. They were opposing forces advancing toward each other in a long, quiet, bloodless war, and the earth would win—there was no doubting that. Only the earth that supported human life would die, but the planet itself, the sphere of rock and fire, would go on until it was consumed by something more powerful. He knew she understood that, perhaps too personally, and the book to her was like a still life painting in a museum, capturing something before it was lost forever. But all of it would be lost. The book, the painting, the museum itself.

She wrote whole passages that were left untouched throughout the book. In essence they had written it together. He had this realization only now, as he stared at the book and the sad remnants of their celebration. He swore the truth of it hadn't struck him before. He remembered how much he struggled to find a way to explain her contribution, and how the dedication alone had crippled him. He'd wanted something poetic, but in the end all he could settle on was the simplest, *for Mariam*, having deleted all the clauses he had attached previously, *my love, my savior, my paradise, my home.*

When he did dare a glance in her direction during their belabored celebration, he recognized a glint in her eyes. Rage. Stifled, but unmistakable.

PART ONE
Mount Belet

ONE

A silky fog had fallen over the hilltop. At four in the morning, after finishing his chemistry lab, John left the science building and made his way down a long series of broad steps to the bottom of the hill. Instead of crossing into the grassy common at the center of campus, he took the long way, walking along the road that looped around the university, because he had never seen it in a fog like this. His mind was tired, half-asleep, but his senses were alive. He enjoyed the light touch of mist on his skin and the diaphanous patches of light from scattered windows and street lamps. He enjoyed the quiet, the softness of his footsteps, until he approached the suspension bridge and his footsteps were drowned by the whitewater thrashing at the bottom of the gorge.

He stopped on the bridge, surprised to see a girl leaning far over the railing. When she backed away from the railing he continued walking, intending to pass her, but she turned to him, obliging him to say something.

"You're not going to jump, are you?"

"I like to listen to the water," she said. "I never get to during the day."

He couldn't see her well. He went to the railing and stood next to her, and together they looked out into the turbulent haze. "I wonder if people ever change their minds, after they jump," she said.

"I'd never go this way," he said. "Why smash yourself against a rock when you can die quietly in your bathtub?"

She had a pretty laugh. He turned his head to get a closer look at her, but all he could see at first was that she wore a white wool cap pulled down to her ears, which were large. Besides that everything was well-proportioned. On her thin face her features were spaced nicely apart, and seemed to belong together. He offered to walk her back to her dorm, and as they walked he told her where he was from and she told him the same. She was from a strangely named town called English Canal, in the center of Sulat Province. He had never met anyone from Sulat before. He wondered if her accent was regional, or if she just had a uniquely lilting cadence to her speech.

"I've heard of English Canal," he said.

"You have?" She was delightedly incredulous. Her step was so exuberant he had trouble keeping up with her.

"Of course. There's a polytechnic there." The College of Sulat Province had a good enough reputation that he'd heard of it in Alexandria, but no one from Alexandria wanted to go there.

"Yes," she said excitedly, "and also a canal, built by the English, in case you couldn't guess. We also have an English Market and an English Tavern."

"Sounds like the English did important work there."

She laughed at his joke.

Besides his knowledge of the polytechnic, which impressed her, he knew nothing else about her province. He did know there had been a military conflict there a few years before they were born. Some men of his father's generation had been sent there to fight. He had grown up hearing snippets about it—it was impossible not to—but he couldn't have discussed the conflict with her with any hope of sounding intelligent. Neither of them brought it up. Thankfully it had no place in this conversation.

Her dormitory was far from his. It had had two wings separated by a central arch with entry doors on either side. He gathered she lived in the east wing, for that was where she stopped him. There, in the faintly lit archway, he saw her more clearly. She reminded him of a woodland animal, her fawn-colored skin and dark brown eyes as wide and curious as a wild cub's. She smiled with a slight overbite of small, crooked, very white teeth. Her name was Mariam.

"It was nice to meet you, John Merchant."

"You too," he said, and he put his hand out. She looked at it, seeming unsure of what to do before she clasped her own hand into his. Their handshake was brief, a clammy meeting of palms, and they each let go in a hurry. He put his hands in his pockets and watched her unlock the door.

She pulled the door open. It looked heavy and he took the handle, holding it open for her. "Goodnight," she said sweetly, and it made him feel lonely, or homesick; it left him wanting for comfort. He must have slipped into a liminal state of exhaustion. There was no more solace in staying awake.

"Maybe I'll see you around," he said, but she was already inside, skipping up the stairs.

He found her again three days later, unexpectedly, at a prized table on the top floor of the library, next to a wide stained glass window. She was asleep, her cheek resting on her folded arms, her thumb dangerously close to her mouth, her lips slightly parted, her eyelids shut and unwavering, and a perfectly soothing yellow light falling over her like a blanket. He sat down across from her and took his books out, marveling periodically at how long she could sleep in that position. After a half hour she lifted her head. He thought she would look at him forever, trying to bring him into focus, but then she recognized him and smiled sheepishly, wiping her mouth with her sleeve.

"You weren't drooling," he said.

"Snoring?" she asked, fearful of his answer.

"You snore like a baby," he teased. "You need coffee."

"This spot will be gone if we leave it."

"Don't worry. I'll find you another place to take a nap."

They went to the all-night coffee bar at the student union, where the coffee always smelled faintly of piss. She took hers milky. They carried their coffee and heavy bookbags into the main lounge, a long vaulted room meant to resemble the great hall of a castle. They walked past rows of narrow tables, lit with banker's lamps, and sat on a bench by the tall windows at the far end of the hall. He loved the view from this window, down the slope to the slate gray rooftops of the boys' dormitories.

"What are you working on?" she asked him.

"Organic chemistry."

"Are you studying medicine?"

"No," he said, "but my father is a doctor."

She waited for him to say more. When he didn't she continued her questioning.

"Is it difficult to be the son of a doctor?"

He thought it was a strange question. Maybe she had picked up some tension in his voice; it *was* everyone's wish and expectation that he become a doctor. "Difficult?" he asked.

"I don't know," she said, shaking her head with a little laugh. "Never mind. That's personal."

"It's all right. It's not that it was difficult. Illness just doesn't interest me. Does that make me sound callous? I think I'd like to be involved in research," he said.

She looked thrilled. "What kind?"

"You know," he said, stalling. "I'm curious about the origins of things." He saw her brows twitch. She could probably tell he was lying, that in these first few weeks of school he had not been curious about much except this sudden sea of unmoored girls.

"What kinds of origins?" she asked.

John had to think. "How the earth formed, for example. How it became habitable." He trailed off, getting bored with his own voice.

She fell into a silence, sadly sipping at her awful coffee. Then she looked around to see if anyone else was listening, and leaned forward so she could tell him something in secret.

"Until this moment it never occurred to me that the earth wasn't always here," she said. He was shocked by her ignorance, but touched by her bashful confession of it.

"It's the kind of thing that doesn't occur to most people," he said.

"It's more than that. I don't feel smart here."

"I'm sure you're smart. I can tell you're smart. You wouldn't be here otherwise."

She blushed. "I should get back to work," she said.

He didn't let her go just yet. He asked her what she'd been reading about in the library, before she fell asleep, and he watched her lips as she tried to explain the French Revolution. He pretended to pay attention, more intent on figuring out if he thought she was pretty or not. She wasn't a ravishing beauty, but she was cute, as only a girl with big ears can be, and there was something in her voice, something melodious and stimulating. As strange as it was to compare her voice to a flower, the word *fragrant* came to him. He could have listened to her all night. It surprised him how much he wanted to be around her, even platonically, without the pressure of sexual attraction.

"The problem is," she said, "I can do the readings in French, but I have trouble conversing. I can't understand the professor's questions. Her French is very fast, and I have to ask her to repeat. My ear is terrible."

"You were reading in French?" John asked. He had not noticed something as obvious as the language of her textbook, during the minutes he sat across from her as she slept. He had always thought himself to be observant.

"Do you have any French?" she asked.

"A little. My German is better."

"I don't know any German," she said, as if she ought to. She was truly lacking in confidence.

"Give me your number," he said forcefully. "I'll call you."

She wrote her number on a napkin and handed it to him. "That's the number for our floor. I don't have my own telephone."

"It's all right if I call you?"

"If you want to. It isn't forbidden or anything."

He called her the next day and they met for a few concentrated hours of productive study. After that, they began to see each other every day. He hoped some of her diligence would rub off on him, but instead he found things about her to distract him. Her clavicle on her right side was more pronounced than the one on her left, for instance. One day he saw that a seam on the side of her dress was splitting, just above her hip, revealing a little patch of skin that otherwise never saw daylight. He put his finger in it and she flinched, like she'd been burned with a cigarette, before she looked down and saw it for herself.

"This is my favorite dress," she said.

Part of him couldn't help but wonder if she hadn't staged this worn seam incident to pique his curiosity, because lately his curiosity threatened to smother him, but she didn't seem capable of that kind of manipulation. From what he could tell she was genuinely unable to tolerate any part of him brushing against her. Every time he tested her boundaries, she would shift ever so slightly, and if he pushed any further she would slink away like a kitten.

On a mid-autumn day that felt like summer, all the students gathered like seals on the lawn. John and Mariam also sat out on the lawn by the obelisk, with the required gap between her right thigh and his left thigh, leaving enough space to avoid any, God forbid, bumping of knees. She commented on the fact that he was reading a novel. He explained that it was for Composition, that he would have to write a paper on it and after much deliberation he concluded that actually reading the book might make writing the paper easier.

A number of student groups were out that day, handing out flyers, pamphlets, and one amateur newspaper after another. John looked over at Mariam, who had collected a pile of flyers and was trying to find a place for them.

"You don't have to take them all," he said.

"I might read them later."

He took one from the top and started reading it to her. *The meek shall inherit the earth.*

"Hasn't that one already been written?" he asked.

She snatched it back and read it silently.

"Something happened to me, recently," she said.

"You lost your virginity?"

"No. Why would you say something like that?"

"I don't know," he said, embarrassed. "What happened?'

"I've known for a while, but finally I am able to admit there is no god."

She ended the sentence with a dramatic exhalation, as if her lungs had been harboring the final stubborn vestiges of her faith. He waited for more. "That's it?" he asked.

"You're the first person I've told."

"How did it happen? How did you decide?"

She thought about it. "I suppose it happened a long time ago. When I was little I had a Catholic nanny. She was very devout. She should have been a nun really except that she fell in love with my father."

John laughed and they got stuck there for a moment. He wondered if he'd heard right about the nanny and her father, and if that was the end of the story or if it went on, and if he should ask her more about it now. After all that thinking he didn't know where to start.

"I wasn't brought up to follow a religion. Religion is complicated in Sulat. My father thought the war was caused by religion but my mother, maybe she would have raised me differently if she had the choice. She was always talking about God. She was always whispering to herself, praying. I wanted to believe there was someone listening to her. I wanted her prayers to be answered. But I knew there wasn't. I know it even more now."

"What did she pray for?" John asked.

"I don't know. When she was young her family fled the war. She must have prayed for peace. For my father to still love her. I know she prayed for me a lot. She was always saying how she prayed for me."

"Well, you turned out all right, so how do you know her prayers didn't work?"

She stared at him with a confused little smile. She had never been this close to him. The hairs on their arms were touching. For the first time he discovered the flecks of gold in her irises. From certain angles they caught the light and made her eyes look impossibly bright.

He spoke very softly. "Anyway," he said, "how does it feel to be godless?"

"I feel free," she said.

Just then she trapped her bottom lip with her front teeth. She released it slowly. Now it was moist and rosy and it filled him with a desire to have his groin strangled between her thighs. All this time she must have been flirting in her own demure way, and now, she had said it herself, she felt free.

"We should celebrate," he said. "We should get hammered. You want to?"

"Hammered. What does that mean?"

He whispered it in her ear. "It means we drink until we can't remember our own names."

She smiled. "Will I remember your name?"

"I hope so, Mariam. I really hope so."

He showed up at her door a few hours later with pastries and an expensive bottle of vodka his uncle had given him for his eighteenth birthday. Mariam greeted him, radiant in a yellow dress that did not suit the season or the occasion. "My roommate's not here," she said.

He'd forgotten about the phantom roommate. He had heard about her, but in a month she had never materialized. He should have invited Mariam over to his room but he was afraid it would have put her on guard. "Will she be here later?"

Mariam frowned. "I don't know, why?"

"Just wondering," he said. He couldn't wait to get drunk. They sat on the floor against her bed. Mariam's side of the room was immaculate and austere. She had not put up anything to mark her place here. Her roommate had decorated her side of the room with posters of the pop star Freddie Mercury wearing different leotards. Last year in his high school, the girls had gone crazy for him. John could think of a half-dozen guys in Alexandria who looked just like him, with equally bad teeth, but none of the girls gave them a second look.

He handed Mariam a pastry and took one for himself. He tossed his back in the bag after a few bites. It wasn't very good and his mind wasn't on eating. She took forever to finish hers, talking in between tiny nibbles, asking him about places he'd been to and things he'd eaten in those places. She was particularly interested in French wine and Russian caviar. Before she was finished eating he decided it was time. He put a little vodka in two paper cups and gave her one. "It'll burn," he said.

"Do I take sips or do I chug it?"

He imagined it both ways. "Just toss your head back and swallow."

She looked skeptical. "Have you ever done this before?"

"Sure," he said. "Not with this vodka. This vodka is supposed to be—," he tried to think of a word other than expensive, settling on "delicate."

"I wish we had some caviar."

"On the count of three," he said, getting impatient.

At three they both poured the vodka down their throats. She swallowed and squealed, throwing her hand up to her neck. "That's vile," she cried. She slumped against the bed, her eyes already brighter, her cheeks flushed. One more drink and she might be ready.

"Want to go again?" he asked. After a second and third round all the sharp edges in the room started to blur. She talked but he had no idea what she said. Her mouth reminded him of a little boat bobbing on the ocean. A little, pretty, pink boat.

She covered the boat. "I think I'm going to be sick."

And just like that she was gone.

He kept on drinking without her, mournfully.

He must have passed out. When he woke up Mariam was in her bed, snoring, and across the room a girl sat on her bed, smiling at him. She was wearing a V-neck sweater and tight white pants. He was sure Mariam had mentioned her name but he couldn't remember it. Maybe because he was drunk, she appeared to be incredibly beautiful.

She lifted an eyebrow. "John?" she asked. He sat up. His name, even as a question, meant Mariam had talked about him.

"Nora?"

"Nina." She pointed her chin toward the bottle on his lap. "Anything left in there?"

He picked up the bottle and shook it. It was about a quarter full. He poured himself another shot and handed the bottle to her. "You can finish it."

"Mariam didn't tell me how cute you are."

"I can't imagine why she would have left that out."

Nina looked over his head, at the bundle that was Mariam.

"She's not of this world," Nina said softly.

"She has yet to decode the sexual behavior of humans," he said, continuing her joke, but Nina looked shocked. "You're awful," she said.

John turned around to make sure Mariam was really asleep. Thick strands of her hair, curled at the ends like the tentacles of a black octopus, fell across her face. He wanted to tuck them back behind her ears. He wanted to wake her up, give her some water, get her out of that ridiculous dress.

"Don't worry, she sleeps like a log. I can do all kinds of things in here and it doesn't rouse her."

He looked back at Nina, feeling strangely timid. She watched his reaction even as she tilted her head back to drink from the bottle.

They talked for a while longer, more comfortably as they finished their vodka. "Are you going to sleep here?" she asked. "Sneak out in the morning?"

"No, I'll go now."

"Good," Nina said. "Mariam might wake up. It would be awkward if she woke up and found us fucking."

He glanced at the door. It was far away.

"I'm just kidding, John. God, the look on your face. As if you don't want to."

"Okay," he said. He was going to say *that's enough* like a middle-aged husband trying to temper his drunken, bitter wife. It was time for him to go. He rose unsteadily on papery legs. The vodka had aged him. He wasn't sure if he could make it home, but he wasn't going to stay here. This girl scared him. It was a terrible night, a terrible waste of a night.

The next day around noon he called Mariam to see if she was all right.

"What did you give me?" she mumbled.

"I'll bring you some coffee. Do you want something to eat?"

There was a long silence. He didn't realize Mariam had put the phone down until she came back on the line. She said, "Nina wants a butter roll."

In less than an hour he saw them both, side by side, and it was as if an experiment had been set up to show him the difference between a girl who lights up a room and a girl who does not, a girl who in fact absorbs ambient light to feed some mysterious light-eating organ in the pit of her body. They were all together in that room, but Nina talked, Nina flirted, Nina sat on his lap and thanked him for the roll. "Are you still drunk?" he asked.

Mariam finally found her voice. "That's how she always is, John."

"Maybe I'm just happy," Nina pouted. "Do you want him Mariam? Because if you don't I'll take him."

"I don't even know what you mean by that," Mariam said.

Nina rolled her eyes. "Can you believe her?" she asked, and John would have said no, he couldn't believe how little Mariam cared to fight for his attention. He patted Nina on the thigh, nudged her off of him, and made an excuse about having labs to do. The room was starting to feel small. When Nina looked at him and whimpered like a puppy, all he could do was stare and smile. Mariam was back in bed, curled into a fetal position and clutching the corner of her pillow with her girlish fingers.

During midterms he tried to keep to himself, but he ran into Nina late one night and brought her back to his room. He didn't know what to call the thing that happened between them, but once she'd gotten started, who was he to put a stop to it? She had a lean, athletic body, and she was beautiful, unbelievably beautiful.

Afterwards, reasonably satisfied with his performance, he was ready for a long, deep sleep, but she wanted to tell him about every sexual experience she'd had since she lost her virginity to her family doctor at sixteen. She said it sounded worse than it was. He was a gentleman, really, and she had been extraordinarily mature for her age.

In the morning, long after she'd left, he found himself craving a cigarette. He got dressed and packed his bag to go to class. On his way out he passed the lounge, where his chemistry lab partner Vic Arora was sitting by himself, smoking. John stopped, fixated on the pack of cigarettes.

"Hi, Vic," he said.

"Hello."

"Can I get a cigarette?"

Vic threw him the box. "Was that your girlfriend?" he asked. "Who snuck out of your room this morning?"

"How long have you been sitting here?" Nina had been gone at least two hours.

"She's tasty," Vic said.

Vic never knew the right thing to say. John lifted an eyebrow, which he did often to question Vic's word choice. He was smarter than he let on, certainly smarter than John and a more meticulous lab partner, but no one liked him. He had a big lumbering body with thick beefy arms. People tolerated him because he looked like he could crush any one of them in a second.

He started talking about the chemistry midterm, tapping his heel so fast and hard against the floor his leg vibrated like a jackhammer.

"Are you trying to get somewhere?" John asked.

"What?"

"Your foot. It looks like you're trying to drill a hole in the floor."

Vic put a hand on his knee to steady his leg. "Sorry," he said. "I haven't slept in three days. Do you know there's a sickness that feels better than being well?"

"No, I didn't. Thanks for the cigarette," John said.

"Sure," Vic said. He didn't try to keep talking, which was unusual for him. He normally didn't know when to wind down the conversation.

After his night with Nina, John avoided the places where he used to run into Mariam, and he wondered if she wasn't also hiding from him. Many days went by and he began to worry about her. He found her in the library during midterms. The half-moon depressions under her eyes, which he had begun to find strangely attractive, had turned a grayish blue. He wanted to settle something there—the tip of his thumb, a light kiss. She offered him the empty seat across from her.

"Where have you been?" he asked.

"In my room mostly."

"I've been looking for you."

"You could have called."

He had been afraid to call. He should have called.

She leaned her head against the wall. "Are you having fun with Nina?"

He didn't know what Mariam knew, what she thought had happened, or what she wanted to hear. "I'm not having any kind of fun right now."

"It'll be over soon. Maybe you can ask her out after midterms."

He couldn't read her at all. Her face was completely impassive, but she looked exhausted and unhappy. "What did she tell you?" he asked.

"She said she likes you. It makes perfect sense," she said. "I don't know why I didn't think of it before. She likes you a lot."

"Think of what?"

"Of you two. You and Nina. She likes you a lot."

"You already said that."

"Don't you think she's pretty?"

"She's a little overwhelming."

"I know what you mean," she said, sighing. "Poor John."

He took his physics book out and tried to work, but he could feel Mariam weighing on him, and he knew he would feel her even after she was gone because she always left something lingering. He wanted to ask her what happened, what he had done wrong. He could love her, but he couldn't for the life of him understand why he would pick a girl so undeveloped, so shrinking.

"Do you understand all those figures?" she asked.

She was looking at the page in his book.

"You mean these equations?"

"Yes, all those lines of numbers and letters."

"They're equations," he said.

"It's so alien to me. All these things exist that I don't feel capable of understanding."

He didn't really know if they were still talking about equations, but he tried to elaborate. "I don't always understand why they're true, or how someone arrived at this conclusion, but eventually I understand most of it."

"How do you know that you understand it?"

"I can picture it. That's what forms first, images, and then I try to describe it."

He almost couldn't go on, suddenly unfamiliar with the shape of her face, as if he were seeing her for the first time.

"Can you describe what the color blue is?" she asked.

"What does that have to do with anything?"

"I read in a linguistics book that none of the ancient texts, including Homer, the Bible, the Koran, the Vedic texts, none of them described the color blue for the sky or any body of water. In most languages it was not its own category but a different shade of green or black. When you said you get an image before you can explain that equation, it made me wonder how I would explain the color blue. I don't think I could get past the images and labels. The sky, the ocean. I couldn't explain what blue is beyond that."

"I guess it would depend on who I was explaining it to," John said. "Someone who never saw colors? Someone who couldn't perceive the difference between blue and green? But honestly I'd have an easier time explaining physics than the color blue. Physics is all about interactions in the material world. It lends itself to description. The color blue is static. What is there to say except it's pretty?"

He wished they could have this conversation snuggled under a blanket outside, under the stars, her body all soft and doughy and naked next to his, but he couldn't imagine it. It wasn't right. It wasn't her.

"Blue, the color of twilight and sadness," she said.

After midterms he slept with Nina again. The more time he spent with her the more he appreciated how pleasant life was when she was around. The most refreshing thing about her was that she had no self-consciousness. She was always willing to risk looking foolish in order to move their relationship forward. He came to understand that he got lucky with Nina, and after a while it didn't feel strange that he was seeing her more than he saw Mariam, to get through a day without thinking very much about Mariam at all.

He hadn't spoken to Mariam in over a week when he walked by the lounge in his dormitory early in the evening and saw that it was crowded. It was an unexpected hour for the lounge to be so populated. The television was showing something of interest, maybe a football match, John thought, but he saw Vic in there, looking agitated. He elbowed his way in until he could see what they were watching. It was a news program showing strange footage, a bright sky full of slowly descending parachutes and a journalist in the foreground speaking over the drone of airplanes and the popping of machine gun fire in the distance. He explained that this was the beginning of an air and ground invasion of Northern Sulat, where rebels had taken over an army base. The camera cut to a scene of men shooting from a rooftop, and then a bomb falling on a block of concrete buildings. When the bomb exploded and the concrete shattered in all directions, one side of the room erupted in cheers and shouts. John recognized Vic's voice booming over the others. He said people who cheered at bombings should get bombed themselves, and of course an argument ensued. In a second Vic was shoved and surrounded by three or four others while the rest of the kids moved aside. John went over to stop him from doing something stupid, but he didn't know if he could. Vic was undeterred by the fact that no one had come to his defense or that he was outnumbered. He kept shouting about the bombs falling on innocent people. His opponents didn't back down either. They claimed none of those people were innocent and they would do the same to us if they had the chance. Then one of them said, "Go back to Sulat, pigfucker." John put his arm between them, barring Vic from charging forward. "Come on," he said, pulling on Vic's shirt. "It's not worth it." He could feel everyone's eyes on him and John got nervous. He wasn't much of a fighter.

Vic yelled, "I'm not from Sulat, you idiot," but at least he was backing away. John kept pulling him toward the hallway and the boys kept calling him a fucker of various animals. John wondered if he would have to keep an eye on Vic all night. He wouldn't be surprised if they vandalized Vic's door or jumped him when they caught him alone. He never imagined Mount Belet students could become so rabid. It seemed to be such an uncivilized response, but a part of him thought Vic had provoked it.

He took Vic back to his room and listened to him rant a while longer. He said the students here were barbarians. Except for John. John was the only decent one.

John was distracted by how orderly Vic's room was. There was nothing on the floor. His books actually lined a bookshelf. Vic took a bottle of whiskey out of his desk drawer. He drank from the bottle and held it out to John. John took it, thinking he could use a drink.

"I haven't been paying attention to the news," John said. "Do you know what that was about?"

Vic was eager to share his idea. "You know what I think is going on? We're trying out our new toys. Don't you remember when the PM was visiting Nixon last year? Do you know at the same time, the foreign minister was in Moscow with Brezhnev?"

John wished he hadn't asked. This wasn't his first time hearing Vic's crackpot theories about politics. In the morning he would read the newspaper instead of filling his head with dubious information from Vic. Then he would talk to Mariam about it. He thought of calling her now to see if she was all right. What if the scene he had witnessed in the lounge represented a prevailing mood at the college? If Mariam felt harassed, or if this invasion spread to the rest of the province, she might have to go home. "I should go," John said. "I think you should stay in your room for the night."

Vic was staring at him. "Where are you from, Merchant?"

John looked at the door. This always happened with Vic. He never understood when someone was trying to leave.

"I'm from Alexandria."

"Where from originally? No one's *from* Alexandria."

That was another one of Vic's ridiculous assertions. Of course people were from Alexandria. It was the largest city in the country and their capital. It was shabby compared to the more famous Alexandria in Egypt, 'the pearl of the Mediterranean,' but one thing they didn't lack was a native population. "For as far back as we can trace, my family has been in Alexandria," John said.

Vic didn't really care. He was only looking for a chance to talk about his own family. "My father's family came from India. My mother's father was born in Syria. What did you think I was? What did you think I was when you met me?"

Many answers came to mind. John said, "I didn't have any idea."

"Do you know that Merchant isn't a real family name?" Vic asked. "People took that name to disguise their religious affiliation, so that they could do business with everyone. Merchants can be Christian, Jewish, Muslim, Zoroastrian."

"How do you know this?" John asked.

"I read it in a book. The actual surname was often passed down as a middle name. Is there a common middle name in your family?"

"No."

"What is your middle name?"

"My parents named us Sonya, John and Theresa. I think we're Catholic. We can put that mystery to rest."

Vic scowled. John said again that he had to go.

"Who's the girl you spend time with? The mousy one."

"What girl?"

"The girl with the ears. With the Anne Frank smile."

John looked at his watch. "It's late. I have a lot to do."

"Are you fucking her?"

"Who are you talking about?"

"The one you don't sneak back to your room. Could I meet her? You already have a girl to fuck in your room. You can share."

When John realized he was talking about Mariam, his palms started sweating. "Leave her alone. She's not interested in fucking, I can tell you that."

"Not you maybe."

"Leave her alone," he said more emphatically.

"She's from Sulat, isn't she? I've never spoken to her but I can tell. I have a knack for picking up where people are from by studying their facial features. I can tell from her eyes and her cheekbones, and from the way she carries herself too." Vic was getting excited. He sounded insane. "Am I right?"

John didn't say anything. Vic smiled. "I knew it. It must be tough for her. I haven't seen any other girls here from Sulat. I can't tell as much with the boys. Boys all look the same, you know, and I don't want to be caught staring at them. I think they go out of their way to hide their identities."

John really wanted to get out of there now, but he had to agree with Vic that Mariam stood out. She didn't quite fit in, and she didn't try to hide where she was from either. "I have to go," John said. This time he departed swiftly. If he'd shown the slightest hesitation, he would have been trapped.

He called Mariam's dorm. When Nina answered, he pretended he had called to see what she was doing. She said she was in the room studying. "Are you alone?" he asked.

"Mariam's with me," she said in a hushed voice.

All he had to do was tell Nina to put Mariam on the phone. There was a pause. He had the opportunity. Then Nina said flirtatiously, "I can come over there."

"I really have a lot of work to do," John said. "Maybe tomorrow." He knew he was digging himself a grave. He hung up the phone, cringing, and spent the rest of the night distracted by waves of self-loathing.

The next morning he read the newspaper for the first time in months. In Alexandria he had to read the newspaper every day at breakfast. His father made him and sometimes it was all they had to talk about. His father was more interested in the major powers, the Soviet Union and America and even China, Germany and Japan, countries that seemed to have the ability to determine what happened in the rest of the world. The main paper in Alexandria printed a lot of international news. Its domestic news was repetitive and depressing, full of political fights in Parliament and violence in the outer provinces. Here at Mount Belet, he'd been freed from that ritual of reading the paper. He hadn't had the time or interest, but this morning, he didn't want to face Mariam uninformed.

The news about Northern Sulat was all over the front page. Not surprisingly, the tone of the article was heavily biased in favor of the invasion, going all the way back to an insurgence in 1949 that began with a massacre of Catholics. Back then, Alexandria staged a military intervention to protect the Catholic population, and after three years the entire province except for the far north surrendered. That region was still under military occupation, twenty-five years later. They referred to it as the militarized zone.

He wasn't exactly an expert after reading one article. There were things that confused him. For instance, why did they need to send in paratroopers if the army was already occupying the area? He decided it would be best to see what Mariam knew and try not to talk very much. He waited for her outside the history building where she had an early class. When he saw her come out, he stood in her path. She was wearing her white wool cap and a thick pullover sweater with a geometric pattern across the chest. She wasn't paying attention and practically ran into him. She looked happy to see him. He asked her if she wanted to walk with him to his class. She said she would like that, and as soon as they started walking, she asked him if he had heard the news. He told her he had seen it last night on television.

"We don't have a television at Curie," she said. "My mother called me yesterday evening. I said I hadn't heard anything and she said that was good, that I shouldn't talk to anyone about it."

"You don't have family in the north, do you?"

She shook her head. "Even people in Sulat don't know what goes on in the militarized zone," she said. "You can't even travel there from other parts of Sulat, and they aren't allowed to leave. It's like a whole other country."

"That's strange," John said.

"What did it look like on television?" she asked. She said she always imagined it to be a very barren place.

"It didn't look barren," he said. "But they showed mostly the sky. It was full of parachutes."

Mariam didn't understand what he meant, and he tried to describe it further, the surreal drifting of the paratroopers.

"But in the paper they said there was an air raid."

"There were some planes," John said vaguely. He didn't want to tell her about the bombing, or the argument in the lounge.

"I read they dropped a lot of bombs. I think it's cowardly to kill from the sky, don't you? My father lost his whole family like that."

John didn't know what to say. In his own family, there were no epic tragedies that he knew of. He couldn't believe Mariam had to carry this burdensome history. Mostly she handled it with grace and innocence but now there was a hint of anger in her voice. He hoped she would follow her mother's advice and only talk to him like this. He didn't think other people would understand her point of view, without knowing her and what her parents had gone through.

"I'm sorry about your father's family. That's so terrible."

"When I was little, I took a train trip with my mother to the south of the province, where my parents are from. You could still see the shells of buildings. You could still see the rubble. I never saw those things in English Canal. My mother had to explain to me that there was a war, that the buildings had been bombed. I didn't know the world could be like that."

"Was there no fighting in English Canal?" John asked.

She didn't seem certain. Either there wasn't much, or whatever was damaged was rebuilt quickly. According to what she knew, it was the northern and southern poles of the province that bore the extremes of the conflict. He thought there was something poetic about that.

"Mariam, I think your mother's right. You shouldn't talk to everyone about this."

"I'm only talking to you. I can trust you, can't I?"

"Of course, you can."

"Do you want me to stop?"

He looked at her, almost grabbing her hand, and said, "You can tell me everything."

She smiled. "You don't have to worry about me, John."

They came to the base of the slope leading up to the science building, its thick Doric columns lifting their eyes to the blue sky. Mariam gasped. "You climb these steps every day?"

"Some days it feels more daunting than others. Today is one of those days. I have a few minutes though. We can sit down."

In reality he had very little time, but he didn't want to leave Mariam. She seemed to need to talk, and he had missed hearing her voice.

They sat down in the grass.

"John, do you mind if I ask you a personal question?"

"Go ahead," he said, eager to hear it.

"Do you ever think about your military service? About what you'll have to do?"

That wasn't the kind of personal question he'd been expecting. He was too ashamed to admit it was one of the first things he thought about as he watched the news footage last night.

"You can refuse," Mariam said. "You go to jail for two years, but two years isn't that long."

"That's easy for you to say."

It was a joke, but she was immediately chastened. "It's true. I'll never have to make a decision like that. Only I've read that people who are sent to do their military service in certain places have to do terrible things. Things they can't live with."

"I'm sure that happens," John said. "But these days, it's not that bad." This is what he'd always been told, that his military service would be easy. It was only ten months, including the six-week training, and he could do it at any time before his thirtieth birthday. But he was always told to get it done quickly, before something happened to break the peace. In wartime the service could be extended for years, and he could be called up at any time. If this conflict in Northern Sulat continued to escalate, it could change everything for him.

It was time for him to go to class, but he suddenly felt the urge to lie down, wanting to feel the cool grass on the back of his head. Mariam watched him, looking a little confused at first, but to his surprise, she decided to lie down beside him. They were almost touching. A heavy silence passed between them.

She began to talk again. This time she sounded nervous, her voice trembling.

"I didn't only see terrible things when I went on the trip with my mother. There were beautiful things too. I still remember when we pulled into Kasbah station at dawn. It was still dark outside and Mama woke me up to look out the window. All the men got off the train and gathered on the platform, and it was completely silent until a man's voice came chanting over a loudspeaker from the mosque. My mother told me it was the *fajr* prayer, the call to prayer at dawn. I've never forgotten the sound of it. I still dream about that station."

John thought it was strange for her to feel so moved by a prayer she'd heard as a child, a prayer she didn't even believe in. Maybe Mariam would always confound him.

"I've heard it," John said. "In Egypt. My parents thought it was a nuisance but I didn't mind it." It had sounded melodic to him, but his mother said it sounded like mosquitoes buzzing in her ears.

Mariam's voice was breathless, full of amazement. "You

never told me you went to Egypt! Have you seen the pyramids?"

"I have," he said, though the experience was wasted on him. He saw filth and commerce and useless things built by slaves. The masses of tourists depressed him and he didn't want to be one of them. He didn't see what Mariam would have seen, the effort and the achievement, the humanity of it.

He had a terrible pain in his chest. Though he had never felt anything like it before he knew Mariam was the cause of it. He thought if he turned and saw the blades of grass kissing the skin of her arms and the tips of her ears, he would start to cry. Every part of his body felt tender and weak.

"I should get to class," he said.

She sat up obligingly and he followed. He stood and was about to offer his hand and help her up, but she said she would sit a while longer. "Thank you for waiting for me, John."

"What do you mean?" he asked.

"Outside my class. I love talking to you in the morning."

God help me, he thought. He was too young to feel this way. There was no shortage of beautiful girls in the world, a decent portion of whom were likely to find him attractive. Yes, he would fight it, the same way she fought it. She was the deceptive one, subversively seductive, and he was the beetle in her quivering web.

During John's final Chemistry exam, bundles of snowflakes settled on the ground. When he stepped outside the world was white. He walked and thought about finding a quiet place, a place for himself, where he could sit and watch the untouched snow, until he saw Mariam standing alone on the bridge, wrapped tightly in her winter clothes, jeans he'd never seen her wear before, heavy boots and a thick ski jacket. Beneath a fuzzy black hat with earflaps sticking out, her face sparkled.

"Here we are again," she said. She took a step forward and

fell into him. It was a shock to feel her forehead pressed against his cheek and the heat of her breath on his neck. "It's snowing," she said. "I'm going home tomorrow."

He put his arms around her. "You're warm," he said. His heart was beating like a hummingbird's wings. "Are you all right?"

Her lips brushed his cheek before she pulled away. She looked over the railing, into the frigid, ghostly mist coming up from the gorge. "We should get Nina and find a place to watch the snow. Do you want to?"

That could not have been what she really wanted. What if he said he would rather take her up to his room and forget about the snow?

"Sure, let's get Nina," he said. "Stay up all night. Watch the sky."

They walked silently to her dorm. By the time Nina came down to meet them he was ready for the distraction, which Nina provided, as usual. She tormented them with snowballs in the face. She was pelting Mariam when John managed to knock her over and pin her down into the snow. The snow was wet and heavy. From a lifetime of winter holidays he knew this snow would harden into milky, undulating sheets, appearing opalescent in the morning sun. Nina took a fistful of snow and smashed it across his face. It stung hard, and when he reached up to touch his cheek he couldn't tell where his fingertips ended and his face began.

He had not heard Mariam's voice for a while. He stood up and looked around for her.

"Did Mariam go home?" he asked.

Nina sat up. "John, look."

He saw her then, not far away, lying still in the snow. He ran over to her, every step a slow heave. When he finally reached her he fell to his knees, lifted her head and brushed the snow off her face. She didn't open her eyes. "Mariam?"

"Is she all right?" Nina called out.

"Go to the call box," he yelled, "Get us a car, quickly."

"Those things never work."

"Just go, Nina, what else is there to do?"

He picked Mariam up and carried her down to the road. Nina was right about the call boxes not working; they had to flag down a car to take them to the infirmary. Nina got into the backseat and waited as he laid Mariam across the seat with her head on Nina's lap. He rode up front with the driver, who proceeded with maddening care along the slippery roads. Mariam was awake now, trembling violently and crying. She said she wanted to go home. By the time they got to the infirmary, Mariam had recovered a little and seemed determined to walk, but a nurse came to the door and practically threw her onto a gurney and took her away.

The infirmary had the look and feel of a monastery, quiet and austere. While Nina filled out paperwork, John stood by a lancet window looking out to a courtyard, mesmerized by the snow still tumbling through the sky. He listened to Nina and the nurse talking about Mariam and her parents, about how to let them know she was sick and wouldn't be getting on a train tomorrow.

After that they sat for a while, waiting for nothing in particular. The nurse told them it was just a flu and she had to sleep it off. They were sent away. He dropped Nina off in front of her dormitory. She was returning to Alexandria early in the morning. "I have an exam tomorrow," he said. "I won't be able to see you off." Actually his exam was at noon. She said she would miss him. "Will you try to see me in Alexandria?" she asked. He said he would try.

The next day, he went back to the infirmary to see Mariam.

"Not now," the nurse said. "Her fever's up again. You can come back tomorrow."

"I'm leaving tonight," he said.

The nurse was unsympathetic.

She smirked when he returned the next morning. As she held the door open she said, "No funny business."

The room was gray and silent. He sat beside the bed and watched her sleep for a long time. She was restless, her skin and hair drenched. There was something so cleansing about fevers, after their break, and that was how she appeared to him, cleansed, wrung out and purified. They had dressed her in a thin, white cotton nightgown. It clung to her body, to the small roundness of her breasts. He could see the dark of her nipples and after a while, ashamed of himself, he lifted the sheet up to cover them. Then he kissed her forehead and woke her up.

She opened her eyes. Her irises appeared darker, obsidian black against the white sterility of the bedsheets. There was a clarity, a lucidity to them, a confidence he had never seen before, and he wasn't even sure she recognized him until she whispered his name. When he touched her cheek she wrapped her fingers around his wrist, and he kissed her burning lips, felt her burning tongue on his. As the warmth of it coursed through his body her nails dug sharply into his skin. It felt like she would never let him go.

The nurse walked in, intrusive with her scolding and sighing, but he managed to stay long enough to kiss the bridge of Mariam's nose. Eventually she closed her eyes again, and let go of him, and the nurse urged him to leave her.

Outside he studied the crescent-shaped grooves her nails had made on his wrist. Slowly the indents filled and the marks faded, but he would never forget the tightness of her grip.

Two

Mariam was nervous about seeing her parents again. She was afraid they would not recognize her, and at the same time afraid they would fail to notice how different she was. Something had happened. At last something had happened in her quiet little life.

Only her father met her at the train station. When she saw him she realized she'd all but forgotten his existence for the last four months. He was both younger and taller than she remembered him, and happier. It made sense to Mariam that her absence would have had a curative effect. Their relationship was always strained, and he'd had a break from it for four months.

"Feeling better?" he asked. His tone was so light she wondered if he was in love again.

"Yes," she said.

"You've lost weight."

"I was sick. I couldn't eat anything."

"I hope you'll eat today. Mother's been cooking all day for you. She was so disappointed when you couldn't come home on time."

On the drive home, she looked out the window at the townhouses lining the canal. They were abandoned and blighted throughout her childhood, but they looked quite nice now, most of them converted into apartment buildings. She loved walking for miles along the canal. She wished she could get out of the car and walk along it now.

When they pulled up in front of the house, her father got out to retrieve her bags from the trunk. Mariam's legs felt heavy as she walked up the path to the front door. Their white bungalow looked the same, neat but dull. She found her mother in the kitchen, vigorously rolling dough into little discs, tossing flour onto the discs to keep them from sticking to the pin. Her hair was falling out of a loose bun and even like this she was beautiful, elegantly beautiful with her high cheekbones and light eyes, a beauty that was out of step with her life.

She stopped in the doorway, trying to separate all the emotions churning inside her. She had missed her mother desperately, and had needed desperately to be away from her.

"I'm here, Mama."

Her mother looked up and remained still for a moment. Mariam could see she had noticed. This girl was not the same one that had left.

With her floured hands her mother came forward and took Mariam into her arms. "My darling, you're so thin."

"I couldn't eat," Mariam said.

"I know, but you'll eat now."

She was sent her to her room to wash up and change out of her travel clothes. "Don't be long," her mother said. "I want to hear all about your friends. You have a letter already."

She ran upstairs to her room. There it was, on the desk, an envelope from Nina. She decided to leave it for later. After she washed up and changed into one of her comfortable old dresses, she went back to the kitchen. Her father was in the house now, sitting at the kitchen table across from her mother who still labored over circles of dough with her rolling pin. How much bread did her mother think she could eat? Her father was reading the paper, holding it up like a shield to protect him from dustings of flour. Mariam had never seen them together like this, simply sharing a room for no practical reason.

"Can I help?" Mariam asked.

Her mother smiled, handing her the rolling pin and turning to the stove to heat up the oil.

There they were, the three of them in a line, her mother frying flatbreads, Mariam rolling them out, and her father reading the newspaper. "How does it feel to be home?" her mother asked, but it was difficult to carry on a conversation over the hissing oil and the rolling pin knocking against the wooden board, and the crackle of the newspaper as her father turned and flattened the pages. "It was snowing when I left," Mariam said. Despite the elevation and the pine trees, English Canal got snow once in a decade.

"Did you enjoy the snow?" her mother asked.

"I didn't get to see enough of it before I got sick, but it was very beautiful."

When the snow began she had waited for John on the bridge. It was cold and she waited a long time. She wanted to say goodbye to him there, in the spot where they'd met, and ask him not to forget her over the holiday. As soon as he appeared she felt ill. She wanted to walk in the snow with him all night but she could barely stand. But he came to her in the infirmary. She was certain he had come, that she had not dreamt it.

Mariam lost her concentration, too aware of her private thoughts. She looked up to see if her father was looking at her. He wasn't. She turned and saw her mother, one hand resting on her hip and the other holding a pair of tongs, suspended a few inches above the oil, ready to swoop down and retrieve the bread when it was exactly the right color.

"Mama," she said. Her father put his paper down.

She tapped her mother on the shoulder and made her turn around. "You're pale," her mother said, laying the tongs down and putting her warm hands on Mariam's cheeks. "Has your fever returned?"

"I'm tired."

"You shouldn't be standing in a hot kitchen. What was I thinking?"

"I'm fine," Mariam said. "I'll just lie down for a few minutes."

Her father went back to his paper, silently.

She climbed the stairs to her room and opened the window. Looking out at the placid canal, she gathered the courage to read the letter from Nina. She ripped it open and read it, her heart racing. There wasn't any mention of John. Mariam was relieved, drawing many conclusions from the letter and changing her mind about them minutes later. Perhaps his attentions were real after all. She had never before been so distracted and exhausted by her feelings. She curled up in her bed and fell asleep wondering.

She waited for a letter from John, but nothing came.

After the holidays another letter came from Nina, a response to a letter Mariam had written. This time Nina talked about John, about spending time with his family and exchanging gifts for Christmas. She talked about his sisters and their annoying habits. The whole letter was about John. She wept against the hard floor and nothing, not even her mother's frantic footsteps on the staircase could stop her.

Soon she was in her mother's arms, surrendering the letter. While her mother read the letter Mariam sobbed convulsively.

"Why are you crying?" her mother asked.

"He was my friend," Mariam cried. "She took him away. She knew what to do with him."

"This boy in the letter?"

"Yes."

Her mother stroked her hair. "Of course, you don't have any experience. Did he encourage you?"

Mariam thought for a minute.

"He always sought me out. He listened to me."

Her mother didn't ask her anything more about it, allowing Mariam to cry until she was exhausted. When she was done Mama said, "He's only the first. There will be others. There are others. When you go back, open your eyes and you'll see them."

Mariam sat up, feeling indignant. "No, Mama, there was one. He found me on the bridge. We talked until the sun came up."

"Let this one go. You have to change how you feel about him, that's all."

Mariam wished she hadn't made a scene. Her mother was not the least bit qualified to advise her on matters of love.

Over the next few days she came to understand that her memories of the infirmary couldn't be trusted. She had clung to something that could have been a fevered hallucination. The important thing was that John had befriended her and saved her from her loneliness. As a test of her strength she decided to compose a letter to the both of them. It was a dull letter about her dull life but at least she had overcome her grief to write it. Afterwards she was able to settle into a routine more easily. She read novels and took long walks along the canal and thought about her future, trying to imagine the kind of woman she wanted to become. She spent time with her parents, who sat together in various rooms of the house just talking about subjects for which she had no context.

She still waited for the postman every day. At last she received something from John, a postcard. It was a painting, a portrait of a girl holding a book. He wrote that he saw the painting in the national museum and thought of her, that he wanted to know how she was, that he was looking forward to seeing her at school and that he missed her. She read it over and over until it became meaningless. When nothing new came, she was unhappy again.

She must have looked pathetic. One day as she walked across the living room, her father turned off his television program and spoke to her.

"Let's go for a walk," he said.

"I don't want to."

"Your mother's at the market. Let's go and meet her there."

"I'm reading."

"It hurts your mother that we don't talk. We ought to make an effort."

Reluctantly she set out on a walk with her father along the canal, toward the market. It was another cold gray day, and the water in the canal was dark, almost black, carrying little more than fallen leaves and rubbish. It occurred to her now that she'd never known where this canal began or ended. She asked her father. Since he was a civil engineer, it would give them something to talk about. He delighted in starting from the very beginning. He told her the canal followed an ancient trading route. It was built by the Ottomans and expanded by the British in the late nineteenth century. They used it to transport marble and other building stones and had planned to extend it as far as Alexandria, but they left before ever finishing the project. It was the canal that had inspired her father to become a civil engineer. He wanted to build "beautiful infrastructure."

When he finished there was nothing more to talk about. They were almost at the market when he took hold of her wrist. She was caught in the shadow of his tall frame, his shoulders hunching over her in utter defeat. His long face, once firm and handsome, was sagging now, deformed. "Are you ever going to forgive me, Mariam?"

"Forgive you for what?"

He didn't seem to have any idea. "For leaving? For Elizabeth?"

"I don't even remember Elizabeth," she said.

"I'm trying, for your mother's sake, because she wants us to get on better."

"You're making it worse, Daddy. You think everything has something to do with you." She had not wanted this kind of conversation. The walk had started with her feeling charitable toward her father. "The truth is I don't even think about you. I forget about you all the time."

"I wish you would tell me what I've done."

"You don't love me," Mariam said. "You don't love Mama."

"I do love your mother. I came back for her."

Mariam knew he was lying. He tried to love her, and that was not the same. "All she does is cook and pray," Mariam informed him. "She thinks she's doing everything right and you still don't love her."

"You were a child, Mariam. You think you know what happened but you don't."

"I know you don't want to be here. It's all I know. It's all I've seen of the world."

Mariam looked out at the canal, trying to stop herself from saying any more. Everything she said now came from her fears about John, not her father, and she wanted to stop before she upset the equilibrium her mother had found with him.

"You're nothing like your mother," he said.

"Thank God," Mariam said. "It was not at all true. She wished she could be as forgiving as her mother."

Her father gave up on their walk. He said he was going back home, and she went in the opposite direction, to the tram stop. The next one came quickly and she rode down to College Street, a diagonal thoroughfare connecting Canal Street to the College of Sulat Province. Mariam had been surprised to hear that John had heard of this place. For a long time, she was afraid it would be her only option. She didn't know what she would have done there. Its humanities and language departments were weak and the curriculum was all about redoing—

rehabilitating, reconstructing, reintegrating a war-torn population. People here were obsessed with the war. They were always anxious even when there was nothing to fear. She had learned this behavior from everyone she'd grown up with and she hated them for it. Mariam had wanted to leave so she could learn how other people lived. How it was to live without the past weighing on you like a leaded smog. That was how John and Nina lived, unburdened.

Still, she loved to visit the bookstores on College Street. She browsed for a while and ran into one of her former classmates sitting at an outdoor café with a boy. Mariam didn't know her well, but she had not allowed herself to know any of her classmates well. She had wanted to get away, and getting away was as much of a mental process as it was physical. After a cordial exchange with her old classmate, Mariam kept walking toward the college library. She spent the afternoon there, distractedly reading articles about the canal as she analyzed her argument with her father. It had begun with him asking for forgiveness, which had enraged her, and she realized it was his approach that was all wrong, the fact that he came to her with a plea, not an offer. She must have been entering a new phase of her life, because nothing felt more important than to be offered something. Yet she was tired of not loving her father. He had survived a difficult life and she wanted to love him.

There was a detailed article about the canal in an international geographic magazine. In the article, it described a time during the war when the canal had become so clogged with corpses it dammed up the water. She asked the librarian to make a photocopy and went home to present the article to her father. She found him in his study. As she came through the door, he pulled his seat up close to his desk and set both hands stiffly in front of him.

"I saw this article about the canal," she said, giving him the photocopy.

His eyes moistened as he read the beginning. "It's about the war so I don't know if you'll want to read it. I know you don't like to talk about it."

"Your mother doesn't like me to talk about it," he said.

"Did you talk about it with Elizabeth?" she asked. She could feel her resentment rising again, and brought up Elizabeth to counter his indictment of her mother. Even if it were true, Mariam was loath to let him forget his transgressions. Later she would realize she'd lost an opportunity to defend her mother, if she had not been so intent on attacking him. She should have told him what her mother had done for him a year earlier, during a period when Mariam and her father were arguing constantly. She had found his every word to be false and cloying and used a tone with him that would have been unimaginable to anyone who knew her outside her home. That period ended only after Mama came up to her room and told her about the stray bomb that had fallen on his apartment block, killing his family—his mother, father, and sister—and all of his neighbors. Her father had narrowly escaped it because he was at the post office sending an application to the University of Stuttgart. He'd left his home as a son and brother, and returned to a pile of rubble and ash. Until then, her father's tragedy had only been alluded to. Mama told her how different it was for her. She and her parents had escaped in the early days of the war, before the air raids, when she was only sixteen, but her father had to endure the fighting for a year before he was able to escape to Germany. The story had not moved Mariam as much as it should have. She thought, with a twinge of guilt, that he was already a young man, not an orphaned child. She didn't know why it was so difficult to feel sympathy for him, and she wished for the coldness in her heart to fade.

For a few months after that, Mariam was delicate with her father. She practiced civility and avoidance, but in that same period her father was often absent, more than usual, and she was certain he was seeing Elizabeth. Mariam couldn't say where. She herself hadn't set eyes on Elizabeth since she was a child, but somehow Elizabeth still permeated their lives. Her scent was still on him. He worked all the time and was sullen when he got home. Again Mariam found him unforgivable, but she was leaving soon for Mount Belet. In a matter of months, she and her father would be free of each other.

Now her father charged past Mariam's question, still seizing a chance to tell her something different about Elizabeth. "She loved you very much, Mariam. She couldn't bear the thought of you not having a father."

"She sent you back, didn't she? She shouldn't have bothered."

Her father placed the article on the edge of his desk for Mariam to take back. "I don't remember her at all," Mariam said as she took the article and threw it in the trash bin beside his desk. "I only remember what you were like when you were with her. I remember the two of you standing over me. Your arms were touching."

Her father closed his eyes, remembering his lover while Mariam stood there. He looked old, his face lined with self-pity, and Mariam was tired. She was tried of watching her parents suffer each other.

"Do you still see her?" Mariam asked gently. On this, she only wanted the truth.

"I haven't seen her in many years," he said. "I gave her up."

For you, Mariam thought. That was what he must have felt, that Mariam by her very existence was the source of his crushing unhappiness. A part of her wanted to say that she was sorry. If it were up to her, she would have rather seen him live truthfully, without losing anyone he loved. They would have all been better off that way, her mother included, but it was too late, wasn't it? Elizabeth was lost to him, and if she said something careless, and her mother was abandoned again, Mariam would never forgive herself. All she could do was leave him alone.

She went down to the kitchen to see her mother.

"What's happened between you?" Mama asked.

"Nothing," Mariam said. "It isn't for you to worry about."

"I thought you were trying. You two break my heart."

They all fell into a weary silence for the remainder of her holiday. She wanted it to end, but she thought of going back to Mount Belet and seeing John and Nina with equal dread.

On the day of her departure, her father drove them to the station and stayed in the car while Mariam and her mother waited on the platform. When the train arrived, her mother tried to hold her, but Mariam didn't want to be held. She said goodbye without looking up and boarded the train, leaning her head against the window and closing her eyes as it pulled away, wishing never to go home again. She did not want to go anywhere she had ever been before.

Three

She had three days without Nina and John. One afternoon she hiked down to the bottom of the gorge beneath the bridge, her hands scraping the rock walls and her feet slipping over ice and pebbles. People died along this path, one misstep throwing them into the frigid rapids below. The wind came in from the north, ripping through the canyon like a bullet train while the waterfalls, fed by melting snow, roared and tumbled into the gorge. She got to the bottom late in the day. Her feet were numb. She wedged her body into a crack in the rock wall, protecting herself from the wind and freezing mist rising from the rapids, and stared at the foaming water. She looked up at the bridge, a hundred meters up, and imagined herself standing over the railing, looking down. With the sun setting and her body stiff from cold and fatigue, she decided it was time to turn around and climb back up the steep path that brought her here. She emerged through the thicket onto the bridge after dark. No one would believe what she had done. She could hardly believe it herself.

On another day she went into town, where shops stretched along a wide avenue for five or six blocks. Her favorite was an old pawnshop, dark, woody and dusty. She could spend hours in there picking up tiny objects, little silver pillboxes, porcelain spoons and porcelain cups, jewelry and many things that seemed to have no use at all. There were shelves crowded with perfume bottles—from a distance they looked like the skyline of a miniature glass city. Under the glass countertop she saw something that looked like a pocket watch with an engraving that swirled from the edge of the circular cover to its center point. She kept going back to the counter to look at it, and finally the shopkeeper took it out for her. He opened it and showed her it was a mariner's compass, not a pocket watch, and it was made of brass. She read the engraving. *The sea that calls all things unto her calls me, and I must embark.*

"That's beautiful," she exclaimed. "Is it from a poem?"

"*The Prophet*," the old shopkeeper said proudly. "It's an unusual piece. We've had it a long time."

"Does it work?"

"I'm not sure. The needle moves, but whether it moves accurately I couldn't say. If you like it I'll give you a good deal."

"How much do you want for it?"

The shopkeeper looked at her kindly. "Twenty-five?" he asked.

Perhaps he would let her put a down payment on it. "Can I have it for fifteen?" she asked.

He winced. "Twenty," he said. "That's the best I can do."

If she bought it, she'd have no money for bus fare, but she wanted the compass. "All right," she said.

As he wrapped it he asked her if she was from Sulat.

"Yes. How did you know?"

"The girls from Sulat are the prettiest. It's been a long time since I've seen a girl from Sulat."

Mariam smiled. She'd never received such a strange and sincere compliment.

By the time Nina returned Mariam was composed, feeling strong enough to handle her. Nina didn't talk at all about John. In fact she was far less talkative than before the holidays. During the first week of classes, after Nina had tried to track him down, it was clear that John was avoiding them, both of them, and only Mariam knew why. He had come to her in the infirmary and kissed her on the lips. She knew this for certain now. Her memory was perfectly intact.

"Have you spoken to him? Have you seen him?" Nina asked.

Mariam shook her head.

"Did something happen? Isn't it strange that you haven't seen each other?"

"It isn't strange," Mariam said. "Why would you say that?"

"You were friends, weren't you?"

"For a while, but then he met you."

Nina looked confused. "What do you mean? You still saw him, after he met me."

"No, not very much," Mariam said. "Hardly at all. And over the break I only got a postcard from him."

"He's moody. I just can't figure him out. One minute he seems so attentive and the next minute he seems to have completely forgotten about me."

Mariam would not have characterized him in that way. He had forgotten her, yes, but before that he had only been attentive, before he met Nina and vanished.

"Why do you like him so much?" Mariam asked.

Thinking about it made Nina smile. "He's cute. He's funny."

"That's all?"

"He's smart."

"Yes, but he's not very reliable, as you say."

"You're right, Mariam. I don't think he's very mature."

"No," Mariam agreed.

"It's just that . . . I believe that he will love me one day."

Mariam thought Nina's confidence was foolish, but no more foolish than her own, she discovered, after Nina did catch hold of John in the days to come. She began to talk about him again, in the present tense, and then from the library window Mariam saw them together. They were walking, Nina

skipping next to him and talking animatedly about something.
They stopped. Nina reached up and put her arms around his
neck. She kissed him for a long time before they parted.

Mariam imagined them discussing the situation, wondering
if they ought to talk to her about the seriousness of their relationship. It was more likely they had never discussed her at all.
That Mariam had fallen away from John's memory as though
her very existence had been erased.

She'd chosen her classes poorly, struggling through each
one in a different way, the worst being her philosophy class.
She should have dropped it when she had the chance, but she
found the professor so hypnotizing she couldn't bring herself
to do it. He was French, visiting for a year from the Sorbonne.
He was dignified and handsome in an academic way, with a full
head of gray hair and deep-set blue eyes, a blue that Mariam
imagined was the color of a tropical sea. He stood close to the
girls, looked at them directly and spoke to them in seductive
tones, though he had a wife who was also teaching for a year in
the French department. Mariam studied his interactions with
the female students much more closely than she did the actual
content of the course.

Before the first paper was due he asked the students to
present their outlines to him privately. As Mariam sat across
from him in his small office, she could hardly breathe. His
presence filled the whole room. His lips twitched as he looked
over her outline. "You want to write about existentialism and
morality?" he asked.

She opened her mouth to speak, knowing her voice was lost
to her. Finally she nodded her head.

"It's a good outline. Do you want to talk through it?"

She shook her head. He stared at her, amused and perhaps
flattered by her silence.

"You can speak English if it is easier for you."

She stared at his knees. "I'm not finished with the outline," she said in French.

"If your argument is that existentialism offers a new morality," he continued, "I will expect you to define morality. I want your definition of morality, what it means to you. Not something copied. Did you understand me?"

"Yes," she said.

"You should speak up more in class. I'm sure you have things to say." He looked back at her outline to remember her name. "Mariam," he said, handing it back to her.

In class Mariam watched him with a girl who seemed to impress him with her comments, though her French was very bad. He called on her a lot, and sometimes their exchanges would last several minutes, as if they were dying to empty out the room so they could make love and talk about Sartre in whatever language suited them. Now during class Mariam's head was full of questions. Would he wear his wedding ring while they made love? Have they been together already? Was the girl a virgin before? The girl was in love with him, that was obvious, but did he love her? What must it be like, to be so desired?

She couldn't sleep and began to take long walks on the outskirts of campus until late into the night. It wasn't safe to wander away from campus after midnight and for some girls it was never safe to walk alone, even on the college grounds, but no one ever seemed to notice Mariam. She was silent everywhere, even in her own room with Nina. If she didn't call her mother she could go days without talking to anyone. Once, when she was about six years old, she had stopped talking altogether. Though it was only for a few weeks that silence had marked her for a long time. For reasons she couldn't have understood yet, her mother had packed her a pink suitcase made just for traveling little girls, and Mariam remembered opening and closing it again and again just to hear the snap of its clasps. Then her father drove up, and her mother put Mariam and her suitcase in that car. Her mother told her she was going to spend the weekend with her father and Elizabeth, and even as Mariam got in the car she was so enthralled with her suitcase she didn't think it odd that her father and Elizabeth would be someplace where her mother was not. It wasn't until she was taken to Elizabeth's flat and saw her father's things there that she began to wonder about her mother. Her father put his arm around Elizabeth and said they were going to get married, that Elizabeth was going to become a kind of mother to her.

The six-year-old Mariam thought having Elizabeth as a mother meant her own mother had been eliminated. How could a child have two mothers? She was so shocked she couldn't get any words out. Her father and Elizabeth asked her to say something. They waited a few minutes, then a few hours and a whole night, until the visit was deemed a failure and she was roughly handed back to her mother the next day. She should have spoken after she was in her mother's arms, but she didn't, not again until she saw her father walking up the front path one morning weeks later. She said, "Daddy's here." It seemed strange now that his return had hastened her speech. In every other way it was disastrous.

She remembered a feeling from that period that she was fading and fading and would disappear altogether, as if her voice was the only thing that made her visible. That feeling was creeping back to her now.

A boy was staring at her one night when she sat on a bench facing her dormitory window. She was waiting for the lights in the room to go out, so she would know Nina had left for dinner and Mariam could go in and try to sleep. She was exhausted and struggling to keep her thoughts straight. When she noticed the boy looking at her she threw her hand up in a limp wave, and after a slight hesitation, he came over and spoke to her.

"I know who you are," he said. "Do you know who I am?"

She smiled, intrigued by his introduction. "No. How do you know who I am?"

"John Merchant is my lab partner. He used to spend time with you. I asked him to introduce us but he refused."

"He refused? How curious." She put her hand out. "And you are?"

"Vic. Vic Arora."

"I like that name."

He kissed her hand gallantly. "And what is your name? It must be something beautiful."

"Mariam," she said. It sounded like a different language when he repeated it.

"Would you like to get a drink?" he asked.

"Right now?"

"Yes, why not? You've been sitting here a long time. I've been watching you."

She looked down, embarrassed by his observation.

He still had her hand and tugged at it.

"I suppose I could get one drink."

He began walking immediately, pulling her along. With every step his pace quickened and Mariam had to run at times to keep up with him. He took her to a pub on a dark street she had never visited, just outside the campus walls. "This is the only place quiet on a Friday night."

He sat her down at a sticky square table and brought her a glass of whiskey. There were no students here, only a few men slumped against the bar. She had only taken a few sips before Vic finished his drink and ordered them both another. He was restless, tapping his fingers on the table. Now that he'd gotten her off the bench, he couldn't seem to make conversation. It didn't take long for Mariam to realize there was something not right about him. She had never seen anyone so trapped in his own body. Her heart broke for him.

"Are you all right?" she asked.

"Wonderful," he said.

"Are you having a good term? Do you enjoy your classes?"

"I love my classes. I feel wonderful in my classes."

"That's good."

"You're sweet," he said. "You have a sweet face."

"Can we go somewhere else?" she asked.

"Where did you want to go?"

"I don't know. Somewhere more comfortable."

He looked at his watch. "We could go to my dorm. But John doesn't usually get back to his room until around eleven."

"Why would that matter?"

"I'm not an imbecile. You want him to see you, don't you? You should hear him and that girl going at it. Really, I don't know when that guy sleeps."

Vic leaned forward in his seat, gripping the edges of the table like he was about to pick it up and throw it across the room. She could hear his foot tapping furiously under the table.

"Let's go somewhere else," he said, thrusting the idea forward like a sword, his Hamlet to her Polonius.

"It's all right. I should go home."

"I know a nice spot," he said. "We can get it over with there and I'll tell John about it later. Don't worry. I'll tell him."

She forced the other drink down. "Are you talking about sex?"

"Of course I'm talking about sex."

"You want to tell John that you had sex with me?"

"Yes."

"Why?"

"Because it would be interesting. It would be interesting to see his reaction."

"Does John talk about me?"

"No. Not at all."

"Then why do you think he would care?"

Vic smiled and his face lightened. He could certainly be charming if he tried.

"You're putting me on, right? Do you want to do this or not? We have to really do it. I'm not a liar."

Mariam couldn't make any sense of what he was saying. She listened and watched his body struggling to move in the world. He had so little control of it, yet she did not find him at all threatening, only strange and awkward and pitiful.

"Let's go then," Mariam said.

He didn't know what to do with her assent. He stared at her and looked down at his large hands, perhaps contemplating the meeting of these separate entities. Then he grabbed her by the arm and pulled her out of the pub. He didn't let go of her until they'd reached the gate of a small park at the end of the street. It was empty, but dark and isolated. She didn't feel safe there.

"I thought we were going back to campus."

"I love this park."

"But it's nighttime. I can't even see it."

"Of course it's nighttime," he said, laughing. "Are you ready?"

Mariam sighed. At least she was here with Vic, who might appear protectively hulking to potential assailants roaming through the park. "All right," she said, and she sat down on the grass.

He was on top of her in a second. He reached into her skirt and pulled her underwear off and before she knew it he had her legs wrapped around him. The weight of him and all the mystery going on between her legs excited her. She could feel his hands there fumbling with his zipper and then the sudden softness of his flesh. She bit her lip and braced herself for the inevitable pain. He kept grunting, but she didn't feel much force. His rubbery penis kept springing away, unable to penetrate. After several minutes he stopped and looked at her. "Are you a virgin?"

"Of course," she said.

"Of course? I haven't been with a virgin in two years."

"Well how hard can it be if you've done it before?"

"It's hard. It's more effort than I want to put forth right now. You used me," he said. "You tried to trick me."

"I tricked you? This was your idea."

He stood up and zipped his pants.

"Get up. Get up, would you?"

"I'll get up when I want to," she said.

"Don't get up then. If you want to be raped stay here. I'm going home."

He waited a while, every now and then taking a few steps toward the gate, announcing, "I'm leaving," and then coming back. She refused to get up, just to spite him. Eventually he was too far away to win. He would either have to come back and force her to her feet, or go home. He chose to go home.

She didn't run after him, but she was too afraid to stay in the park on her own. After his footsteps faded she walked briskly back to campus and didn't see him again.

A few days later Mariam fell asleep at her study carrel in the library and woke up to find a note scrawled on a scrap of paper and placed at her fingertips. It was only three words, written in John's assured handwriting. *I miss you*, it said. Mariam closed her eyes and held the paper to her lips.

When Mariam got back to her room, she found Nina crying bitterly. For John's birthday she was going to rent a car and take him to a vacation cabin for a weekend. "Was it too much?" she asked. "When I told him about the car he said he wanted to be alone for his birthday."

"That's not so bad."

"He doesn't think we should see each other anymore."

Nina wrapped her arms around Mariam's waist and cried. Mariam didn't know what to do with her hands. She patted Nina's head a few times. "Why don't we have a drink?" Mariam asked. When Nina lifted her head she was able to extricate herself. "We can celebrate John's birthday without him."

Nina smiled, a watery, childish smile. "All right."

"What can we drink?"

Nina went into her closet and pulled out a small box filled with bottles, some of them empty. "I feel like some brandy."

The brandy went down more easily than John's vodka. It didn't take long for the heat of it to rise into Mariam's cheeks, and Nina's cheeks were also beautifully pink. She began to entertain Mariam with tales of her romantic misadventures. She had experienced so much at such a young age. Mariam listened, but her thoughts wandered to John, to what he had been thinking and feeling over the last few weeks. All she wanted was to know his state of mind.

"You'll find someone else," Mariam said.

"I know," said Nina.

Mariam felt encouraged by Nina's confidence. She always seemed to have the expectation that something exciting was about to happen. In a way, it was contagious. Just now, Mariam felt it too, that something in her life was certain to change.

On the morning of John's birthday Mariam skipped her first class. After Nina left, the telephone in the hallway began to ring. Someone answered it. Then there was a quiet knock on her door. The girl told her through the door that a boy was on the phone for her. Mariam put on her slippers and shuffled into the hall. She picked up the phone and said hello. It was John. He asked her if she was having a good morning. She said yes, she was finally having a good morning.

"It's my birthday, Mariam."

"I know. I have something for you."

"Will you bring it to me?"

She got ready and wrapped her gift with butcher paper and a ribbon, and she ran down the hill to his dormitory, carrying the box in her coat pocket. It was a blustery day, cold and gray, and when she arrived he pulled her into the room, covered her ears with his hands and kissed her before she could give him the box. Nothing in her life could ever come close to this, the warmth of his lips on hers. He didn't want to let her go. He kissed her over and over and over again.

His room had a fireplace and there was a fire crackling in it, and outside the branches of a tree shuddered in the wind and tapped his window hauntingly. She made him sit in front of the fire and open his present. As he held the box he looked sleepy and sweetly unkempt, his thick black hair sticking up in every direction. She had always wanted to touch his hair. It was so straight yet wild. She wanted to fill her fist with it and pull.

He opened the gift carefully, untying the ribbon, peeling the tape away, unwrapping the paper and lifting the cover, staring into it before taking out the mariner's compass she had found in the pawnshop. He examined it, holding it up to the firelight and lifting his flat hand up and down like a balance scale to feel the weight of the treasure in his palm. He turned it over and read the words engraved in the brass.

The sea that calls all things unto her calls me, and I must embark. He read it aloud, his deep voice seeping into her skin. She moved closer to him.

He turned back to its open face and watched the needle waver and settle.

"You picked this out for me?"

"I've been waiting to give it to you."

He kissed her again. "Are you cold? Don't you want to get under the covers for a little while?"

"How can I say no to you on your birthday?"

"You can't."

She stood, letting her coat drop to the floor as she stepped out of her shoes. He watched her unbutton her dress. She pulled the dress over her head, awkwardly, but left her slip on.

"You don't know what you do to me, Mariam."

"But I haven't seen you in weeks," she said.

"I've seen you," he said. "I always fell apart."

"Did you come to me in the infirmary?"

He touched the lace hem of her slip.

"You came to me, didn't you? Then I waited. I waited for something to change and nothing changed."

"I was afraid," he said. "Weren't you afraid?"

"Yes," she confessed. He pressed his forehead against her knee and she ran her fingers, at last, through his hair.

"Stay here with me. Let's never leave this room."

She pulled away and got into his bed. Though her heart was racing she lay very still, resisting any urge to cover herself, while he came to the side of the bed and looked down at her body. If she was still long enough she thought she might fade into the dust, into the light. "I was a ghost until you found me," she said.

Then she turned away. She stared at the wall and felt his weight unsettle the mattress. She could feel his warm breath on her shoulders, his bare arms over hers, his rough leg parting her legs. He got as close to her as he could. "I only want to hold you, Mariam."

She settled into his arms and closed her eyes.

She could not remember what woke her up, whether it was a dream or the wind or his lips on her neck. Because the day-light was still a solid gray, she wondered if she had only dozed off for a few minutes. John was awake, with his hand on her stomach. She could feel his erection. His hands crept up to the neckline of her slip and slid down to her breast, where his fingers grazed her nipple. She turned her head and kissed him. If only she could explain her conflict. She wanted him, but the brute force it would take to break into her body was terrifying.

Something caused him to lift his head and look into her eyes. His eyes were full of fear and wonder. She wished he could see what he saw at that moment, to think what he thought and know what he knew.

"I'll be right back," he said.

"Where are you going?"

"I'll be right back," he repeated before scurrying out of the room.

She stretched and looked at his bedside clock. It was eleven o'clock, still morning. It felt like she'd been sleeping for hours. Without the heat of his body the room was frigid; the fire had gone out. She sat up, waiting for John to come back so they could go eat something. She was starving.

For the first time she noticed the telephone on his bedside table. She was wondering if all the boys had their own telephones when he swung the door open and slammed it shut, startling her. "It's Thursday," he said.

She thought about it. "Yes, it's Thursday," she said.

He threw her dress at her and looked for his own clothes. "What's wrong?"

"I missed my biology exam. I forgot about it."

"You forgot?"

He turned away from her and zipped his pants. "It's because I haven't slept in days. I've been thinking about you," he said.

She got out from under the covers, shivering, and put her dress over her head. She tried to fasten the buttons, but her fingers were cold. Before she knew what was happening there were tears falling into her lap. Everything she attempted seemed to end in disappointment. She felt like the world was written in code and she couldn't decipher it. "I wanted you to have a nice birthday," she said. Her voice was scratchy and childlike.

"I was having a nice birthday," he said softly. "Too nice." She was being pitiful, and now he felt the need to be delicate with her.

"I'll call you later," he said. "We'll have dinner. I have to figure out what to do about this exam."

"All right," she said, wiping her eyes and reaching for her shoes. She couldn't help acting this way. Being invited and sent away, both without warning, was a shock to her body and her nerves were firing in all different directions.

She stood up and wished him luck. Once she was out the door, she hurried out of the building and ran back to her room, where she fell into her bed and wept. She had an afternoon class but she didn't go. Even after she had cried enough, she stayed in bed, her mind drifting from one thought to another.

The phone in the hallway rang all afternoon. She got up each time to answer, taking messages for the other girls in her wing and delivering them to their doors. After a while, she realized that her self-pity was an excuse to stay in her room and wait for John to call. Her stomach was growling with hunger and she decided, not without a lot of anguish, to go down to the dining room and eat without him.

She was gone from the room for less than an hour. The phone was ringing again as she returned to her room. More of the girls were back now, opening their doors to get to the phone, but Mariam beat them to it. She picked up the receiver and said hello, triumphantly.

It was John. "Did you eat?" he asked.

"I'm sorry. I was hungry," she said.

"It's all right. I ate too."

"Oh, good," she said, relieved to know they'd both had the same thought.

He asked her to come for a walk, and in ten minutes, she

met him at the Obelisk. They walked from there toward the suspension bridge. He walked quickly, with a purpose. There was a particular spot he wanted to take her to, a rock shelter just off the suspension bridge. They didn't cross the bridge. He veered off before they reached it, onto a hiking path that was smoother than the crumbling rocks on the other side of the gorge. It led to a ridge that ran parallel to the gorge. They walked along it until they had a view of the first waterfall. This was the water they could hear from the bridge, but she had not come far enough to see it before. From there he took her hand and led her down a steep path for a short distance, and before long they were on a wide ledge where the rock had receded into a shallow cave. He took his jacket off and spread it out onto the floor of the cave. "The seating's not very comfortable," he said, and she said it didn't matter. They sat close together on top of his jacket, gazing at the curtain of water ahead of them.

He told her that he'd gone to his biology professor's office and more or less told the truth, that it was his birthday and he'd overslept. He said he would accept a lower grade but could he please take the exam, swearing he was prepared for it. The professor gave him hell. He made him sit down and answer questions orally. He grilled him for an hour on things that weren't on the exam, berating him along the way, and then gave him the written exam.

"Do you think you did all right?" Mariam asked.

"I think so. Who knows?"

"You're not missing another exam right now, are you?"

He smiled. "I'm sure I'm not. Are you?"

"I might be. I haven't gone to classes in weeks."

He laughed. Of course she was only partially joking. Physically she had been present in her classes, but her purpose for being there had eluded her. She was afraid her grades would not be good enough for her to continue at Mount Belet.

As far as this new development with John, she wasn't sure if it would help her focus again or throw her more off balance.

He kissed her cheek timidly. She kissed his lips. She didn't want him to wonder what she wanted. She realized their stalled romance had not been his fault alone. She had not been open about her feelings for him.

"Have you been unhappy here?" he whispered. She said yes, she had been very unhappy.

"I'm so sorry," he said.

When it was getting dark, he walked her back along the ledge and helped her back up the rocky path. They strolled back to her dormitory, as they did the first time they met. He said now that he'd had the birthday he wanted, he could go back to his room and concentrate on studying. "I have to try not to lose my head," he said.

"Me too," said Mariam.

They took their time saying goodnight and parted slowly.

When she got back to her room, Nina was standing by her bed, her arms crossed. "Where have you been? Your mother's been calling." She picked up a notepad from Mariam's bedside table and read from it out loud. "Your mother called. Mother again. Mother, urgent."

"I wasn't gone that long," Mariam said.

"I think something's wrong. You have to call home, now."

Just then the phone rang in the hallway. "I'm sure that's for you," Nina said.

Mariam went out and answered it. It was her mother, just as Nina said it would be. She didn't sound at all like herself. "For God's sake, where have you been? We almost called the police."

"I'm sorry. I was studying. I was only gone an hour or two."

"Your father's had a stroke."

"Is he all right?" Mariam asked. She had not really absorbed what her mother said. She had to repeat the words back to herself, like she did in French, in order to understand. She didn't see how it could be true. He wasn't even fifty. Her mother had told her now and again that he had a weak heart, but she had always understood that more figuratively than literally.

"Your uncle is on his way to pick you up. He'll be driving all night. Don't make him wait."

"I have to come home?"

"Of course you have to come home. Your father's had a stroke."

Mariam hung up the phone and went back to the room. She pulled her suitcase out from under her bed and took an armful of dresses out of her closet.

"What happened?" Nina asked.

"My father's had a stroke," she said, mimicking her mother.

Nina began to help her, taking the dresses off the hangers and folding them carefully.

"Don't pack everything. I'll send you whatever you can't fit," Nina said.

"I'm sure I'm coming back," Mariam said.

"I know. Of course," Nina said, backing away. Mariam looked at her. She seemed nervous and unsure of herself. Mariam wondered if she had guessed what was going on between her and John. She didn't come forward again, and Mariam continued packing on her own.

She didn't know what time her uncle would be arriving. He had been in the army and never lost his military punctuality. Her parents used to joke that he had two speeds, fast and stop. Mariam could never work out his exact connection to her father's family. He was not a blood relative, but he and her father had been very close when they were young. He lived two hours outside of English Canal and about four hours from Mount Belet. He could arrive before midnight.

Mariam wanted to call John, but she couldn't, not with

Nina hovering. She thought better of it anyway. She wanted him to study, to not lose his head. She would be home by morning and would call him from there. As she finished packing, she asked Nina if she would tell John what happened, and say goodbye for her. Nina promised that she would.

"You've been a good friend to me, Nina."

Awkwardly Mariam embraced her. In her life she had not embraced many people. Since childhood, perhaps no one but her mother, and John. It wasn't the contact that was difficult as much as the anticipation of parting. Nina held on to Mariam's hands, her head lowered, her eyes downcast. "I knew what he meant to you," she whispered. "I'm sorry, Mariam."

"You have nothing to be sorry about."

Her uncle arrived around midnight, demanding a swift exit as he heaved the suitcase off the bed. "Is this all you packed?" he asked. He carried it out without waiting for an answer.

"He looks like a barrel of laughs," Nina said.

Mariam smiled. She looked at her bed, wondering if she would ever see this room again. Her mother would not have called her home for something temporary.

When she was home, and saw the condition of her father and her mother, she knew she was never going to return to Mount Belet. She couldn't get a minute alone to call John. She needed to be in the right mindset, now that she understood how final her goodbye would be. By the time she could call, it was already late afternoon. There was no answer. She wondered if Nina had already told him. Maybe she had gone to him last night, and stayed until the morning.

But in a few days she received a letter from him. He said he hadn't believed Nina when she told him what happened. He said he couldn't recognize himself in the mirror. She had taken pieces of him with her, and he wanted to know when she would return them.

Mariam wrote him back a letter describing her father's con-

dition in detail, so that he could understand the impossibility
of her return to Mount Belet.

After many weeks went by, she had to admit a sense of relief
at being home. She was where she belonged, no longer having
to fit into an alien society. And she had no idea if John would
have been constant in his attention if she had remained at
Mount Belet. Now there was a rhythmic predictability to his
letters, and she didn't have to worry about what he wanted and
how fast she could give it to him.

Not that it was easy by any means to watch her mother working so hard, to know her father was trapped in his body, with
memories and feelings and maybe even a full comprehension of
language but no means of communicating. Once, when she was
trying to get him to take a spoonful of broth, she said to him, "I
would never have wished this upon you." She had been wondering if he remembered how they were together, if he feared
her ill will or thought her incapable of sympathy toward him.
His lips moved very slightly. She put the spoon to his mouth
and he sipped the broth, looking grateful as he swallowed.

Only sometimes she felt equally sorry for her mother.
Sometimes she thought that if things had worked out the way
he'd wanted, it would be Elizabeth taking care of him now, not
Mama, and that irony seemed very cruel to her.

In a few months, her mother had his care well in hand, as if
she'd been doing this all her life. She gave Mariam a few of the
easier chores, at Mariam's insistence. It would have been useful for her to learn how to drive so she could take her father to
his various appointments, but there was no time for that and
the money they got from selling his car helped pay for some of
his treatment. The real reason for her coming home was clear
only after many months. She needed to get a job. Her father
started receiving a pension, but it didn't come close to replac-
ing his salary.

She was lucky to find a job at the college library a few miles from her house. She did well there and they told her she could earn a library science certificate in one year while she worked. Once she got her certificate, she would be promoted, and then the money would be decent. Mariam thought it was an excellent opportunity. Her mother was more somber about it. It wasn't what she'd had in mind for Mariam's education. "You'll continue your education as soon as we can manage it."

"At least I'll be in a scholarly environment," Mariam said, trying to get her mother to see the bright side. She was lucky to get a job at the college at all. "I can take other classes later."

Mama didn't look convinced. "I suppose there's a chance. I was younger than you when I went to work. I had dreams of being a scholar once. Can you imagine?"

"Couldn't you go to school in Germany?" Mariam asked. Her mother was only sixteen when they left, surely young enough for high school in Germany.

"How? We left with nothing. We had to take whatever work we could find to survive."

Mariam wanted to know more. It was rare for her mother to talk about Germany, aside from her father's courtship there. She spoke about that with a somewhat pitiful nostalgia. Mariam asked her what work they did, and she was surprised to hear that her grandmother had worked in a sewing factory, that even Mama had worked there for a short while. "Your grandfather had to work in an aluminum factory."

Mariam was shocked. "An aluminum factory? That must have been so difficult for him." Here her grandfather had been a lawyer, quite a well-known one from what her mother told her. Mariam never knew the exact reason they fled the country so suddenly, and why they went to Germany, to a place where the scars of war must have been so visible. Now, hearing all this talk of factories, she wondered if Germany's borders were open because of labor shortages.

"Luckily I was able to get a better job," her mother went on. "I was very pretty, you know, and my German was excellent." For the first time in months, her mother allowed herself a little vanity and smiled. She seemed to have forgotten the point she was trying to make about her education. Mariam thought it was a strange coincidence that both of their educations had come to such an abrupt halt. For how many generations had that happened to the girls in her family? Mariam wanted her mother to know that she wouldn't give up.

Mama seemed pleased. "Good girl. Don't make the same mistake I did."

Her mother went on to say something that puzzled Mariam. "Don't pin your hopes on a romance. They never get you anywhere." She didn't know if Mama was trying to draw some analogy to her situation with John. She thought she'd been discreet about him. Sometimes she kept his letter sitting in the mail pile for hours, as if she was in no hurry to read it, and Mama had never shown any curiosity about his letters. Mariam concluded that her mother was speaking only of herself, still pondering her aborted education.

At the college library, Mariam found her calling. After she earned her certificate, she was put on the research floor, where she displayed a certain intuitive gift for developing a productive chain of resources, regardless of the discipline. Her main task was to take research requests from the patrons and draw up lists of sources with the pertinent information that would likely be found in them. She was like the spinner at a spinning wheel, thinning the rough tangles of information into a fine workable thread. She always did a thorough job and won praise for it, and as she handed over her findings there was often a look of tender gratitude, as if the recipient had momentarily fallen in love with her. If she had stayed at Mount Belet, her gift would never have flourished. She would have strived like the others toward higher levels of academic thought and she would have failed.

She expected at any time that the letters from John would become less frequent and die off, but they kept coming. They had a feverish quality, as if writing to her was a compulsion he couldn't control. Though he never mentioned other girls, she could read between the lines. When he said things like, "A few of us went swimming in the gorge," she imagined his hand on some girl's naked thigh. It was confusing to her, of course, but it would have been absurd for him to make any promises. She herself had no idea what they were to each other. They were everything and nothing to each other. That was the only way for her to understand it.

It went on like this for a long time. He said he sometimes needed to hear her voice and he began to call her late in the evenings after dinner, infrequently but enough to cause her mother to disapprove. She asked Mariam to finally explain the nature of their relationship. Mariam couldn't.

"I don't like that, Mariam. Why should it be so complicated?"

"Because I'm here and he's there."

"So what? Is he courting you?"

Mariam laughed. "No, Mother. No one does that anymore."

Mama was annoyed. "It wakes your father when he calls. You'll have to tell him to call at a different time."

Mariam said she would tell him. "We're just friends, Mama. Try not to worry."

"Maybe there are young men here who would like to be your friend."

"I don't see them knocking down our door," Mariam said.

"Well, obviously you have to show some interest."

The truth was that she was asked out on a few occasions, invitations that she declined as politely as she could. The more suitable the boy seemed, the more she resisted. She felt it was unkind to lead someone along unless she could resolutely say nothing would go further between her and John. To go out with someone now would make her feel unfaithful, both to John and to the other one. And most of the time, the men who pursued her were not suitable. They were married, or old, or disgusting in some way.

For instance, there was a widower who had been trying to make conversation with her at the tram stop on College Street. Even though his wife was barely cold in the ground he appeared every day until Mariam began to suspect that he was following her. He was courteous, though obviously stricken with lust. She shrugged him off until one day she was in a bad mood, growing impatient with John's stalling. Somehow a decision had been made that they would not see each other until he graduated from Mount Belet. She didn't recall having any part in the decision-making. He simply announced that he would come and see her when he graduated, implying that he would not see her anytime before that. His graduation was still a year away. She wasn't even ready to see him again, but she felt, as probably her mother had feared, that she was being used and taken for granted.

So this widower had caught her at an opportune moment. After a few conversations in which he paid little attention to her dull answers to his dull questions, he confessed his undying devotion. She had allowed it because she was finally ready to be done with her virginity, and this man, perhaps in his early forties, was not horrible to look at. Above all he persisted. He endured. He asked her out for coffee. As they drank their coffee he asked her out to dinner. She said, "If you want to sleep with me we can do it now." He might have wanted more from her but in his position, who could blame him for taking what he could?

"Do you have condoms? I'm not getting pregnant."

"No," he said. What he had were four children. They were all at his mother's house, leaving his own house temporarily available.

"Fine. I'll get them and meet you." She had been observing how to do this, in case she ever needed them. They were behind the counter at the pharmacy. She would have to ask for a box and risk being shamed with a look or, worse, a prying question, but it was perfectly legal for her to purchase them.

"You have to be quick. The children are back at eight."

She picked up the condoms at the pharmacy without making eye contact with anyone and met the widower at his house. She passed through it into his bedroom, took her clothes off, got on her back, closed her eyes and let him stroke her and rub his bearded face all over her breasts. He graciously put the condom on and stuck her with his cock a few times, indelicately, efficiently, and it was done, her ponderous virginity shed at last.

She thanked him.

"When can I see you again?" he asked.

"We can't see each other again. You've been a perfect gentleman, but you have to forget about me."

He didn't give her any trouble. She got the sense all of this was too much for him. She said goodbye and rushed home to write a letter to John, the only one who needed to know. In the letter, she all but came out and asked him what his intentions were. She knew he never wanted her to save herself for him. He hinted often that she shouldn't shy away from certain experiences. Like that crazy boy, Vic, he apparently had no interest in sex with virgins. She was convinced this news would change something for them. It would be unexpected, something to rattle him out of his complacency.

John called her when he got the letter. He asked her if she was all right and Mariam began to cry. She had no idea losing her virginity would make her so sad.

FOUR

After graduation, John decided not to delay his military service. It was hard to tell Mariam that he would spend the summer with his family in Alexandria and start his training in August. They had talked about seeing each other in June, but they had not decided if he would travel to English Canal or if she would come to Alexandria. He knew the time had come for this to end. They had to meet, and either consummate their relationship or allow each other to fall short, to be who they were and not who the other imagined, and finally let their paths diverge. All they needed were a few days, but as soon as he got home and thought of making the arrangements his heart knotted up. He wasn't ready and the summer passed quickly. He called and told her he just needed to get his military service out of the way. It was all he could think about.

Mariam sounded weary. "Are you trying to avoid making a decision about me, John?"

It was a fair question he didn't know how to answer. "Have you made a decision about me?"

She didn't answer him either.

The morning before he was to leave for his training he escaped from the house and went to the call center. Because his parents and his little sister were always hovering around him he could barely get time alone to write a letter, much less have a private conversation. They would want her to be explained, Mariam, who couldn't be explained.

"Are calls to English Canal going through?" he asked the

clerk, who told him no one had tried yet that morning. He tried, but his call did not go through. He went home to finish packing. The last thing he packed was the compass she had given him on his nineteenth birthday. Every time he held the compass he remembered that morning, how he had asked for her, knowing she would come.

The compass was always cold. It made his palm ache. He only wanted to handle it when he packed it, yet he always packed it. He wouldn't dream of leaving it behind.

From the training camp he wrote her two or three times a week to keep her from worrying. He described the monotony of his days. The morning siren sounded at five, followed by a bunk inspection, company formation, and a five-mile run before breakfast, then three hours of physical conditioning, infantry school, and weapons maintenance. Lunch. Afternoon training varied from day to day, ranging from moral education lectures to poison gas simulation, team challenges, dinner, barrack and camp chores, and finally an hour of personal time before lights went out. It was a kind of managed hardship, unpleasant in the moment but not without its rewards, and made easier by its well-defined duration. During the physical conditioning, when he felt like his lungs were going to cave in, he thought about his body getting stronger, about the human body and its evolution, its beauty, and he welcomed the exhaustion at the end of each day. It was an orderly and dispassionate regimen, with none of the warmongering Mariam had feared. He told Mariam he was unlearning a lifetime of self-serving individualism, that this was an important part of becoming a man. He wanted her to understand this, but in three weeks he didn't get a single letter in return. Her silence was alarming. He was going to give up his one weekly phone call to get in touch with her, instead of his parents, but before he got the chance he was called in to see Staff Sergeant

Abraham, a man built like a silverback gorilla, with eyes too close together on a broad, flat face. The staff sergeant told him to sit down. He held a manila envelope, its bottom bulging. He began by saying the commanding officers had praised John for his discipline, and John thanked him for the compliment, thinking this must have been a routine evaluation. The fact that they had noticed his ability to stay collected and alert under pressure filled him with some measure of pride.

He kept glancing at the manila envelope, which Abraham now tapped with two fingers.

"You have a most ardent admirer," he said, smiling with one end of his mouth. He widened the opening of the envelope and let John have a glance at the contents. Little white envelopes, Mariam's envelopes.

"I wasn't aware that you screened letters, sir."

"Only if there's a cause."

"Have I done something wrong? I thought I was allowed to receive letters here."

Abraham leaned back in his chair. "Do you know anything about this girl's family?"

John didn't know if this was a real question. He didn't want to answer. "I don't understand."

"Do you know anything about her province? About her people?"

That seemed like an entirely different question. "I've never been to Sulat, if that's what you're asking."

"This girl's grandfather was a radical. He was a socialist and a separatist."

"Was he?" John asked. He knew immediately he'd made a mistake. It sounded snide, like a challenge. Abraham squinted, his eyes becoming oblong slits. "I didn't know that," John clarified. "But I've never heard her talk about her grandfather. Did she write something about him in her letters? I would be surprised by that, if you don't mind my saying, sir." John was nervous.

He told himself to keep quiet before he said something that got either of them in trouble. He wondered if they had intercepted his letters as well, if she had received any of them. If she had not received a single letter from him, he was afraid she would give up on him completely.

Abraham couldn't get off the subject of Mariam's grandfather. "He started a war and left the country. He left the mess for the rest of us to clean up. It was a savage rebellion in Sulat. Didn't they teach you anything about it in school?"

"A little," John said.

"You would be a good candidate for a posting in the militarized zone. Do you know where that is?" Abraham asked.

John swallowed, his throat tightening. "Northern Sulat?"

"We send our best reserves there. Would you like to be posted there? Close to your sweetheart?"

"Are you saying that's where I'm being posted?"

"I don't know where you're going to be posted. I'm only asking a question. Tell me truthfully."

"I would prefer not to go to the militarized zone."

"Why not?"

"Because it's militarized. I'd rather serve in a different capacity."

Abraham chuckled. "What exactly do you think the militia does? Give out blankets? Your job is to maintain order. You'll do that wherever we tell you to do it."

"I understand."

"But I don't blame you. I wouldn't want to go that shithole either."

Abraham dismissed him, throwing the manila envelope into a pile. John stood up and saluted, but before he reached the door he turned around. "Is there any chance I can have the letters, sir?"

"I don't have the authority to give you the letters. They go to Document Review."

John stood there until Abraham looked up, visibly irritated. "I said you're dismissed."

As he walked back to the barracks, he tried to make sense of the meeting. He had not expected, in return for his loyalty and outstanding performance, to be subject to secret surveillance and veiled threats. He was certain he was being sent to Northern Sulat. Lately the reserves had been talking about the best and worst assignments. There were a few places no one in their right minds wanted to go. The militarized zone was one of them. They said if you were sent to Northern Sulat, you were technically at war. The militia was getting blown up there all the time.

He wasn't allowed to call Mariam until Sunday. He was afraid she would be at work and he would somehow have to give her mother a message. Her mother never said anything to him besides hello but still he was terrified of her. He managed to catch Mariam just as she was leaving for work. He told her quickly there was a problem with the mail service and she shouldn't send any more letters until he was settled at his post. She didn't have time to ask any questions. He wasn't able to find out if she'd received any of his letters.

The morning he was to be given his assignment, he went into the latrine and threw up. No one at his table could eat their breakfast. They had to look for their names on a list pinned to a wall inside their barracks, in the same way some of his professors at Mount Belet posted their scores after an exam. John almost cried when he saw his assignment, a post in the Golpat Desert on the eastern border. The other reserves teased him mercilessly, saying vulgar things about his sisters, saying they must have sucked Abraham's cock to get him such an easy assignment.

* * *

Despite all of his communication, Mariam couldn't say she had a sense of how John was doing. In his letters, he kept saying how good it felt to be pushed beyond his limits, as if he'd been training for the Olympics. Then there was his strange phone call on a Sunday only to say that there was a delay in the mail service. These days she was hardly at home on Sundays.

All summer, it had been rumored that the library was about to acquire a large collection of documents from the War Crimes Commission. Currently they were housed at the Governor's Office until their rightful home could be determined. Mariam followed the story closely. She had never witnessed an archival acquisition and was interested in the process, and she wanted to see the documents. She was too afraid to approach the head of research about it, so she asked her friend Misha if she had heard anything.

"It isn't official yet," Misha said. "It's all politics, you know, but this is the most neutral place, unless they send the papers abroad. To Geneva or some place like that."

"Are they considering that?" Mariam asked.

Misha smiled. "Of course not. Why would Geneva want them? You're so simple, Mariam."

Misha enjoyed telling Mariam how simple she was. Mariam was sure it was meant to be a compliment, or at the very worst a benign sort of teasing. She laughed agreeably and went on with her investigation.

"Have you ever seen a collection like this come in? Will we be cataloguing them or is that already done?"

"It's all a big mess, from what I hear. Why? Are you interested in cataloguing?"

"Yes, I think so."

"I can pass your name on. You'd be good at it. I for one don't want to do it. It's so bleak."

A few days later Misha came to Mariam with a stack of bound papers—*Rules for Archival Description, Volumes I, II, and III*. "It's official," she said. "Here's some bedtime reading." There were six hundred and seventy-five pages.

She had to be interviewed, but the head of research already liked her and Mariam had no trouble conveying her enthusiasm for the project. Then there was a two-week training, including background on the War Crimes Commission and how they collected their documents. The training was in part to teach the rules of archival description, which they practiced with a number of dummy documents, but it was also to build an overall context for the project, to give them a sense of its purpose. The most important thing was to give each document equal weight. Every testimony had to be searchable and navigable, and the archivist had to relinquish all preconceptions, all opinions about the war and become completely objective. These documents would reveal the truth of this war for many years to come and had to be catalogued exquisitely.

She couldn't write anything about this in her letters to John. Besides the fact that she had signed an oath of confidentiality, it seemed unwise to write letters to a military camp about her cataloguing of war crimes. Her letters were as mundane as ever, and she kept writing them even after he told her to wait until he knew where he was posted.

After her training, she was given a study room dedicated to her documents. She had to keep the documents locked up and discuss them with no one but the project supervisor until the archives were on the shelves. It was a tiny room, with one small work desk and a wall lined with shelves and boxes. A ceiling lamp flooded the room with yellow light, but if the door was closed and the light switched off, the space filled with an interminable blackness.

At first she thought she was going too slowly. Each item required several levels of description, and she found it impossible to follow the content of the document and fulfill the myriad descriptive tasks at the same time. She had to read each document many times, more than anyone else, she imagined, because she was so worried about the procedure. In those first few weeks, troubled by the mechanics of archival description, she absorbed little of the war itself. It was months before she noticed that in her waking hours she was constantly interacting with two worlds, the one that was moving in front of her eyes, and the one in her head, looping like images from a slide projector. She saw students reading in their carrels, and she saw people exhumed from concrete burials whose skin and clothing were covered in limestone dust. She saw Misha gossiping with the girls on the reference floor, and soldiers raping women and throwing them into the canal to drown. She saw military squads racing each other to execute whole neighborhoods of people. They were rewarded for clearing neighborhoods, these boys in uniform who were ordered to wander like bands of marauders, and when they were older, if they survived, they had to face the monsters they once were. Mariam imagined the dour court reporter transcribing hours of testimony, and witnesses answering endless questions about one incident in front of a panel of people whose stake in the truth was unknown. Sometimes she thought these efforts at documentation could elevate human consciousness and put an end to all war. Then she remembered how big the world was, how pregnant it was with war at every moment. This was not the first attempt to understand a war, and none of the historical mining of previous wars had prevented this one.

If she was already in a fragile emotional state, it was best for her to avoid the work that day. After a while, she found it soothing to stand in the room with the light switched off, to let the darkness envelop her, before reentering a world that was so strangely ignorant of what she had just learned.

* * *

John enjoyed the eighteen-hour train journey to his desert post. For the first time in six weeks, he wasn't surrounded by reserves and had time to think about other things besides drills and postings. He had never been this far south and he stared out the window at the ever-changing landscape. There were mountains dramatically eroding, their slopes left chipped and shredded. The landscape appeared all but barren, but there were a few unexpected pockets of life, grasses tufting up from fissures in the rock and purple, heathery shrubs surrounded by herds of mountain goats bleating at the passing train.

They got stuck in a tunnel for a few hours. He fell asleep and woke up as the train staggered forward and they emerged from the tunnel to see the sun flashing off crystalline specks on the rock face. The terrain eventually became more feminine, less angular as they traveled further east. When it was too dark to see anything more out the window, he fell asleep again and was awakened by the train conductor. He had to get off the train and walk a few yards away from the platform to meet another reserve like him standing by a military jeep. The kid was talkative. He said the desert was boring as hell. He dropped John off in the middle of the night near an aluminum shack and said, "That's your barrack. Good luck." Next to the shack, there was a man sleeping by a dying campfire.

John turned on his flashlight and went into the shack. There was no one in there and he didn't know which of the four bunks was his. He went back outside, threw more kindling into the fire and crouched down in the sand until the fire died again. He looked around in all directions into the darkness that went on and on. Then he wrapped himself in his sleeping bag and lay down on his back, looking up for the first time to see the infinite sky dense with stars, the whole universe bearing down on him.

In the morning he found out the other man sleeping next to the fire was named Sherod. Sherod was a twenty-nine-year-old cook. All through his twenties Sherod had looked for ways to avoid his military service. He thought he'd be long gone from the country by his thirtieth birthday, but things did not work out and here he was, avoiding a prison sentence. He was a fan of American westerns and especially the famous actor John Wayne. Sherod tried to say John's name with an exaggerated American accent but he could only achieve it by sneering and talking through his nose. "Jaaaan," was how it sounded. When they weren't at their posts Sherod drank. Every time he drove into the nearest town for provisions, he mailed letters for John and brought back cheap bottles of moonshine. It burned like acid and John, much to Sherod's relief, did not drink much of it. They shared the shack with the two night sentries, Tamer and Nasir, whom Sherod strangely nicknamed Flaco and Gordo after some Mexican characters in a western movie he'd seen. Flaco was the thin one, and Gordo a bit fatter though still skinny, and John did not actually know which was Tamer and which was Nasir, but John only ever saw them when they were changing shifts.

At their posts they were supposed to inspect trucks and other vehicles heading to and from the border, but there was little traffic here, with one road slicing a hundred miles of desert in half. John was given the watchtower, from which he could see for miles the stillness of the desert. On most days the only vehicles that passed were military or commercial trucks with permits to pass through their checkpoint. The few unauthorized vehicles Sherod did intercept were let go with a small bribe and permits that he had forged through a friend. Sometimes Sherod would radio the next checkpoint twenty miles away and tell them to look out for a truck with a false license plate number. Of course that truck would never appear, and just talking about them waiting for it entertained him for hours.

One morning, before dawn, John heard gunfire and ran from the shack to find Sherod standing over a dead goat. The goat must have fallen off one of the transport trucks and wandered over from the road. Sherod had come upon the little creature bleating mournfully and decided to put him out of his misery.

It took all day but they skinned and cleaned the animal and dug a pit, and then roasted him right there in a makeshift oven they dug in the sand. Flaco and Gordo abandoned their posts for the feast, and after they ate they sat outside the shack drinking, chain-smoking, stargazing, and conversing. Flaco and Gordo were young, both eighteen. They didn't seem to know what to make of John. They had never traveled far from their rural homes and had never met someone born and raised in Alexandria. They asked him many questions, which he answered with great care, feeling tremendous pressure to represent the city realistically. He tried to tell them that even he, having grown up in Alexandria, didn't know everything about life there. He only knew about the life that had been handed to him. Undaunted by John's vague answers, they kept up their questioning.

"Are the girls in Alexandria pretty?" Flaco asked.

Sherod balked. "Idiot! There are millions of girls in Alexandria. How can they all be pretty?"

"But in general," Flaco said, standing firm. "Girls from there are prettier."

Sherod laughed. "How would you know?"

"The girls at home look like bulls," Gordo said.

Flaco was not one to be thrown off course. "Do you have a girl? Do you have a picture of your girl?"

"He has a girl," Sherod said. He grinned and winked. "He sends her letters. She gave him a pocket watch."

"It's not a pocket watch," John said.

"Whatever it is, he plays with it at night."

Flaco and Gordo were curious. "Let's see a picture. Is she sexy? She must be sexy."

"I don't have a picture," John said. None of them could

understand why. He couldn't explain how it never occurred to him to ask her for one. And it wasn't as if Mariam had spent the last three years snapping pictures of herself. "Anyway, she isn't from Alexandria."

Flaco and Gordo didn't care. "What does she look like? Tell us."

John tried to describe her, the gold flecks in her eyes, and her silky hair, how the ends of it curled just a little at her shoulders. They looked disappointed.

"What about her tits?"

John said he didn't want to describe Mariam's "tits." They were all silent for a moment. Then Sherod had a revelation.

"He hasn't seen them! You haven't seen them, have you?"

The three of them fell over laughing. John took the ridicule, happy to let that be the end of it. In the morning when they were all hungover, only he seemed to remember anything they talked about.

Sherod had already been in the desert for six months when John arrived, and after three more his military service reached its successful conclusion. He would go home and celebrate his thirtieth birthday. On his last night the four of them drove to the nearest town twenty miles away and drank until they couldn't see straight. John woke up in the middle of the night next to a girl who looked too young to be on her own, a girl he didn't remember meeting, and he went down to the street looking for his companions. He walked up and down the street several times, but figuring he'd been ditched he walked into a pub that was still open and asked if there was a telephone he could use. There was one in the back, the bartender said, but it didn't always work, and they would charge him regardless of whether or not the call went through. They agreed on a cash amount, which John somehow put together with bills tucked inside his socks, before he stumbled to the telephone hanging on the wall in a back corridor. He had no idea what time it was. He dialed Mariam's number. It only rang once before she answered. He said he was sorry for calling so late and he didn't have much time so he had to get right to the point. "Are you awake?" he asked her.

"I'm awake. Are you all right?"

"You haven't written any more letters, have you?"

"I haven't sent them. I was waiting for you to tell me where you are."

"I'm in the desert. Miles from anywhere. The sky at night . . . Mariam . . . I wish we could lie under it."

"Where in the desert? Are you drunk?"

He straightened up, hoping a more sober posture would improve his speech. "I miss you, Mariam. They took your letters."

"What do you mean?"

"They took your letters away from me. I didn't get to read them."

"They took them? You said there was a delay."

"It was a bad delay," he said. He told her to hold on a minute and dropped the receiver. He went to the bar to ask someone to write down the name and address of the pub.

He hurried back to the phone. "You can write to me at this pub. I'll tell them to hold the letter." He read the address to her several times, thinking each time he'd made a mistake. "You got it?"

"I think so."

"It'll get here. There's nothing else . . ." He was going to say in the vicinity but there were too many syllables.

"John, you don't sound all right."

"I've been drinking because it's Sherod's last night and tomorrow he's going home. I liked him so much. He was like a friend to me."

"I'm glad you found a friend."

"I want to see you, Mariam." He hoped he sounded more like himself. "Are you still there?"

"I'm here."

"I'm going to marry you."

"John, stop."

"I love you, Mariam. I do. When the time is right I'm going to come and marry you."

She laughed. "When will that be? When I'm eighty?"

He could see Mariam as an old lady, frail and beautiful with her gray hair in a bun. "When we're eighty we'll live by the sea," he said. "Then we'll get into a little boat and float away."

"You're drunk," she said.

Someone called out that the pub was closing. "I have to go, Mariam."

"All right. Will you remember any of this tomorrow?"

He thought she was being funny. "Why wouldn't I?" The bartender told him he'd owe more money if he didn't hang up. "I have to go now. I have to go."

After he hung up he realized she hadn't said goodbye. Neither had he, for that matter. He wanted to call her back, but the bartender had begun tossing stragglers out by their collars. John sidestepped him and ran out the door.

At the end of the street, he found Sherod, Flaco and Gordo, each as drunk as the other, and they celebrated heartily at their reunion. Eventually their conversation turned to making their way back. The plan was for Sherod to drop Flaco and Gordo back at their posts, then go back to the shack and pack for his departure. They almost made it, but in the headlights, as they approached the watchtower, they saw a Military Police truck parked on the roadside. "Shit, shit," they said. "We should run. We should keep driving."

"Let me do the talking," Sherod said.

The MP came up to their jeep, staring into the backseat at Flaco and Gordo, who were supposed to be on duty. "Can you two goatfuckers tell me why these posts are abandoned?"

"It's my fault," Sherod said. "It's my last night. Really my service ended as of midnight, but I'm not shipping out until the morning."

"Did you order these men to leave their posts?"

"No, no," they all objected. "It wasn't like that."

They had to exit the jeep and get on their knees,. Their wrists and ankles were shackled and the four of them were thrown into the back of the MP truck. As they sobered up they each shared stories of their night, what they could remember of it.

Finally, Sherod said, "I'm sorry. This is all my fault."

They all balked. Gordo said, "It was worth it, for me."

"I'll get you out of this," Sherod promised as he was pulled off the truck. By then they were all sober, and Flaco was crying.

"Stop crying," Gordo said. "Do you know what they'll do to you if you cry?"

As far as John knew, they were all put in the hole for a week of solitary confinement, but since he never saw any of them again he couldn't be sure. After his solitary, he was given an extra three weeks of service penalty and transferred to a new post. John didn't know where he was being sent. He was put in the back of a transport jeep that traveled steadily for about two hours. He was convinced again that he was heading for Northern Sulat, but he was let off in front of some barracks marked with a sign that said Menud Fort, and John suddenly wished he'd been sent to Sulat. Menud Fort was a military prison, another one of the assignments all of the reserves had feared. The only reason to be there was to learn advanced interrogation methods. To become a torturer.

He was lucky, then, to only be given transport duty, driving detainees from various points to the facility. He never saw the inside of the prison and never had to handle the prisoners himself. All he did was drive, let the checkpoint guards open the back of the truck, and drive away. He never stayed to watch the struggle behind the prison gates. There was always a struggle. To get a detainee behind the gate, he either had to be outnumbered or unconscious.

He tried to write to Mariam as soon as he was transferred, but the only thing he could think to write about was the prison, the monster in the middle of the desert, and the men he sacrificed to it.

* * *

The letter she wrote to the pub came back to her unopened. She'd written it on a single sheet of onionskin paper, late at night with her impulses firing, her handwriting so small it was perhaps not even readable. By the end it was overflowing with lovesick entreaties. *Every day I think only of you and wait and wait and wait.*

When the letter came back, she called his house in Alexandria. His mother answered. Not knowing what to say, Mariam asked if John was home, and of course his mother said, "He's finishing his service. He won't be home until summer."

"And he's all right?" Mariam asked.

"He's doing fine. Who is this?"

"It's Mariam."

"Mariam?"

"Yes."

"A friend from school?"

"Yes, from school."

"Call back in the summer. You can speak to him then. Or I can tell him you rang. He calls on Sundays." She didn't wait to hear what Mariam wanted before she hung up.

At least he was all right, she told herself. But in her heart she knew what was happening. She knew that she was being forgotten. She was thankful to be so busy, though sometimes at night she couldn't sleep and she wanted to know that her whole life would not be like this. That John, or someone else she could love, would help her sleep.

One morning, Mariam and her mother were drinking coffee before the sun came up, as had become their private ritual. Mariam was silent that morning, preoccupied with a transcript of testimonials about a bombing in the south, in Belarive where her mother had grown up, in which a school with sixty-three children inside was leveled to the ground. Forty of the children died, many were maimed, some escaped with no injuries, and three of them, mysteriously, were never found. Most of the testimony dealt with the intent, whether the bombing was accidental or part of a military strategy targeting civilians. The commanders of the operation said they'd received deliberately misleading intelligence that the building no longer operated as a school but as a rebel base. They swore under oath that the rebels knew the attack was coming and did nothing, that they had sacrificed their own children for their immoral crusade. Mariam wanted to ask her mother about the school. She would have been in Germany already but she must have known some of the children's families. She must have heard about the bombing from her family that was left behind. Mariam wanted to talk about it, to get it off her mind, but she had signed an oath and didn't want to betray it, even to her mother, who would not have told anyone of importance.

Mariam broke her silence. "Do you know what I've been thinking about lately? Our trip to Belarive when I was little."

Mama smiled. "How can you remember that?"

Mariam did remember it clearly, even the train ride. For a long time there was nothing but fields of grass and wheat, then hills and streams, made by God, her mother said, unlike the canal, which men had built. They had seen storm clouds in the distance and Mariam knew there would be rain before the rain came down, and this delighted her, the possibility of knowing what would come before it happened. She and Mama curled up on the cot and slept through the downpour and then woke up at Kasbah Station, to the melodic call of the *fajr* prayer. It came over a loudspeaker from the mosque near the station, and Mama told her about the minarets, the tall towers from which the imams would call out the prayers in the olden days. The platform of Kasbah Station filled with men who kneeled and bowed in unison. Later that morning, they pulled into Belarive, still in ruins ten years after the war, the ground strewn with rubble that had tumbled from the now skeletal buildings. But Mariam had not seen destruction. She saw a happy lot of children who had climbed a mountain of rubble. They were at the summit, jumping up and down and waving to the train, and Mariam had waved back, wanting nothing more than to join those children on that mountain. Now she wondered if that had been the remains of the school.

"I should never have taken you there," Mama said. "I wanted to see my family, but everyone had changed. It seemed we could never understand each other again, the ones who lived through the war and the ones who didn't. The only thing that mattered was that I had left."

"That wasn't up to you. They couldn't have blamed you for it."

"Maybe they didn't. But nothing was as I remembered it. It was a difficult time for me, Mariam. I thought it would help me to go home." Mama shook her head. "It didn't help at all."

Mariam remembered that her father had not accompanied them. It was Mariam and Mama alone, and they stayed in a large house run by her great-uncle, her grandmother's brother, a house where many people lived, though none of them children Mariam's age. The house was so large she sometimes lost her mother in it. She would walk through the house crying until Mama was found. In her memory the house was a cement box, bare and cold, with little furniture and everyone sitting in chairs pushed against the walls, as if the rooms had been cleared for a party that never began. Her mother was sad, her smile artificial and discomfiting, and Mariam had been afraid of being left there forever. It was probably only a week before they took the train home to an empty house.

"It must be better now," Mariam said. "We should go back. I'd like to meet my family again now that I'm older." Her uncle died some years ago but her mother still kept in touch with her cousins. Sometimes Mariam heard her laughing on the phone with one of them.

Mama didn't jump at the idea. "Go and get ready," she said. "You'll be late for work."

As Mariam was getting ready in her room, she looked up and saw Mama standing at her door. She was clutching a framed photograph. "If you have a few minutes, there's something I want to show you."

"I have time," Mariam said.

Mama entered cautiously and sat down on the bed, asking Mariam to come and sit next to her. She showed her what she had carried in. It was her grandparents' wedding picture, which had always been in its frame atop a tall bureau in her parents' old bedroom next door, the room they abandoned after her father's stroke.

"Do you remember this photo?"

"Yes," Mariam said, but she had never looked at it this closely. Her grandmother was beautiful, wearing a white dress with a high neck and long sleeves, her hair covered by a lace veil, and her grandfather was equally handsome. She could just make out the traditional embroidery of his white wedding shirt. Their expressions were somber in the way of all old photographs but there was some confidence, some brightness in their eyes. It was still a joyous photograph, as if they were assured of their happiness and the happiness of their children.

"This is your grandmother. She wore hijab," Mama reminded her. "Do you remember one time I showed you a picture and you asked if she was a nun?"

Mariam did remember. She remembered how it had made her mother laugh, just like she was laughing now. It was a perfectly reasonable question at the time. No one in English Canal wore hijab, and she had only seen nuns cover their hair. She knew her grandmother gave it up in Germany, maybe out of fear or shame. She knew a fair bit about her grandmother, come to think of it, little things Mama had told her over the years. She knew her grandmother was very intelligent, though not highly educated. She was a lover of card games, and ruthlessly competitive at them. It was the only time she raised her voice, playing card games. And Mariam knew some of her dishes, which Mama struggled to replicate. She knew she died shortly after Mama's own wedding.

"This is your grandfather, Suleiman Momin," Mama said, pointing to him. She paused and took a long breath. When she spoke again her voice was airy and weak. "He died when I was seventeen. We hadn't been in Germany a year. He hanged himself in the middle of the night."

"I'm so sorry, Mama. I didn't know." This had been her mother's war, and she had lived it for a long time.

Her mother clasped her hand. "These last few weeks, I see a change in you, Mariam. You're so grown up all of a sudden. I've wanted to tell you this for a long time, but I never knew the right time."

Mariam smiled. "This is the right time, Mama. I'm glad you told me."

"To tell you the truth, I never wanted to come back here. Your father wanted it. He said he wanted to restore order and beauty to his true home."

"Beautiful infrastructure," Mariam said.

"Yes," her mother said, surprised to hear Mariam repeat

her father's phrase. "I didn't agree to come for him. It was for my own father. If he were alive it would have meant so much to him, to know it was possible to come back. But coming back doesn't heal anything, Mariam. It causes new wounds."

"You were a good daughter," Mariam said, but Suleiman Momin had relinquished his right to a dutiful daughter. Therefore, Mama had done it thanklessly, on behalf of the dead.

One day, at work in the document room, she saw her grandfather's name as a subject heading in the index of a newspaper that was no longer printed—Momin, Suleiman—and it looked so uncanny to her, as if he had been waiting for her to discover him there. She looked up each reference and printed a small collection of microfiche articles, which she arranged in chronological order to piece together a frame of a narrative. The early articles were about his work as a lawyer. He had argued an important case that had moved through the provincial high courts, attempting to overturn a ban on the niqab, the veil some Muslim women wore to cover their faces in public. Her grandfather said the ban would further segregate the province into Catholic and Muslim ghettos, setting neighbors who had lived side by side for years against each other. Another set of articles was about his involvement in the New Sulat Democratic Party, the NSDP, a party of social democrats whose chairman was Peter Moses, a Catholic. There was a photograph of her grandfather and Peter Moses talking to each other at a podium. According to the caption, Peter Moses was about to deliver a speech to a crowd of ten thousand on the occasion of the prime minister's visit. In his speech he compared the prime minister to other foreign interlopers, the English, the French, the Ottomans, and others even before them who had tried and failed to create permanent outposts in Sulat. In the early days of the war, Peter Moses was arrested and killed in military custody. After the death of Peter Moses, the leadership of the party collapsed quickly.

She tried to tell her mother what she'd discovered, thinking how little her mother at sixteen must have understood the circumstances of their exile. Here was an explanation. Her grandfather would have certainly been arrested and probably executed if they had stayed. But her mother showed little interest. She said her father was indeed an important man. He was always going off to meetings and demonstrations. There were always a lot of men passing through their home. She told Mariam that she had perfectly understood, even at sixteen, their reasons for leaving.

* * *

On Sunday mornings, John did the transport runs by himself. He got to sit by his truck with his coffee and a newspaper and watch the sunrise. He was almost finished with his military service, almost home, and he decided before he did anything else he would go and see Mariam.

He couldn't wait to see her now. These were his Sunday mornings. Everything was clearer, and easily decided. It was on one of those Sundays, the start of his last month of service, that he was called to a checkpoint on the hospital road.

"How many?" he asked.

There was only one to be transported. As he drove up to the checkpoint, one of the guards ran toward him, flagging him down and stopping him before the gate.

"We'll bring the prisoner here," he said.

The protocol was to drive all the way up to the detention area. There was too much that could go wrong while transferring detainees on foot. "Where is he?" John asked, squinting at the road in front of him. He saw the other guard standing by a car several feet in front of the checkpoint. "I need to pull up," he said, and he kept driving.

As soon as he stopped, the guard who'd been chasing him opened the back of the truck. He'd never seen them in such a hurry to load up. He watched the two guards lift the prisoner, whose face was covered with blood, and John was so intent on watching them he almost didn't see that the car up ahead was occupied. John got out of the truck and approached the car. He saw the unmoving figure of a woman in the front passenger seat and slowed down. The guards had loaded up the prisoner and were calling to him to come back. John already knew the woman was dead, there was nothing more to be done, but he kept going and stopped by the side of the car. He stared into the backseat. There was a little girl, dressed in a pretty frock, with her chest shot open.

In a daze John opened the back door and put his fingers on her wrist. Next to her tiny hand, his fingers were monstrously large, engorged. He felt around on both wrists, unable to find a pulse, but he couldn't say for certain she wasn't alive. Her face held all the serenity of a sleeping child. Her fingernails were painted with bright pink nail polish.

The guards were still yelling at him to come back. John looked in the front seat, at the woman he'd seen from a distance. Now he saw that she was pregnant, far along judging from her size. They had fired into her abdomen. He wondered if she had been in labor.

One of the guards was behind him now. "What the hell happened here?" John asked him. This guard, a kid John had seen every day for the last three months, looked no different today than he did yesterday. He had an unmemorable face with inexpressive eyes, still, even now.

"They're waiting for you," he said. "Don't worry about this. Someone's coming."

"Who's coming?"

"We went through the proper channels. Someone's coming."

"You need an ambulance."

"We've already called it in."

The guard walked him back to the truck. John got in and

gripped the steering wheel to steady his hands. The two of them were watching him now. The other one looked nervous as John drove away.

He drove a little further and pulled up on the side of the road to call an ambulance himself. He was sure his prisoner needed a doctor, a proper doctor, not a military doctor. He picked up his radio to call an ambulance but before he had a chance to figure out what to say, the prisoner, who must have been unconscious for a while, began to wail like a wild animal. He was pounding on the divider, so hard it made the front seat quake, and John realized the man was not restrained. His pounding lacked a distinctive metallic clink.

John waited for the pounding to subside before he got out. "I'm going to open this door," he said. "I'm not going to hurt you. I just want to talk to you."

Not a sound came back to him. He opened the door, expecting to see a huddle in the back corner of the truck, but before he knew what was happening the prisoner leapt out, pushing John to the ground and squeezing his hands around John's throat. The man's thumbs were lodged into his neck. He was incredibly strong, made stronger by grief and rage, and just when John was about to give up fighting, the hands around his neck slipped. He moved quickly, pushing the prisoner off him with all his strength and slamming his head into the bumper until his whole body went limp. Fresh blood poured from the man's head into the dirt, but he was still alive, still breathing. His eyes still blinked. Tears spilled out of them, making tracks in his dirty cheeks.

John could have left him there. He could have called the ambulance, as was his intention. He could have concocted a story about being knocked out and disarmed by a prisoner who got away, but it did not occur to him anymore to do those things. He went into the glove box for a spare pair of handcuffs. By the time he came back, the man's eyes were closed.

He was unconscious, and John hoisted him into the truck. He drove to the fort and deposited his prisoner, looking so damaged himself they sent him to the infirmary. When they'd finished wiping the blood off him, they'd discovered none of it was his own.

In the canteen that night he saw the two checkpoint guards sitting together, not speaking. They caught him staring and forced John to look away, and that was all that ever passed between them.

On his last Sunday he sat in his truck, gazing at the sunrise. All of this space and solitude had led him to make a decision about his future. He took his compass out of his pocket and read the engraving. *The sea that calls all things unto her calls me, and I must embark.* Mariam had chosen this for him. She had waited for him to find his courage and watched him open this gift with sweet anticipation. In turn he had given her nothing. A few fervent kisses and some promising words from a distance—scraps—that was all he had given her, and with certainty he would fail her again. He could never be the man he wanted for her. Mariam was something extraordinary. She had no idea of her own worth, yet he knew exactly what he was.

He went to the side of the road and dug the heel of his boot into the dirt until he'd made a deep hole. He put the cool brass against his lips before he threw the compass into the hole, sealing it into the tightly packed earth.

When he got back to Alexandria, he sat down to write her a long letter. All of the things he wanted to say were there on the surface of his mind, the terrible things that had happened since they last spoke and what he learned from them. Theirs was a country of firm boundaries not meant to be crossed, or rather, he didn't have the strength to withstand the difficulties of crossing them. He knew what he wanted to say, but when he began writing, the words escaped him. In the end, the letter was brief. It only needed to help her let go of him, so that she could carry on with a fruitful life.

> *Dear Mariam,*
> *I know it has been many months since you've heard from me. As you've probably guessed, my military service is over and I'm back in Alexandria. Over the last few months, I had a chance to do a lot of thinking about my future. I've decided to pursue a doctorate in Geology, which will be strenuous and time-consuming, and I'm afraid it isn't realistic for us to move forward. You need to stay close to your parents and I can't be of much help in your situation. We have to accept that fate was not on our side in this lifetime. I wish you all the happiness in the world, Mariam. You're in my heart, always.*

It wasn't the letter he wanted to write. Still, it brought tears to his eyes.

Her response was two words written on a slip of paper torn from a notepad. *I understand.* He squeezed it into a tight ball and held it inside his fist. It's done, he thought. It was finally done.

He lost himself in the text of James Hutton's *Theory of the Earth* and worked on his application. In the entire country there were three doctoral programs in Geological Sciences, one at Presidency College in Alexandria, one in Sulat, and another one at Mount Belet. Sulat was out of the question, with Mariam there, and he could see no reason to go back to Mount Belet. In January, he began his studies in Alexandria, happy for his mind to be occupied again. He found his chosen discipline to be utterly absorbing. In a way it was like falling in love, and this love consumed him for many years.

* * *

His final letter arrived. She came home from work and saw

THE PATHLESS SKY · 119

it on top of a pile of mail on the kitchen table. Her mother was sitting at the other end of the table, peeling potatoes, and they were both eyeing the letter at the same time. Mariam tore it open and read it right there. She knew, from his mother's polite detachment and the months of silence, that this was coming, and it would make no difference if her humiliation came in the privacy of her room or in the kitchen in front of her mother. At least he was saying goodbye. A part of him must have wanted to simply slip away and fade from her memory.

Her mother had long stopped what she was doing. Neither of them said a word. Mariam put the letter back in the envelope and went upstairs to her room.

A few weeks later, she saw the widower again. He grabbed her elbow as she walked down the street and asked if he could take her home. He must have been watching her long enough to see that she'd lost all her confidence. She went with him, right then, and all afternoon made him the object of her furious desire. After that, they met every Saturday until the end of winter. At the end of winter he asked her if they would ever be more than this. He said the neighbors were beginning to talk, that they had noticed her coming to his door every Saturday like an expensive prostitute, and if it got back to his children he would never forgive himself.

Even though she cared nothing for the widower, she cried all the way home. Like her mother, it wasn't her privilege to be wanted. Once she accepted it, after more time went by, she was able to realize that she wasn't unhappy. Her days had a certain rhythm that pleased her. She enjoyed her work and found tranquility in her home life. Best of all, her father had turned a corner. He was speaking and walking with more confidence. He was moving about the house and carrying on rudimentary conversations. One day Mariam came home from work and saw a photo album sitting on the kitchen table. "Your father had me rummaging through boxes looking for that," Mama told her.

"It's his album from his student days. He wants you to look at it with him."

Mariam was touched. She took the album to her father in the living room. He sat up when he saw her, and she joined him on the sofa with the album open across their laps. There were pictures from all over Europe, some of himself but mostly of his friends, strapping Germanic lads with broad grins, young women with blond hair that fell in curls to their shoulders. He pointed to the pictures, trying to say the names of the people and places, and in some cases his pronunciation, especially of the German cities, was perfectly clear. Munich. Stuttgart. Berlin. Mariam complimented him. "Your German is very good."

They came to a picture of her father and mother together, sitting in an outdoor cafe. Her mother's hair was windswept, wisps of it falling across one cheek. He was sitting close to her, his arm behind her shoulders. They made a stunning couple.

"She could have been a film star," Mariam said.

"Yes," he agreed, tapping the photograph. He had loved her then, and Mariam imagined their buried grief to be a kind of magnet, pulling them together, even if it was that same grief pulling him away years later. Suddenly, Mariam was moved to do something she had not done since she was a child. She leaned over and kissed her father's cheek.

"Mary," he said, patting her hand. He called her Mary now because "Mariam" was too difficult to pronounce, something about the shortness of the syllables. They stopped trying to correct it a long time ago. He couldn't say his wife's name anymore either—Arifah—but now he called her "love," and it was beautiful when he said it.

She didn't mark the passing of time, but it passed quickly. In three years, the war archives were catalogued and prepared for public use. At the end of it, Mariam was proud, but she fought off a sense of mourning having once again lost something that had enthralled her. She was twenty-six years old, and just beginning to think of her future. She wanted to find her own path before it was too late. She wanted to go to Paris. She wanted to fall in love again, but properly. She wanted to continue her studies, perhaps in library science or in a different field. She realized there was so much even in her own country she hadn't seen. She had never been to Alexandria, for instance.

One afternoon she was dreaming like this, thinking about Paris, when she noticed an old man waiting for assistance at the reference desk, a slight little man with crinkly eyes. He must have been trying to get someone's attention for a while.

Mariam approached him. "Is anyone helping you?"

"You, I hope," he said amiably. "I'm Dr. Malick. Head of Geology."

"Of course. I recognize the name."

He seemed delighted by that. "I have a reference packet I need compiled as soon as possible. I'm taking my students to Alexandria for a regional conference. I'd like them to know who they're meeting."

"Sounds important," Mariam said.

He passed her a paper with his handwritten notes. "Forgive me if my writing is unclear. These are articles I want to include. Is this all right?"

"I can figure it out," Mariam said. There were about eight articles, all with multiple authors. None of it meant anything to her until she came upon one name, *Merchant*, and the initial after it.

"Do you know all these authors?" she asked.

"I do."

"This *Merchant, J*, is he around twenty-six, from Alexandria?"

"He is. Do you know him?"

Mariam smiled. "I think I did know him, at Mount Belet. I was there for a short time."

"It must be him," Dr. Malick said. "He's at Presidency now. Bright young man. Quiet."

"What a coincidence," she said.

"Was he interested in geology even then?"

Mariam hated to disappoint him. "He was eighteen," she said. "He was interested in many things."

That amused the old man very much. "I think I get your meaning. And what is your name?"

"Mariam."

"Mariam, shall I tell him you said hello?"

"Yes, please."

"Anything else?"

Mariam couldn't think. "Tell him I'm doing well, if he asks."

"I'm sure he will ask," he said.

After he left, Mariam ran to the stacks to look for the journal containing the article. She was eager to read it, to see if she could hear John's voice in it. Once she read the first paragraph, she couldn't continue without laughing. Not a word of it made any sense, yet somehow it did sound like him.

PART TWO
Alexandria

FIVE

D r. Malick of the University of Sulat Province was a spry, wiry man in his fifties, with thin strands of hair that seemed drawn to some heavenly body wanting to lift him upwards. His papers were mostly technical, minor in scope. He seemed to relish the practice of geology, the tools, the products, the meditative fieldwork, the craft rather than the theory, as if he wanted to know only what was there and capture it with an artist's hand, with little interest in the forces that created it. His talks were so tightly focused, so fixed on one object, in this case a single, intensely detailed map of English Canal illustrating the difficulties of mapping around an urban center where the geology is often obscured, that he often left his listeners wondering if he'd been speaking in a long, extended metaphor and they'd failed to grasp it.

In this seminar he led a debate on the continued use of manual plane-table mapping, despite the new technologies that made it obsolete. He argued as well for the remapping of regions as the understanding of the geology of those regions evolved. In the end, there was no denying the beauty of his hand-drawn maps, and the depth of the story they told. "A map is never truly finished," he said. "It can't capture the whole story but it is an endeavor, a labor of love, and no satellite picture can compare to that."

John liked that description. Something about the tenderness of it moved him, and yet it was so expected. "Sulat is for lovers" was a phrase they used at Presidency to belittle their

126 - CHAITALI SEN

method. John's own graduate program, at Presidency College, was more theoretical, tailored for those whose overwhelming ambition was to emigrate, and as such it often felt rootless. The program at Presidency was about testing what could be known, about stretching into the far reaches of time or geography in order to know what was intuitively thought to be unknowable. At Presidency every question about the earth's evolution was worthy of research, whether or not it was useful, whether or not there were sufficient resources for conducting the research and actually reaching any viable conclusions. Then there was the Mount Belet program, growing rapidly but underrepresented in this seminar room. Mount Belet was for the capitalists, the sons of industrialists who wanted to expand their wealth. They were not scientists so much as gentleman pirates.

And over there in the outer-province of Sulat was Malick, toiling away on his maps. John was certain the insult of the refrain, *Sulat is for lovers*, would be lost on Malick. Wielding enough influence to bring together the country's three academic geological programs, with all of their philosophical differences, Malick had proven the utility of love.

When the seminar ended, John's advisor, Nehemia, asked him if he was coming to lunch. John watched Malick as he carefully rolled up his maps, while everyone around him stood up and fled the room.

"Yes, you go ahead. I'll bring Malick." John liked Malick. He was interesting, and he and John had developed a certain rapport.

He'd only met him six months earlier. From the beginning John had watched him with too much intensity, heavy with curiosity about this man and his home in English Canal, the place he inhabited alongside Mariam. It was ridiculous, after three years without a word between them, to look at him and think of Mariam. She was lost to him now. That was the choice he had made, for good reason, but his body never did come to understand it.

Now, the room had emptied out and Malick spoke up. "Are you going to sit there staring at me or are you going to help?"

John got up to help, holding up the long tubular cases so that Malick could place his rolled-up maps inside and seal them up.

"You look tired," Malick said.

"I didn't sleep last night." He had not been sleeping, not for weeks. "I was working on my dissertation." For his dissertation he was analyzing the formation of the metamorphic bedrock along the Alexandria uplift in order to map the peaks and elevation of the crust that had once stood above it, a mountain range as high as the Himalayas. Now it was all numbers that ceased to make sense.

"It isn't going well?" Malick asked.

"I think most of my data is wrong. I think it's all wrong."

"What does Nehemia say?"

"He said I should figure out what's right about it, get it done and move on."

"He has a point. I don't even remember doing my dissertation. I know the topic. I have it somewhere in a box. But I don't ever look at it or think about it. Hardly anyone continues to pursue their dissertation topic after they have their doctorate."

"I can't imagine abandoning it," John said.

"You find another angle. Good research takes years, John. You don't have that kind of time. Finish it. Get your doctorate. Then you go on to the study that's going to make your career. Can we lock these up somewhere?" Malick asked.

"Leave them here. I'll lock the room."

Malick agreed and stood up. Suddenly his whole demeanor changed. His hands flew up in an animated flutter. "I almost forgot. I met a young lady last week who said she knew you at Mount Belet."

He must have said Mariam's name. It happened so fast, her name like the flapping of wings. He imagined her talking to Malick, remembering her lovely mouth. He wondered if she had smiled or blushed, or if her voice had carried any signs of loss. "Where did you see her?"

"At the library," Malick continued. "I asked her if you were interested in geology even then, and she said you were eighteen, that you were interested in many things." This had Malick in stitches. "I told her you were very bright and quiet."

"Quiet?"

"She seemed proud to have known you."

John waited for more but that was all. Malick had nothing more to add.

"Did she say anything else?"

"She said hello. She said to tell you that she was doing well, in case you asked."

They walked in silence out of the building and down the street toward the restaurant where the others had gathered for lunch. They were almost at the door.

"Maybe a change of scenery would help me," John said, pretending to go back to the problem of his dissertation. "Are you working on a map this summer?"

"I am, in Luling Province."

Luling was more remote than John had in mind, nowhere near English Canal.

Malick noted John's disappointment. "You said you wanted a change of scenery. You can meet me there."

"Maybe I could come to English Canal," John offered. "I could help you there. I could work with the summer students."

"That would make trouble with Nehemia."

"Nehemia will be out of the country."

"You're not going with him?"

"It isn't for work. He's visiting family."

Malick stopped and inspected John.

"I need help in Luling," he said. "Come to Luling with me and then we'll see."

That night John thought about going to Luling with Malick. What would it achieve? He could go to English Canal now and find Mariam at the library if that was what he wanted. He could write her a letter. He could call. Or he could stall again, make a map with Malick and spend more time delaying things.

John decided he would go. He decided he had to go, as if Malick knew a trick that would set him right.

As soon as he and Malick worked out the details of their mapping trip, John went to see Vic at his apartment where he lived with three other students. It was subsidized student housing, affordable, but filthy and crowded and Vic was miserable there.

Vic had not been at Presidency for long. A year after John started his doctoral program, he found Vic sitting in a coffee shop near campus. Even after John approached his table he still wasn't sure it was Vic. His features were all familiar, the curly hair, the broad chest and hulking body, but his posture, his whole way of carrying himself was entirely different. Vic stood up and shook his hand. "John Merchant. I can't believe it. How long has it been?" John sat down with him and waited for some flashes of the Vic he knew at Mount Belet, the boisterous pontificating, the awkward outbursts, the constant fidgeting, but none of these manifested. John accepted that they were older, and looking back he couldn't believe how young they really were, how much like kids in a playground, and it wasn't fair to allow himself to mature and not attribute that same capacity for growth to Vic. It was only that Vic had been such a large personality. Brilliant in many ways, but stunted and confrontational, even more so as the years went by.

John and Vic had gone through the same coursework at

Mount Belet. Sometimes John got the eerie sense that Vic was following him, always watching. By the end of their four years they knew each other well, though John would not have wanted to call him a friend. Yet he was happy, surprisingly happy, to run into Vic that day in the coffee shop, because he had been feeling lost in his own body for some time, feeling untethered, disconnected even from his family. Vic's recognition of him made something inside of him click, if only briefly.

Vic said he was looking at some doctoral programs at Presidency, and John had asked him unwittingly what he'd been doing for the last two years. He assumed he would have said working, or traveling. He didn't actually know what he expected Vic to say, but when he said he'd recently gotten out of prison, John didn't believe him. Vic had to explain how he'd run away from the barracks during his military service and got caught. While he was in prison he'd received a medical diagnosis from a military doctor. He was put under the care of a psychiatrist and released after two years.

Stunned, John said, "You didn't have to tell me all that."

"There's no point in lying about it."

What doctoral program was going to take Vic, who was incapable of lying about his prison record and psychiatric disorder? Vic said he was interested in Climate and Atmospheric Science, and John said it wasn't his department, but he could talk to Nehemia, who could talk to the head of that department, and they could see what happened. Perhaps it had helped a little but in the end Vic got himself admitted to the program, and had so far proven himself to be a serious scholar. He expressed his gratitude to John often, perhaps disproportionately to anything John had actually done for him.

Now he saw Vic often. Vic brought John into his impeccable room, a retreat from the chaos just steps away. He got a bottle of whiskey off the bookshelf and filled two glasses.

John told him he was going away for a few weeks, possibly

for the whole summer. "You can stay in my apartment, if you want."

"Are you serious?"

"Why leave it empty? It's quiet. You can get some work done."

Vic made a feeble protest, but the offer was too good to refuse.

"Where are you going, anyway?" Vic asked.

"Just following Malick around for a little while."

"Malick? Why? Is Nehemia spying on him?"

John didn't say any more about it. They drank their whiskey, talking a little about Vic's coursework.

"You're going to see Mariam, aren't you?" Vic asked suddenly.

How could Vic have known that? They had only talked about Mariam once, nearly ten years ago.

"You know it's a bad idea," Vic said.

"Why?" John asked.

"Obvious reasons," Vic said. "Whatever made you let her go once is still a factor, isn't it?"

John considered Vic's point, but lately he felt like he was coming out of a long illness. The person who severed Mariam from his life was a fevered version of himself.

"I'm not trying to change your mind. I'd like to get out of this dump for the summer so the longer you stay the better for me."

"Good." John felt it was settled.

"I didn't know Mariam well," Vic said.

"Right. You didn't know her at all."

"No, I did know her a little. You broke her heart every day, I think."

"You didn't know her. What do you mean? How would you have known her?"

Vic smiled. "You see, John, how much it all matters? Look

at you. It might as well have been yesterday. How will you contain your disappointment when you see she's not the same girl?" He leaned forward. "She belongs in the past. That's where you left her."

John stared at Vic. He had to remind himself that Vic was certifiably insane. No matter how much sense he made, he had no real understanding of people.

One day he would ask Vic what made him run from his barracks in the middle of the night. What couldn't he stand to do? Every day, without fail, John saw a little girl in a car, her tearstained face and blood-soaked dress, her little button nose, little polished fingernails the size of peas. Every day he wondered who had painted her nails that candy pink color. He could imagine the girl, lively and small, showing off her fingernails everywhere she went, distracting her mother, tugging at her father, soliciting the attention of neighbors and workmen, and after everyone else had seen them, giving them a good look herself. Tucked into bed, before she falls asleep, she can't stop smiling at her own hands. Vic had three years in prison, but John had this, a girl, her mother, her father.

"You have to be able to fix your mistakes, Vic."

"What do I know about it?" Vic said. He lifted his glass in a kind of surrender.

John took an overnight train to a town six hours north of the cabin where he and Malick would set up base. Malick picked him up in an old van and they drove, starting off along a sheered-off hillside through a massive section of blue-hued limestone. The laminations ran horizontally for a while, but then they curved, buckled, undulated, and turned sharply toward the sky, the layers of rock like the spines of books placed vertically on a shelf, evidence of drifting, collision, and compression. In a matter of kilometers they moved millions of years up the time scale, through siltstone and shale, thinly bedded marine mud. Further still the rock became coarse and cobbled, like a poorly assembled stone wall, a conglomerate mess deposited by an ancient river system.

It was a spectacular road cut that made Malick philosophical. "Geology and roadbuilding are two chain-linked human endeavors," he said. John had nothing of value to add, but quoted his first geology professor at Mount Belet. "Road cuts are a geologist's X-ray machine." They both chuckled. So far Malick seemed delighted with his company.

The cliffs tapered. The land flattened and sprouted a windswept pelage of tall yellow grasses. That too faded, and the road became as rough as the fields around it. The van pitched until the road forked and they came to a town where a cement factory stood like a fortress over a limestone quarry. They stopped at a small cafeteria to eat lunch. It was hot and everything was bleached from a dusting of limestone powder, making the sky brighter and the sun more blinding. The cafeteria was cooled by a number of standing fans blowing toward the middle of the room, but only a few tables caught the moving air. They took the only available table by an open screened window. John sat there sweating over a glass of chalky, tepid water. From here it would be another two-hour journey.

They got back in the van and Malick drove laboriously out of that barren white basin. They reached a range of rounded hills and John dozed off for a while, jerking awake when the van turned off-road to climb a rocky path, where the brush had been sloppily cleared away. The low branches of the shrubs tapped the sides of the van.

"We're here," Malick said. A small adobe shelter came into view, a beige cube so congruent with the geology of the place it appeared to be thrust out of the ground like some habitable outcrop.

The cabin had to be cleaned before they could unload their

equipment. John found the old water pump and filled a tin pail with cold water. He put his mouth into the stream to relieve his parched throat. The water was rich in iron and had a bloody aftertaste that coated the back of his tongue.

After Malick swept the dust off the floor, John mopped it down with a wet rag. When he was in the military he enjoyed this sort of collective, ritualistic cleaning. By the time they were finished cleaning and unloading the van, it was almost sundown. "Let's drink," Malick said. He opened a provision pack and pulled out two small glasses and a bottle of whiskey, a box of crackers, a ceramic bowl, and a tin of sardines his daughter had sent from Italy. "There's a charcoal pit out back," he said. "Tomorrow perhaps we can procure some meat."

The mere mention of meat ignited John's hunger. He watched Malick roll open the top of the sardine can and empty it into the bowl. He broke the sardines up with a fork and then mashed them into a paste. John looked sadly at the small bowl, wondering if Malick had any more food tucked away in his pack or if this was to be their evening's ration.

Malick measured out a thumb-sized portion of whiskey for each of them, and they clinked their glasses. "A small drink. We have a long day tomorrow."

Malick asked him about the fieldwork he'd done with Nehemia, but John didn't have much to report. Nehemia's guidance was more theoretical. Malick obviously disapproved, surely already knowing Nehemia's lack of field orientation, and John realized too late he'd been set up for a lament. Prolonged study in the field was the only way to achieve an intimate knowledge of the earth. What *was* geology if not fieldwork? John nodded, silently disagreeing.

"My training was all in the field," Malick explained. "These days young people want to see everything through a machine. When I was your age, younger actually, we mapped the Lake District in Northern Sulat. Even then the region was heavily militarized, but we had clearance. Have you ever seen pictures of the Northern Sulat Lake District?"

"I've seen maps," John said. "Not photographs."

"I worked on those maps. Lake District is a misnomer, makes it sound clean. It wasn't clean. It was hell."

"A complex system of waterways," John remembered.

"Limitless. The easy part was paddling the canoe, but most of it was portage over rocky hills in unpredictable weather. It took the whole summer, and when we were finished, there were three of us, we were sick with respiratory infections. I still have complications from that trip, but we were over the worst of it and returning home when my friend Samir said he had to relieve himself. We pulled over next to a grassy field, thinking nothing of it, and waited while he went to take care of his business."

Malick paused for a moment to retrieve a kerosene lantern. The daylight in the cabin was vanishing rapidly, and soon John and Malick were like two apparitions glowing in the dusk. Malick continued his story.

"We didn't even have time to smoke a cigarette before we heard the explosion, coming from the field. Samir had stepped on a land mine. I was frozen, terrified. A part of me wanted to drive off but somehow we forced ourselves to step into the minefield to look for him. It felt like years passed before we found him. He'd been thrown further in, away from the road. Because he hadn't cried out we were sure he was dead, but he was alive, staring at the sky with a strange smile on his face. He was in shock. His leg was gone. I mean completely. There was no right leg. We carried him, trying to retrace our steps, thinking any moment might be our last, and then we drove like lightning to the checkpoint, but he'd lost too much blood already. He died there, just after they pulled him out of the vehicle."

Malick looked shaken, as if this had happened not twenty years ago but last week.

"No one warned you there was a minefield there?"

"We had a defense map, but it was not accurate."

"What a pointless death," John said.

Now past the distraction of his land mine story, Malick took a cracker and dipped it into the sardines. "If I had more energy, I would have made you endure more hardship on this trip."

"I'm amazed you still come out here, practically on your own. Why?"

"It's the only thing I know how to do. And why are you here?" Malick asked. John almost misinterpreted the question before Malick elaborated. "Why did you choose to become a geologist?"

In the beginning people asked him this all the time, but not lately. John tried to remember what he used to say. "I like the scale of it," he said. That was all he could retrieve and his mind went off on a different tangent. "A part of me believes an understanding of the earth will always give me a feeling of belonging, a sense of home anywhere in the world, no matter where I find myself."

Malick laughed. "That's the strangest answer I've ever heard," he said, pouring another sliver of whisky into their glasses. "Isn't it the people that make a home? The culture, the language?"

"Ultimately, I suppose."

"The land itself is not important. We attach meaning to it, but the land is important only because of humanity, because it serves us, because it helps us evolve. The idea that you can feel you belong somewhere because you know the composition of the land, I don't think I agree."

John tried again. "Maybe 'belonging' isn't the right word. I meant because I study the land I have a purpose for standing on it, and that sense of purpose negates the alienation of being a stranger in a new place."

"You're attached to your home," Malick remarked.

"No, not particularly."

"You are. Only you don't realize how much."

John corrected him. "I'm attached to a feeling of home."

That night, John slept soundly, exhausted from his travels and soothed by the utter darkness of the cabin. He repeated to himself what he had said earlier to Malick—he was attached to a feeling of home—and he was satisfied, having at last revealed something of himself that felt conclusive.

The next day they hiked to the broad, flat summit of a low mountain with their awkward packs of surveying equipment. This was the best place to begin, giving them the widest overview of the topography, a range of long and narrow hills, beds of granite under a carpet of soil and grassy vegetation. The range was bound by a moderate fault in the east and the Luling uplift to the west and north. "There is incredible diversity here," Malick said. "We could map this for years. That irregular hill that looks like a lion's head consists of alternating intervals of glauconitic sandstone and glauconitic skeletal grainstone. Over here we have Precambrian granite and schist." There were two major transgressive-regressive sequences, telling a story of rising and falling sea levels. "If we get enough good days like this we'll be able to capture quite a bit of complexity."

John's limited experience with mapping had taught him more about reading a map than making one. The mechanics and concepts of the task were not difficult to grasp. He knew how to level the plane table and tape down the Mylar sheet, first by the centers of the long sides, then the short sides, then the corners, and then all around to keep dirt and moisture from seeping under the sheet, and he understood how to measure and tape off a baseline, setting up the plane table along it. The mathematics of it, the procedures for calculating and recording vertical and horizontal distance and slope length and measuring the strike, dip, and dip direction of a geological feature, was all basic trigonometry, but he couldn't immediately grasp how Malick made the big decisions—which points to use as controls, where and how far apart to place the stations, and later, which features to include and which to ignore.

He worked slowly, stooping awkwardly over the plane table until his back hurt. In the afternoon sun he frequently had to stop and wipe the perspiration off his face to keep it from dripping onto the Mylar sheet. At certain angles the sun blinded him, and his head hurt, and he was hungry, and after he had been working a long time and Malick told him to take a break, he looked down at the map and saw nothing but a blank sheet marked with a few light pencil lines. He could not imagine it turning into anything that could capture the truth of this landscape. Malick kept saying, "What is on the ground must be reflected on the map," but there was so much on the ground. And as their terrain got rougher, over the next few days, the work became more physically demanding and John's exhaustion more profound. He would fall asleep each night still reading the crosshairs on the alidade, still sketching, still seeing the lines and swirls of the map. They appeared to him like thumbprints and the delicate tracks of inky caterpillars.

At the end of the first week, Malick said he was pleased with their progress. They were seeing the beginnings of a regional synthesis. "Are you satisfied with your work?" he asked John.

"Yes, I think so."

They sat on a boulder eating sandwiches, looking out at a silver stream coiling through the valley. These rare moments of rest made Malick wistful.

"You remind me of my son," Malick said. "Though he's older than you. He's thirty."

"Not much older. Does he live here?"

"He's in Germany, working. He hasn't lived with me since he was little. My wife died of cancer when my son and daughter were young. They were raised by my sister."

John wondered how they'd come to that decision. "And your daughter lives in France?"

"Yes, married to a French boy. She's thirty-one. They tolerate me like they would a persistent uncle."

Malick sounded weary. Perhaps it hurt him to think of his children for too long. John wanted to ask him more but he thought better of it. They sat for a while longer. John was silent, gathering words that could explain his reason for being here.

"Do you remember that you told me about Mariam, from the library?"

"Of course," Malick said.

"Did she seem happy?"

"Happy? Yes, I suppose. Was she someone special to you?"

John didn't know how to answer. It was uncomfortable to sit here discussing his past, though he had asked for it. "We haven't seen each other in almost eight years."

"Something occurred to me after meeting her," Malick said. "I believe I knew her father. I was a consulting geologist on one of his projects."

"You must have known him," John said. "He was a civil engineer. What was he like?"

"Difficult, and brilliant, a man with great vision but always distracted. He had left his wife. We all thought he was crazy for that alone. Talk about a beauty, my God!"

"He went back to her," John informed him, but Malick was lost for a moment, perhaps reveling in the memory of a beautiful woman, or simply the idea that he was once young enough to get caught up in the life of a difficult colleague.

John felt he should get to the point. If the conversation went on too long, he didn't know what he might end up confessing.

"I thought if you gave me a reason to be in Sulat, I would have more time to explain myself to Mariam."

Malick looked worried. "You need to explain yourself? What did you do to her?"

John felt defensive. He wanted to talk to Mariam about it, not Malick. "She seems to have forgiven you, John." This was a kind enough statement but John took it as a subtle attempt to discourage him. Like Vic, Malick seemed to think he should leave her alone.

"I need to go whether you invite me or not. I don't know what I'm still doing here, really. What I'm trying to say is I have to follow you home."

"I was sure you wanted to get out of Alexandria to avoid your dissertation."

"I didn't have to leave Alexandria to avoid my dissertation," John said.

Malick laughed and patted him on the knee. "Let's take a break from this tomorrow," he said. "There's something else I want to show you."

They set off early the next morning. When they reached the area Malick had wanted to show him, John didn't know what to look for. They parked off the road and hiked for a long time over boulder-strewn hills until they came to a place where a number of larger, more angular boulders were scattered in all directions. They were in the Luling greenstone belt, a geological rarity containing remnants of the earth's early continents, small swatches of Archean rock which by chance had survived the forces of erosion and subduction. The rock here was among the oldest still found on earth. It was a gift to have within their borders. The exposed bedrock was grayish green and craggy, its edges jutting out of the soil at steep vertical angles. "We've mapped this area quite thoroughly," Malick said, "but last summer I brought some students here, just to take another look. In a few places, here and a bit further out, there is a layer of spherule-rich ocean sediment. The spherules were impact-derived. Their age coincides with the formation of these angular boulders, 2.8 billion years."

All at once, John tried to look surprised, intrigued, and confounded. Choosing one would have required more than an elementary knowledge of the Archean era. Impact-derived spherules pointed to an asteroid strike. "Is there any other evidence of a strike from this period?" John asked.

"I don't know," Malick confessed. "If you had been thinking for some time about the evolution of continents, and then happened upon this evidence of an asteroid strike embedded in this rather small outcrop of Archean rock, how would you proceed?"

John was tired, his body ached, and he couldn't see the point of this mental exercise. "I suppose I would try to figure out the size and quantity of the impacts, try to find out if this was an anomalous event. I would look for everything that's been published on asteroid impacts in the Archean period, learn everything about the composition and distribution of the spherules. That would be a good start. Do you agree?"

Malick nodded. "I asked my students the same question, but none of them were interested in pursuing it."

Who could blame them, John thought. No one in their right mind made the early continents a focus of their study. It was too difficult, the few greenstone belts around the globe had been picked over, and there was no gratification in it. John was willing to bet that at least half of the country's geology students didn't even know this region existed.

"I feel I've run out of time."

"You still have another twenty years," John insisted. "You're not dying, are you?"

"Not that I know of," Malick said. He began to think out loud, composing a lecture on continent formation, muttering on about repeated cycles of cooling and melting and lighter materials separating from denser ones, about the creation of a buoyant crust. John wondered if the problem was not one of time but self-doubt. Malick was formulating a question. The issue wasn't whether there was an impact or how large it was. It was deducing, from all that, whether the impact helped or impeded the beginning of a continent. It was a far cry from making maps.

"You can help me," Malick said. "Gather some literature for me. It will give me an idea of whether I should pursue this or not."

"Right," John said, but he was confused, unsure of what he'd just agreed to.

Malick slapped his back. "So you're coming. To English Canal. Beg your sweetheart to forgive you and do a little work for me. All right?"

There were eight weeks left in the summer. Eight weeks could be enough. Malick's invitation was sincere. "Yes, all right," he said. Suddenly he couldn't keep still. He felt like he could run for miles.

SIX

It was impossible to find a room in English Canal on short notice. He was stuck with a musty house far from the campus, where his temporary landlady, an ancient, cantankerous woman, hobbled around in a yellow housecoat and talked to herself in a raspy death rattle of a voice. She seemed to resent every interaction with John, including the one in which he paid her money to rent a room. She took the money sneeringly and put it in the pocket of her housecoat. The old woman, and the house around her, smelled like urine and disinfectant. His room was upstairs, in the attic, and had the same smell but plenty of windows, which he opened to let in a redemptive breeze. The view was nice, pitched roofs and tall pines.

He left the house and walked along the canal to the College of Sulat Province. He almost lingered among the cafés and booksellers on College Street, but instead continued walking until he came to the campus, a small cluster of twelve buildings around a long grassy common. The library was a white townhouse with tall windows and black shutters, a simple, beautiful building that made his nerves rattle. Mariam was inside and he wanted to be past this reunion, yet he evaluated the architecture of the library for a long time.

The lobby was bright with marble. He looked at the directory and took the elevator to the top floor, the research department, and approached a young woman standing behind a long, curved counter. She said, "Good afternoon" in a voice as wispy as a cloud. When he told her he was looking for Mariam, her decorum floundered. Her mouth hung open for a moment before she answered, "Mariam's in the map room."

"I see. Where is that?"

"You can't go to the map room," she said. By then she was smiling with a delirious look in her eyes. "Would you like to wait here?"

She pointed to a seating area nearby with wide leather armchairs. As he sat down another woman joined the first one behind the counter and a secret conversation began. John looked away, but every time he heard footsteps his head jerked as if he were on a leash. He studied the dark wood panels lining the walls. They continued all the way up to a wood-coffered ceiling, from which there hung a large chandelier resembling the helm of an old ship. It was a strangely calming focal point. He looked up and breathed in, trying to think only of his admiration of the chandelier.

Afterwards, all he could remember was that she was not there, and suddenly she was, standing nearby and staring at him with her lips parted. That was where his eyes fell first, on the sliver of darkness between her lips. She wore a sky blue dress that lifted the blue from her pale brown skin. One side of her hair was pinned behind her ear, those ears—now jeweled with small pearl earrings. His imagination had failed him. Now his body was numb and his voice, a coiled rope.

She asked him to follow her. Somehow he rose, walking weakly behind her. She led him to a study room, far from the inquisitive glances of her colleagues, and behind that door, they fell into a silent embrace. He could feel her trembling and suffering, like him, and he kissed her ear, her cheek, her eyebrows and lips.

An invasion of voices in the hallway pulled them apart. As the voices passed she collected herself and backed away. He leaned on the table behind him, trying to hold still.

"What are you doing here?" she asked.

"I'm working with Malick for the summer."

"Dr. Malick," she said. "I met him a few weeks ago. I asked him to say hello."

"He did. Can you get away?"

"I can't. I have to work until eight today." She didn't offer an alternative.

"What about afterwards?" he asked, sounding desperate. Already this transaction was slipping away from him.

"I suppose I could meet you after." She glanced back at the door. "I won't have much time. The last tram is at ten. There's a place near the tram stop. I could meet you there. It's called English Tavern."

He grinned. "English Tavern," he said. "It's still here."

She understood him and smiled, at last.

"I'll find it," he said. "You'll be there?"

"Of course," she said. Her hand was on the doorknob. "I'll see you there."

The tavern was easy to find. He got there fifteen minutes early and was relieved to see Mariam sitting on a bench by a streetlight, reading a book. "Did I have the time wrong?" he asked.

"I got off a little early. I didn't know how to contact you." She closed the book delicately and slipped it back in her bag. Then she stood up and they walked together into the tavern. There was a great deal of noise from a billiards room in the back, but the front room was empty and quiet. By a window facing the street, there was a small table. They sat across from each other and he ordered their drinks, two gin and tonics, which they finished quickly as they made small talk. He ordered two more and they talked for a little while about other things, other people. He told her about his mapping trip with Malick. She told him about her father, about his slow recovery.

She asked him if he stayed in touch with people from Mount Belet. He said not many. "What about Nina?" she asked. Of course Nina would have been the only one who mattered to her.

"No. You?"

"I get a postcard from time to time. She lives in Brussels. She married a doctor. Did she ever tell you she lost her virginity to her family doctor?"

"Don't tell me she married him."

"No," she said, smiling. "But she must have had something for doctors. Even sons of doctors."

He didn't want to talk about Nina anymore. Nina was someone he forgot about constantly.

"I never really bought the story about the doctor," he said.

She picked up her glass and held it to her lips for a long time before she took a sip.

"I did then," she said. "I believed everything everyone told me back then."

He emptied his glass and looked around, feeling unsettled without a drink. He either wanted another or he wanted to take Mariam somewhere quieter. He knew they would have to talk about the past. It was the reason he was here, to talk about it and then bury it.

"Do you remember the last time we spoke?" she asked.

"A little," he said. He remembered that he had called her from a strange pub in the desert, that he had talked about stars and a boat. For John, the memory of that night carried a heavy weight. It was Sherod's last night, the night that put him in the hole and got him sent to Menud Fort. It was the night that derailed him. He couldn't guess what it was for Mariam, if it was a time that held onto her and wouldn't let go, or if it was simply a logical place to begin their conversation. In a way, it was the beginning of his abandonment.

"After you hung up I had a terrible feeling that I would

never see you again. I wrote you a letter. I sent it to the pub like you told me to and it came back to me. I was so worried I called your mother to find out if you were all right."

"She wouldn't have known anything," he said.

"No, she didn't know anything. She didn't even know who I was."

He knew he had to offer her something. "I was sent away that night, Mariam."

"Sent away?"

"I got into some trouble and I was sent away."

"To where?"

"I know that I owe you an explanation. I have one, Mariam, I do, but can it wait a little longer? Can it be enough that we're here together right now?"

"You don't owe me anything," she said gently. "You told me the truth. You said goodbye and I accepted it."

"I didn't think I could take care of you. I couldn't imagine you in Alexandria and I couldn't imagine myself here."

"You were right, John. I understood."

Of course, he thought. That was all she had said then, that she understood.

"What I don't understand is why you're always the one that decides. You decide when it's over and when it should start again." She pulled her shoulders up into a deep shrug. "Now it looks like I was waiting for you all this time."

"I know you weren't waiting," he began, searching for the right thing to say. "I just needed to come and talk to you."

"Why? Why now?"

He was nervous. Mariam seemed rightfully distrustful of his intentions, and alarmingly willing to send him away. Whatever confidence he'd had at the start of the evening had vanished. He was afraid everything he said would come out sounding insincere or self-centered. He was here now because Malick had given him a message, but how could he explain that to

Mariam without acting as if he only came because he'd been summoned?

It was no use. There was nothing he could say. He reached across the table and took her hand. Encouragingly, she didn't pull away. Her fingers curled beautifully over his thumb.

Her attention was drawn to the street where the high-pitched bell of the tram signaled its arrival. A few passengers got on it. They took their seats and the door closed. "That's the last one," she said.

He didn't know if she had another way of getting home. He could walk with her or put her in a taxi, but neither of those was an acceptable end to the evening. "I have a room in a boarding-house," he said. "We could go there and be alone for a while."

She was still looking out the window. When she looked back at him, her eyes were alight, both troubled and excited by his proposal. He warned her that it didn't smell very nice and the landlady was unpleasant, and Mariam said, "Let's go."

They left the tavern and strolled to the street where he thought he would find the boarding-house. It wasn't there. He was lost among all the streets that sloped in the exact same way. After they wandered for a while, Mariam asked what street it was on, and took him right to the house. There was a flicker-ing blue light in the side window, the television blaring through the walls. He put the key in the door and got it open just as the laughter from a comedy program invaded the hall-way. He gestured to Mariam to wait at the bottom of the stairs, while he walked down the hall to the television room where the old woman had fallen asleep on the couch. He thought about tiptoeing past her to turn off the television, but it would have been horrendous to wake her. He shut the door, went back to Mariam, and took her up the stairs.

Thankfully the breeze had freshened the room in his absence. Mariam went to a window and looked out. "Do you see the canal?"

He stood behind her, looking in the direction she was pointing. "If you follow the canal east, it goes straight to my house."

He put his arms around her waist and they were silent, watching the pine branches bounce lightly in the wind. After a while he kissed her neck. She turned around and leaned against the wall, unbuttoning his shirt as she kissed him. Her dress frustrated him. He searched for an opening, something to help him peel it away from her body. She was burning up in that dress.

He didn't want it to happen here, cheaply, against the wall, so he carried her to the bed and dropped her onto the sagging mattress. He gave up on the bodice of her dress, content to feel the shape of her breasts through the fabric, and moved his hand down to the skirt, which he raised along her warm thighs. She lifted her hips to help him get her underwear off. He unzipped his pants, then shifted, awkwardly tugging to pull his wallet out of his pocket. When it was free he opened it with one hand and looked for a condom he knew was in there, but a light scrape of her teeth on his earlobe made him fumble. The wallet fell to the floor. "It's all right," Mariam said, holding him back. She reached into his pants, and he kissed her gratefully.

She flinched a little when he slipped his hand between her legs. As soon as she whispered something into his ear, a lewd and unmistakable command, he lowered his pants and entered her, full of awe and disbelief, as if he hadn't expected all of their fondling to lead to this. They made love slowly and silently, taking up enough space to fill a coffin. She took his collar into her mouth, biting it, salivating on it. Just watching her suck on his collar made him want to explode. Finally she let it go. She found his tongue and he felt her rise and break, her eyes squeezed shut, her whole body tightening. He was so struck by her climax that he came inside her without warning and fell over her like a heavy drape. She held his head against her chest, their hearts beating discordantly until their pulses settled.

After a while he became conscious of her captivity. With some effort he rolled off her, immediately bristling at the withdrawal of heat and flesh, her sudden absence. He got on his back and let the breeze cool his face. She slipped her hand into his.

When he woke up, it was not dawn yet and Mariam was lying next to him, curled up on her side with her back to him. Here they were again, waking up after a brief slumber, but they were more clothed this time, more heavily armored. They'd gotten the sex out of the way but the sex hadn't settled anything. He could finally see the zipper running down the back of her dress. He tugged on the metal tab.

"If I knew you were coming I'd have worn a different dress."

"How do you get this blasted thing off?"

It took both of his hands but he finally got it. Once the zipper gave way the dress opened, down to the small of her back. He ran his fingers down her spine. He unclasped her bra and watched her slip out of it while he took off his own clothes, his constrictive shirt, his undershirt, his long unzipped pants and his cotton shorts, his stupid socks, until he was naked and unfettered, and Mariam was almost there, except for the dress which still clung to her hips. She turned onto her back to get a full look at him. Her final disrobing, a slow slinking exit from that blue yoke, was so captivating he didn't dare reach down to help her. "We don't know each other anymore," she whispered.

"We know each other a little," he said. This time, they weren't concerned with being quiet. The bed creaked and hammered the wall.

When the sun was up, they got dressed and snuck out of the

house, moving apprehensively out into the world, distrusting its ability to give them the sustenance they needed. Coffee and breakfast brought them slowly closer to the reality of their surroundings. She cheerfully confessed she had forgotten to put on her underwear, and fidgeted quietly while he smoked a cigarette.

Back in his room, they stared at a pile of papers he had stacked on a desk.

"I have to go," she said. "My mother will need me, and you have work to do."

He sat on a rickety wooden chair as she searched for her underwear. She found it in the bed and made a show of putting it on, lifting her skirt as she slipped it up her thighs. When she was finished she smoothed down her skirt, grinning at her bawdy performance.

"It's a strip tease in reverse," she explained. "I wish I had a sweater."

He stared at her in wonder. She moved restlessly under his gaze, running her fingers through the tangles in her hair, waiting for him to say something, to get up and walk her out, to look away.

"Do you still have the letter you wrote to the pub?" he said. He didn't know why he had a sudden longing to read it, to hear the voice of the girl he used to know.

She laughed. "I have it but you'll never see it."

"Why not?"

"It's horrible. It's pathetic. Pages of me begging you to love me."

The mood changed. They were back again in that place, where she had thought herself unloved. It was time for him to correct her old perceptions. He leaned forward, signaling to her that he had something important to say. She noticed and sat down on the side of the bed, prepared to stay and listen. He had not expected to want to tell her all this so soon, but he couldn't bear the thought of her leaving already.

"That night that I called you from the pub," he said, "We had abandoned our posts. When we were caught, I was given a new posting in Menud Fort. Do you know about Menud Fort?"

"I've heard of it," she said.

"It's a military prison. I did transport runs delivering men from the checkpoints to the prison. Sometimes I didn't even get out of the truck. The checkpoint guards loaded them into the back and the ones at the gate took them out. Do you see what I'm trying to say?"

She said, "You were given a job and you did it."

"I wanted to get out of there. So that I could put it behind me and come see you. I thought about you, all the time."

She nodded, seeing that he was getting off track. "What happened there, John?"

He described it as if he had memorized a script, listening dispassionately to his own voice while trying not to see the things he described. In that way, the right words came out in the right order. "One day I pulled up to the checkpoint. The checkpoint guards were jumpy. They had a prisoner who was barely conscious, and past the checkpoint, there was a car with its doors open." He was trying to explain to Mariam that nothing had seemed right, even with everything he had come to accept about that place. The whole scene was charged with something that compelled him to get out of the truck and see if the car was empty. "There was a little girl, no more than six," he said, "shot in the chest. She had tiny fingernails with pink nail polish. Her mother, in the front seat, was pregnant. They were on the road to the hospital and it was possible she had been in labor."

He had not looked away from Mariam, forcing himself to watch her reactions. She listened, steadily holding his gaze, as if she had been trained to hear confessions like this. Her eyes were warm and full of compassion.

"Do you want to know all of it, Mariam?"

"Yes," she said.

"I went back to the truck. The prisoner had been loaded into the back and I drove off. In a few minutes, he started shouting, kicking and pounding his fists, and I could hear that he wasn't shackled." That one detail, the missing metallic sounds of a prisoner's chains, caused her brow to furrow. But she recovered and he went on. "I stopped the truck and opened the back. As soon as I opened the door, he knocked me off my feet. He put his hands on my neck and there was a struggle."

She waited. For the first time, she averted her eyes. "Did he make it?" she asked calmly.

He told her what he knew, that he'd hit the man's head against the bumper until it bled into the sand, until he stopped moving. "Then I put him back into the truck and took him to the gate."

He felt he had told her enough. This was who he was. It would never leave him. For the rest of his life he wanted it to be a secret only Mariam knew. She was free now to decide if she wanted that burden.

"You've suffered with such terrible memories," she said. "I don't blame you for not telling me then."

She didn't say why. If she thought she would have judged him, he was certain she wouldn't have. She would have tried to soothe him, and he had not wanted to be soothed.

"I want them to let me go," he said. He didn't realize he was thinking out loud until he heard her respond.

"I hope they will, John."

Much later, she told him about a project she had worked on at the library, which required her to read thousands of pages of testimony for a war crimes tribunal. It made sense to him, then, that she had listened to his confession without flinching. While he became consumed with a discipline in which human history mattered as much as a handful of sand, she had spent hours alone in a locked room, reading stories that gave her nightmares. He couldn't really understand why she would want to submerge herself in a sea of brutality, but this is where they met again, both acquainted in their own way with the horrors of the world. Before she left him that afternoon, in their first twenty-four hours together, they had gotten that out of the way. He could be happy again, thinking of all the peace and beauty to come.

SEVEN

It was raining. Mariam stood by the window facing the
canal, and John sat next to her, in his lonely chair, leaning
over with his forehead on her hip. He wanted to make love
to her with the windows open, with the sound and smell of the
rain coming in, and if he was persistent enough she would
probably give in, but then the whole cycle would start again. It
was easy for them to be similarly reckless their first night
together, in his room at the boarding-house, but in the following days, their togetherness still confined to this room, they
proved to be similarly practical. Mariam wanted to get on a
contraceptive pill, after she was sure she wasn't pregnant. It
would take two weeks for her to be certain, a long time in a
short summer, but John agreed it would be a mistake for her to
get pregnant. He said he was sorry he hadn't been more careful. He had thought, when she told him not to look for the condom, that she was already protected. The truth was that she
didn't want him to use a condom with her, not then or now,
that it made her feel insecure in a way she didn't want to admit.

In a way they needed two weeks of abstinence. They had
been apart for eight years, the last three a complete mystery.
There was so much to fill in. She didn't even know where he
lived now, and was surprised to hear that he lived in an apartment that belonged to his family, on a quiet street close to the
garden district of Alexandria. He told her he had a friend staying there for the summer. "You know him from Mount Belet,
in fact, or at least, he knows who you are."

She couldn't think of anyone it could be.

"Vic Arora," he said. "Do you remember ever meeting him?"

"Oh," she said, feeling ill, "I do remember him."

"He wouldn't tell me what happened with you."

"Nothing happened," she said quietly. "He made me sad. He seemed so uncomfortable."

John understood. "He was strange then, but he's grown into himself. He wasn't comfortable being eighteen."

"We spent a little time together," Mariam said. "Maybe an hour or two."

John frowned. "Did he hurt you?"

"No. He didn't hurt me. I wasn't afraid of him. Maybe I should have been but I wasn't."

John told her how he'd run into him a few years ago and had been moved enough by his ordeal to help him. When he talked about Vic she felt she learned something important about both men, and about the world of men, which was so alien to her. She learned that Vic had more courage than anyone knew, and that John wanted to reward him for it, even if no one else did. She felt tearful listening to John talk about Vic, his friend that he spoke of more lovingly than he had of anyone else in Alexandria, even his parents or sisters. About his parents and sisters John spoke with great affection and mild irritation, but not admiration, not reverence, not even the kind of familial devotion that he had for Vic. She realized she would be safe with John if he loved her. How would he sound, talking about Mariam to Vic? Would Vic come to admire her, simply from the way John told her story?

When she wasn't with him, she was constantly distracted. She evaluated all of their interactions, cataloguing her shifting feelings of security and insecurity. She inserted herself into her idea of his life in Alexandria, trying to envision a future with him. Most of all, she could not forget his story of the murdered family in Menud Fort. A curiosity about them kept resurfacing. She believed John had told her everything he could, everything that he knew and could face, and still she wanted more. She didn't know where this desire came from, if it was habit from working on the war archives, or if there was a greater purpose to it besides a satisfaction of her own curiosity. She kept forcing it down, and it kept floating back up. She didn't want to cause him more pain, but the girl whose fingernails were pink, the mother who was in labor, and the father who had fought John in the sand—all of them had names.

He came to meet her parents after she started taking a contraception pill. She didn't want a fear of pregnancy to be on their minds, and they needed some time to come together, to shed some of their separateness. As a unit they presented themselves first to his unpleasant landlady, and then to Malick, and to Misha and the others at the library when John came to look at maps and read journals and allegedly work on his dissertation in a study room.

She was nervous, of course, about what he would think of her home and her parents. She timed it so that he would arrive during her father's afternoon nap. She didn't want John to be overwhelmed by both of them at once, by her mother's curiosity and her father's confusion. This was a good decision for she had not quite prepared him for her mother. Her beauty startled him, and Mariam had forgotten how it was for people when they first met her mother. No one could reconcile the outward glamour of her appearance, those striking eyes and high cheekbones, with the drudgery of her circumstances.

Her mother was also awkward, frazzled and absent-minded. Mariam had never brought a man home before, and certainly her mother had not expected this one, the one whose letters had stopped so brutally. It was two in the afternoon and she began to open a bottle of wine John had brought for dinner. "Mama, not now," Mariam said. She took the bottle away and ordered her to make a pot of tea instead. Once the tea was set, Mariam cut a plum cake and they sat down. John and Mariam sat next to each other, facing her mother's interrogation from the other side of the table.

"How are you finding English Canal?" she asked John. "It must feel very small after Alexandria."

"It's charming," John said. He looked at Mariam. "It's very charming."

"Mariam tells me you're working with Dr. Malick. She doesn't remember, of course, but her father used to know him."

"Malick mentioned that," John said. "They worked on the highway project."

"And you're writing your dissertation," Mama said with forced enthusiasm. "What is the topic?"

John and Mariam began to laugh. It had taken him many attempts before he could explain his dissertation to Mariam in a language she could understand. The basic idea was simple enough, but his execution of the idea was so complex he'd lost sight of the simplicity of it. Poor Mama looked back and forth between them, waiting painfully. Mariam could see he lacked the confidence to explain it again now, and decided to rescue him.

"I think it's like this, Mama. The bedrock of Alexandria and the central metropolitan region was formed beneath an ancient mountain range that was once as high as the Himalayas. John is studying the characteristics of the rock, and from the amount of heat and pressure that would have been required to form it he can figure out what this range looked like, what the highest and lowest peaks were, things like that."

"How interesting," her mother said. She turned to John and asked him, "Did Mariam represent it correctly?"

"She has stated it perfectly," John answered.

"Mariam understands a great many things that I don't. This has some modern application, I imagine."

"What do you mean?"

"I mean there is a compelling reason to know about this mountain range?"

"Not really," he said cheerfully.

"It certainly reminds us of the impermanence of things," she offered.

John and Mariam nodded in silent agreement and her mother sighed. "It's time to wake my husband from his nap. Why don't you two take a walk along the canal?"

"I thought I'd show John the house first," Mariam said, but Mama looked stricken. "The house?"

"Just upstairs," she said. She felt like a little girl, wanting to show her room to a new friend. Mama was relieved and excused herself, disappearing to the back of the house while Mariam took John out of the kitchen. They breezed through the living room and she pulled him up the stairs, but he kept stopping to look at the photographs that hung on the wall, pictures of Mariam during various stages of her childhood, including some awkward ones she tried to cover with her hand. When she begged him not to look, he took hold of her and lifted her away from the wall, pretending to look at all of the pictures as he carried her thrashing and squealing to the landing. They tumbled into her room, the door slamming shut behind them, and they devoured each other on the floor like mute savages. It was over in a few thrilling minutes. They were safe now, protected from the tyrannous biology of reproduction.

As soon as he recovered he was up walking around the room, endearingly curious about her possessions, riffling through the jewelry box on top of her bureau and picking up the book on her bedside table. "Les Fleurs du Mal," he said.

"I'm trying to keep up my French," she said. "The only

time I get to read is when I'm going to bed, and invariably I fall asleep. I think now my brain associates French with sleep."

"We read a lot of geological texts in German."

"You converse fluently in German?"

"Only with geologists."

Something coincidental occurred to her. "Maybe you and my mother can talk to each other. My parents met in Germany."

"I remember. I remember you told me that once."

"My father too," she said. "He might remember some of his German." She told herself to shut up. He'd only just met her parents and already he was saddled with responsibilities.

There were no more objects in the room to occupy him. He stood by her bureau with his hands in his pockets. She was still lying on the floor, a slovenly mess and her body not quite solid again. His composure embarrassed her and she sat up. "I want to show you something," she said. She went to her bedside table and opened the drawer. The only thing inside was a hardbound notebook, which she had wanted to fill with information about her grandfather. It was not even a quarter full, but every now and then it interested her again and she found something more to put in it. At the beginning of the summer, she had added a letter from one of her grandfather's close comrades. She had tracked him down in Marseilles after a series of frustrating communications, wrote to him with limited hope and was surprised to receive his reply within two weeks. He said he would like nothing more than to sit with Suleiman Momin's granddaughter and recall him, but he asked her to come quickly, because of his age and poor health. He was over eighty and his penmanship was large and heavy, like a child's. After reading his letter, though she was sure he was confused about the distance she would have to travel to get to him, she took it as a sign that it was time to go abroad. She started planning a trip to France, and might have had her passport and visa and her ticket booked before the end of the summer, but John came and her curiosity shifted. In truth she had forgotten about Marseilles. Why did things happen like this, in competing pairs?

John sat down to look at the notebook with her. "I haven't shown this to anyone until now," she said. "Not even my mother. My grandfather killed himself in Germany and broke my mother's heart." His eyebrows shot up, casting deep lines across his forehead. His forehead was so expressive, so sympathetic. "Suicide? Why did he do that?" John asked.

"My mother said he wasn't made for a life of exile."

"How old was she when it happened?"

"She was seventeen," Mariam said. "My grandfather had been a lawyer here. Then he got involved in politics." She showed him the information she'd collected in the notebook, crudely trying to narrate her grandfather's story. John listened without interruption, but he got stuck on the photograph of her grandfather with Peter Moses. He kept her from turning the page and squinted at the picture as if he'd seen it before.

"I know about your grandfather," he said, sounding far from certain.

"What do you mean?" she asked.

"When I was at the training camp they took your letters. I never got to read them. They said something about your grandfather," he said. "Did I ever tell you that?"

"You told me they took my letters. You think it was because of my grandfather?" He was being vague, and she found it hard to believe her grandfather's actions would have held much consequence so long after his death.

"The commanding officer called me into his office and showed me the stack of letters. I remember his face clearly. He looked like a wild pig. He said something about your grandfather, and the war."

"What did he say exactly?"

John looked hopeless. "I don't remember. That he was a

troublemaker, something like that. All I could think about were the letters. I was hoping he would give them to me."

"But he didn't?"

"No," he said. He seemed distracted now, pulled away by his fragmented memory. She was torn between wanting to know more and wanting John to remain here with her, in the present.

She put her notebook back in the drawer and didn't say anything more about her grandfather. "Let's go see the canal," she suggested. They washed up and went outside, walking along the canal toward the Market Bridge. She told him how the canal was being drained slowly. When it was empty, they would fill it with cement and turn it into a wide boulevard. They stopped at the Market Bridge and looked over the parapet into the tranquil water. "It's so peaceful here," he said. They stood there for a long time with their bodies overlapping. It was amazing how long they remained there without moving. Mariam couldn't remember the last time she'd been so still. Then Mariam wanted to help her mother prepare lunch, and they walked back, talking about everyday things regarding her father and mother and their plans for the afternoon. By the time they reached the house, her father was up and sitting on the sofa in front of the television, feeding himself a small meal of rice and minced beef. He looked at John curiously, trying his best to keep his food on the spoon at the same time. "This is my friend," Mariam said. Her father tilted his head toward the seat next to him, and John sat down. There, she thought happily, they were already communicating well. She left them and went to the kitchen.

Mama was surprised to see her alone. "Don't leave him in there," she scolded. "What will he do when your father starts asking questions?"

"He'll handle it," Mariam said, though she didn't want to witness it herself, John straining to understand and her father giving up in frustration. She got busy snapping the ends off dozens of string beans. "What do you think of him?" she asked.

"He's good, darling. I prayed for him to be good."

"I knew he would come, Mama. I always knew it."

"Did you, Mariam?"

"Yes."

"Well, then, thank God he did."

They began to talk about the end of the summer. He said he would not return to Alexandria without her. He wanted to get married here, and not tell anyone until it was done, and she agreed. She didn't want a long engagement. She didn't want letters and telephone calls. She wanted to take this chance at happiness even if she felt ill-prepared for it. There was only one thing she needed to know before she committed to the idea without fear. She needed to know if she could always be herself with him. After a little effort, she had received a packet from the headmistress of a government school in Menud Fort. It contained a detailed letter explaining how often children from her school disappeared for various reasons, but for the dates in question, there was only one child it could have been, a five-year-old girl named Rohana Bul. Rohana Bul had a twelve-year-old sister they hoped had escaped, but she was found dead later, in the field, a short distance from the checkpoint. She had been violated, the letter said. Also killed on that day was Rohana's pregnant mother. The fate of her father had never been determined. The headmistress enclosed a copy of the child's enrollment form along with her school identification photo. The reproduction was small and grainy, but solid enough. All of their names were there in the packet, but the picture was only of Rohana.

Mariam took the envelope to John. She sat on his bed, holding it in her lap. "What is that?" he asked.

"I've done something, John. I don't know if it will make you

angry. But I've done it and I don't want to keep it from you."
He watched her take out the picture of Rohana Bul. She
handed it to him without explaining it. She could tell from his
look of confused sorrow it was the same little girl he'd found
in the car. It seemed to cause him great pain, and in the
moment he might have felt betrayed by her. He might have felt
unsafe, but Mariam was certain it was better for him to see it,
and better to know her name. He stared at the picture for a
long time, and in the days following, he told Mariam he had
dreams in which Rohana was a living child, and in those
dreams it felt like she was their own daughter.

At the end of the summer, he came to the library and signaled her toward a private study room. He had to wait by the
door, since she was with a student who was taking a long time,
but as soon as she could get to him and unlock the door and
bring him into the room, he grabbed her and kissed her fanat-
ically. "We can do it tomorrow," he said.

The next morning she left the house without seeing her
mother, which wasn't so unusual. Sometimes she was in a hurry
and her mother was occupied in the back of the house. Mariam
wore a white dress printed with periwinkles, a little bit of lace
at the hem. She went to the courthouse and waited for John,
and he appeared a few minutes later, dressed handsomely in a
dark blue suit, running up the steps and catching his breath
when he reached her. He asked her if she was ready. They
stood at the main entrance, waiting for the doors to open.
There was no one in front of them or behind them wanting to
get married that day and once the doors opened it was all fast
and efficient. The magistrate seemed weary of romance and
eager to finish up. They had to stand across from each other
and repeat an oath, and when the magistrate asked if there was
a ring Mariam was about to say no, there couldn't have been a
ring, but John reached into an inside pocket of his suit jacket
and pulled out a ring which he slipped on her finger, a sweet

silver ring with a small round stone that was the faintest of blues, the blue of a glacier. "This stone is aquamarine. It comes from Sri Lanka. There are four diamonds," he began, but she kissed him and he couldn't say another word.

"All right, all right," the magistrate said sternly. "You're married now."

It hit her slowly, as they signed their marriage certificate, that she had done something irreversible. It wasn't that she wanted to undo it. She wanted nothing more than to be married to John, but if there was any chance to do it differently, it had passed. Walking out of the courthouse she got a sick feeling in her belly. "I have to go tell my mother."

"We'll tell her together," John said, unburdened. What a surprise his parents were in for.

"No, I have to tell her myself. Come for supper. I'll make something nice."

"Don't worry, Mariam. She wants you to be happy. Show her how happy you are."

With that advice she left her new husband and walked home along the canal to prolong the journey. By the time she got home she had convinced herself of how well it would go. Her mother would be relieved to hear the news, to have her prayers answered. Surely she prayed for the end of Mariam's solitary life?

Her mother was alone in the kitchen, buttering toast for breakfast. Mariam had forgotten that it was still early in the day. Her father would have been trying to dress himself. He would appear in the doorway any minute either needing assistance or pumping his fist triumphantly, ready for his next challenge. Her mother looked up, still busy with the toast. "You haven't left yet?"

"Actually, I took the day off. I just came back."

"Back from where?" she asked. Mariam had not meant to hold out her hand yet. She was looking for the right words and

166 · CHAITALI SEN

looked at her hand instead, at the ring, as if it might tell her
what to say. Her mother saw the ring and locked her eyes on it,
even after Mariam lowered her hand.

"Don't be upset, Mama."

"Why would I be upset? What mother wants to be invited
to her only daughter's wedding?"

"We didn't tell anyone," Mariam explained. "Not even his
parents know yet."

"What was the hurry? Are you pregnant?"

"He has to go back to Alexandria."

Her mother made a strange, snickering sound. "To chase
the ghosts of mountains," she remarked. It wasn't like her to
be so belittling.

"You said he was good. That's what you prayed for,"
Mariam said. Of course it was possible Mama had lied when
she said that. Mariam wondered now if lying wasn't the thing
her mother did best.

Her mother went back to buttering the toast. She bored
holes in it with her furious scraping.

"I expected a longer engagement. Usually there is some
kind of engagement."

Mariam couldn't see the point of an engagement. Hadn't
she waited long enough? Did her mother have no sympathy for
her, no understanding at all of her desires?

"He's going back to Alexandria next week," Mariam said.
"I'm going with him."

Mama didn't respond. She tossed the butter knife into the
sink and turned to the stove to get the kettle.

"I know it's soon but we can hire a nurse," Mariam continued. "It's what Daddy needs anyway. We'll send you money.
Maybe in a few years you can move to Alexandria and he can
have the best medical treatment."

Her mother refused to turn around, now preoccupied with
filling up the kettle. Her silence was hostile, saber-sharp and

piercing, and Mariam was becoming shrill. "You can't really think that I should stay here, when I have a chance to go?"

This time when her mother looked at Mariam, her eyes were soft and pleading, desperate to try a different tactic. She squared her shoulders and lifted her chin, dignifying herself, taking care with what she might say next. Mariam was prepared to hear something important, something more reasonable. "Mariam," her mother said with gentle love and condescension, "marriage is not some kind of escape."

Mariam stared. "Believe me, Mother, if anyone has shown me that, it's you."

For a second her mother resembled a cowering dog, but she hardened again and Mariam backed away, ashamed of herself and wary of how much farther this confrontation could go. Before she could apologize her father showed up at the door with his shirt more or less buttoned. Her mother ordered him to sit down and slid a plate of toast in front of him. "You should learn to butter your bread," she said. "It's not too difficult. I think you can manage it."

Her father puckered his lips. He did that with his lips a lot, and Mariam had never figured out if it stood for ambivalence or defiance. A shrug or a grimace? He might have thought his attempts to communicate physically were clear, but they were painfully unclear.

"Mariam is married. She did it this morning."

Her mother lifted Mariam's hand and showed him the ring. "She's going away. She's leaving us." Her voice broke as she said it. She laced her fingers through Mariam's and regarded the ring one more time, running her thumb over the blue stone.

Her father patted her ringed hand, and therefore her mother's hand too. "Good girl," he said.

The kettle began to shriek. Her mother let go of her and went to the stove, and Mariam, after taking a breath, got three cups down from the cupboard.

EIGHT

I n Alexandria, the foliage was varied and everywhere in late summer there were window boxes overflowing with flowers. John lived in an elegant building on a boulevard lined with imported ginkgo trees, their branches lush with prehistoric, fan-shaped leaves unlike any leaves Mariam had seen before. They went on many walks through artful neighborhoods, and in the evenings they went up to his rooftop to look over the city of white domes and silver spires, miles of domes and spires until they faded into the sky. John pointed in a different direction each night, teaching her the geography of the city. To the south, on a clear day, they could see the river that tore the city in half and the jeweled bridges that mended it.

She met his parents and sisters at their house in Cypress Gardens. All she could say was that she had spent a weekend with them and survived. She survived his father's kindness and his mother's reserved manners, survived his older sister Sonya who was so enthralled with her ten-month-old son she hardly noticed Mariam, and she survived the baby, Nathan, whom John devoured every time he came near. Nathan was a fat and sweet baby and Mariam didn't dare pay him too much attention. She even survived John's sister Theresa, who was ten years younger, only seventeen, just starting her final year of high school. She was the most heartbroken by John's sudden marriage, as if she had thought she was going to marry him herself.

When the weekend was finished and they were finally

home, Mariam didn't know what to say about his family. She missed her own mother and the restful tedium that comes from an unquestioned sense of belonging. As she wearily got ready for bed, John said, "Don't let them intimidate you." It was true, she had been intimidated, and she'd spent the whole weekend in a panic, terrified of him leaving her side.

"I'll do better next time," she promised.

"You did fine. That's not what I meant."

"I'll get used to them."

"And they'll get used to you," he said. "They'll love you."

She knew his family was unhappy about the marriage, but she also got the idea that it wasn't completely unexpected for John to go away and come back with a wife. There were things about him they could not predict or understand, and they adored him for it.

Her next trial was a department party hosted by Nehemia and his wife, who lived in an apartment in the Jewish Quarter, one of the oldest parts of the city. The taxi got lost in the maze of dark streets and narrow cobblestone alleys barely wide enough for a car. Almost an hour late, they stopped in front of a stone building with a large mahogany door. The area was faintly lit with gas lamps and sconces. John tapped an iron doorknocker and the door was heaved open by an elderly doorman.

Mariam squinted into the deep yellow light saturating the mirrored lobby. They climbed a winding marble staircase to a third-floor landing that fanned out like a river delta, where one red door punctured a curved white wall. Behind the door was a tangle of voices and Mariam gripped John's hand, hoping he wouldn't abandon her too quickly.

John rang the doorbell, and after a shuffling of footsteps the door swung open and Mariam was pulled into the apartment. She was grateful for the dimness of the main room, a long salon lit only with a scattering of Tiffany lamps. She met Nehemia first, who was younger and less intimidating than she expected.

He had a salt-and-pepper beard and large soulful eyes, and then his elegant wife came up beside him, dressed stunningly in a full-length brocade gown. Mrs. Nehemia and John kissed each other on the cheek. To Mariam she offered her hand and smiled. "How lovely," Mrs. Nehemia said to no one in particular. Mariam was introduced to more people whose names and affiliations she could not remember.

Vic appeared suddenly, like a bear in the woods. Without any warning he took her into his arms and squeezed her. He muttered into her ear something about his cock being bigger than John's. "That must be why you couldn't get it in," she said, and he pulled away, laughing. Mariam was relieved to have it past them; it never again needed mentioning. John was staring at them, his mouth a little bud, and Mariam went back to him in a hurry. "You bastard, you've done it now," Vic said to him, giving his arm a punch.

"I need a drink," John said. He pulled Mariam to a table-top collection of glasses, rounded wine glasses and conical martini glasses, tumblers for whiskey and flutes for champagne. An adjacent table held bottles of clear and amber liquor arranged neatly in rows, punctuated with bowls of lemon wedges, olives, and shockingly red cherries. Mariam didn't know what to do with any of it, but before John could make her a drink Nehemia came and took him away to meet a new doctoral student.

Mariam knew not to follow him. She walked over to a triptych of French windows and looked out. It was too dark to see anything but an old wall and a park behind it, more darkness and the shadowy limbs of some hulking, ancient tree.

She felt a gentle hand on her shoulder. It was Mrs. Nehemia, trying to hand her a martini. Mariam took the glass and stirred the martini with the skewer of three olives. She took a sip.

"It's my specialty," Mrs. Nehemia said. "Is it too strong?"

"No," Mariam said emphatically. She picked up the skewer

of olives and put it indelicately into her mouth. While Mrs. Nehemia stepped away to retrieve her own drink, something pinkish with a cherry floating in it, Mariam popped the first olive into her mouth and let the juices burst on her tongue. Amusedly Mrs. Nehemia watched her savor the olive. What a stylish woman she was. Her earrings were opal.

"You're the reason my husband's been in such a terrible mood," she said at last. "He thought Malick was stealing him. We were so relieved when we found out he'd only gone off to get married. How do you like Alexandria?"

"I think it's beautiful."

"It must be difficult, experiencing a new marriage and new city all at once." She asked Mariam about her home, which Mariam described with a warm feeling that surprised her.

"It sounds quite modern," Mrs. Nehemia said. "In Alexandria, people tend to think the rest of the country is so backward."

"Backward?" Mariam balked. "No, we have everything. It's not as developed but that's because of politics, not the people."

"That's very true," Mrs. Nehemia said. "I like the way you think. You should talk to some of John's colleagues and correct their attitude."

"You should visit English Canal," Mariam said. "Even John liked it."

"The way you describe it is quite different from what I expected. If you ever pass through the neighborhood by Victoria Park where the Sulatis live, most of the women are veiled." Mariam nodded. She had not known such a neighborhood existed. "Is that common where you live?"

"Not where I lived," Mariam said. She didn't want to say more. She was ignorant of too many things to get into a reasonable conversation, such as what Mrs. Nehemia meant by veiled, and where in Sulat it might have been more common, or who had migrated to Alexandria from Sulat and for what reasons. She tried to remember the women on the streets in Belarive, but she was only six and had not taken careful note of the passing women. She knew for a fact her mother walked outside without even a headscarf, but most of the women probably wore some kind of covering. Mariam did happen to know why it wasn't common in English Canal. She had found out from reading about her grandfather's cases that English Canal had been one of the municipalities banning "garments that obscured the face," as far back as the 1920s. It had surprised her to find out the college had taken an active role in supporting the ban. "These things are so complicated," Mariam said, sounding like she was too feeble minded to think about them, and Mrs. Nehemia said she was fascinated by the differences in people. Mariam smiled. She thought Mrs. Nehemia was endearing and kind, and the drink she had given her was relaxing.

"Your home is lovely," Mariam said. "And this neighborhood, there's so much history here!"

Mrs. Nehemia boasted that her family had lived on this street for five generations.

"Do you ever feel like an outsider in Alexandria?" Mariam asked. "I mean, being Jewish?"

Mariam hoped she hadn't overstepped. Mrs. Nehemia looked surprised, but not offended. "You know, I used to, every time I left the neighborhood. But I suppose when you get older, you learn what to expect and you adjust yourself accordingly."

"I see."

Mrs. Nehemia studied Mariam, looking amused. "No one's ever thought to ask me that before."

"I hope it wasn't rude," Mariam said.

"Not at all. You're very charming."

Mariam felt she might be monopolizing Mrs. Nehemia's hospitality and looked around the room for John. In the center of the room there was a long sofa and a stylish wooden coffee table, and matching wingback armchairs at either end. Every seat was occupied. Throughout the room there were more intimate arrangements, and in one corner a cluster of women, seated in a huddle, were talking and sputtering with laughter. John, Vic, Nehemia, in fact all of the men were gone from the main room.

"Who are the women over there?" Mariam asked.

"Wives," Mrs. Nehemia answered. "Like you. Do you want to meet them?"

"Do you think I should?"

Mrs. Nehemia looked back at them. "They're gossiping at the moment. I don't think you will enjoy them."

Mariam finished her drink and looked woefully into her glass, and immediately Mrs. Nehemia replaced it with a fresh drink. Mariam took a sip, but the effects of the first martini suddenly overwhelmed her. If she drank a second one, she'd be falling down. How mortifying if she got sick in front of John's department.

Mrs. Nehemia took the drink away. "You must eat something now," she said, and led her across the room to a table of exquisite hors d'oeuvres, figs stuffed with soft cheese, four varieties of olive including a home-cured green olive that tasted less briny, more fruity, and darling little chicken croquettes, fried herbed almonds, and grapes to cleanse the palate. Her hostess went off to tend to new guests, and Mariam ate more olives. She couldn't get enough of them.

When she was full she wandered away from the table. She followed the sound of men's voices and found her way to the terrace. John was there, drinking whisky and talking to his colleagues. He put his arm around her and went on talking about something she couldn't understand. Mariam rested her head on his shoulder. The men teased her, offering their own shoulders instead. They made some crude jokes about foreign women and John, calling them terrible names, told them to shut up. Mariam, feeling truly drunk now, didn't know which foreign women they were talking about.

They were among the last to leave. When they were departing, Mrs. Nehemia held Mariam's hand and said, "Take care of her. I like her very much." Now flush with affection, Mariam leaned forward and kissed her cheek, and everyone seemed to be laughing. "I like her too," John said. In the taxi going home, he slipped his hand between her legs. He was also drunk. "I'm the envy of the whole department. Now they all want to go to English Canal and come back with a wife."

Once the new term began, Mariam had more time to herself. She set her mind to finding a job, putting in an application at the Presidency College Library. John was sure they'd have a position for her but there was nothing open in the Reference department, and Mariam did not want to go back to Circulation. It didn't matter; there were so many interesting libraries in Alexandria. The one that caught her attention was the Library of the Antiquities in the neighborhood called Old Alexandria. Mariam looked on the metro map. It was a little far, requiring a transfer at Parliament Square, but she could do it. She would have to learn, anyway. What was the point of leaving her home if she was going to remain trapped inside another one? Surely John would want her to be independent. He hadn't put any restrictions on her job search.

She called and had a lengthy conversation with the director. Mariam was excited to talk about her experience and her work on the War Archives and the director sounded very interested. She said their specialty was preserving older documents, but if Mariam was interested, they had a one-year internship and training course in document collection and preservation. She thought Mariam would be an excellent candidate. It didn't pay any money, but the training was free. Mariam said she would think about it. She didn't know how John would feel about an unpaid job, though they didn't need the money. He claimed she saved him money, which was probably true considering his apparent inability to open bills or use a stove.

She was excited when John got home. Before he could get his shoes off she'd told him all about her conversation. He misunderstood. "You went there by yourself?"

"No, I called. I spoke to her on the phone. But what do you think? It doesn't pay. Did you hear that part?"

He didn't know where it was. She showed him on the map. "That's far," he said. "I don't want you to go through Parliament Square. There are bombings there all the time."

"Bombings?"

"Well, bomb threats. Evacuations. But once a bomb did go off in a trash can. There are no trash cans there."

Mariam laughed. "What do you mean there are no trash cans? You don't want me to go because there are no trash cans?" She knew what he meant but she still thought he was being ridiculous.

"Parliament Square is dangerous. Read the newspaper."

"All right. Maybe there's a different way I could go."

He thought about it. "I guess we could go this weekend and see how it is."

"She asked me to come in tomorrow. John, I have to do this on my own. I can't depend on you for everything. It's a good opportunity. The only problem is the money, but it's only twenty hours. I can still get a part-time job."

"Then I'll never see you."

"You'll see me, don't be silly."

He didn't argue any more. He said he would take the train with her to Parliament Square in the morning and she could continue on from there. If she still wanted it, he wouldn't stop her.

Mariam thought that was a very reasonable solution. She was pleased with the way they had talked things out.

"Listen," he said. "I wasn't going to tell you this until it's final, but there's a good chance we're going to Copenhagen in March." He told her they had submitted a paper for the World Geomorphology Conference and Nehemia got unofficial word that it had been accepted. They were waiting for the invitation letter. Depending on the department funds, they would only have to pay for Mariam's plane ticket.

Mariam couldn't believe it. They had talked about traveling the next summer, when things were more settled. Copenhagen in March sounded so wonderful she could hardly believe it. She had to tell herself this was her new life and she should get used to announcements like this.

"But you'll be working. I won't be in your way?" she asked.

He raised one eyebrow. "I hope you'll be in my way."

She could barely contain her excitement. "I don't have a passport. Does it take long to get one? Should I apply for one now, just in case?"

John nodded. "Everything here takes a long time."

Mariam had so many more questions. How much would the plane ticket cost? Would it be snowing in Copenhagen in March? Would Mrs. Nehemia or any of the other wives be going? He didn't know the answers to any of her questions.

She said, "I'll take the job in Circulation, then. We're going to need travel money."

"Traveling can be expensive. What about the Library of Antiquities?"

She pretended to think about it. "Maybe I'll still go, just to see it." She was aware of how masterfully he had steered her away from something she thought she wanted. She didn't know how she felt about that part, but in this case, she felt she could accept defeat.

The next day she went to the passport office to fill out her application. She showed the clerk her marriage license and her residency card. He said it was better to have a birth certificate but Mariam explained that she never had one. It wasn't unusual to not have a birth certificate, especially in Sulat, and the clerk didn't seem concerned. He said birth certificates weren't standard until 1965 and Mariam said, "Really? How interesting." As she filled out her application, her fingers were unsteady. She had to put the pen down repeatedly to wipe her hand on her skirt. She realized she had been waiting for this all her life. She had been waiting for the world to open up.

"Do I need to have my picture taken?" she asked.

"Not yet. You'll get an approval letter and then you bring the photographs."

"How long will it take?"

"Three months."

"No longer than three months?"

The clerk hesitated. "Not usually."

"We're traveling in March," she said.

"You'll have it by March, no problem."

That same week, Mariam took a job in the Circulation department at the Presidency College Library. It was dull but easy, and within a month she was able to send more money home to her parents.

She told her mother about the trip to Copenhagen once it was official. Mama said, "That's wonderful, darling. You'll have to send me a postcard."

"There's no reason why you can't come to Alexandria for a little while. We can pay for a nurse. Or you can bring Daddy with you." She'd had this conversation with her mother before.

"It's such a hassle, Mariam."

"Don't you want to see where I live?"

"I have such a lovely picture of it in my mind."

"But I miss you."

"Oh, stop, you don't miss me at all. Don't tell lies."

She swore her mother was getting more impossible by the day.

By the end of the fall term, four days past the three month mark, Mariam still hadn't received her passport letter. John had already purchased their plane tickets. Their hotel room was booked. Everything was set but the passport.

"Stop worrying," John said. "When they say three months it means four."

At last, the letter from the Passport Office came at the end of December. It was a short letter, three sentences. Mariam held it in her hands for a long time. Her name was printed clearly, Mariam Merchant (née Azim). Everything about it seemed to be correct, written in bureaucratic language, on official letterhead, except for the most important thing, the promise of a passport. The letter said her request had been denied.

John came out of the bedroom, asking Mariam where she'd hidden his blue tie. He stopped when he saw her. "What is it?"

She handed him the letter. She watched him as he read it, hoping he would say there was no problem, that there only a little missing information that they needed in order to finish processing the request, and she would know that she had misunderstood the letter completely, but she could tell from his expression of vague panic that he had not been expecting anything like this.

"Let's go to the passport office now," John said. "I'm sure this is a bureaucratic mix-up. They do this kind of thing all the time."

"They do?"

He looked at his watch. "Hurry up and get ready. My class is in three hours."

She didn't believe it was a bureaucratic mix-up, and since there had been no reason given for the denial, the reasons were left to Mariam's imagination. In the taxi, she made a mental list and narrowed it down to three possibilities: her grandfather's political activities, her letters that were intercepted during John's military service, probably still in some government file somewhere, and her work on the war archives. She thought that had to be it. She had intricate knowledge of war crimes, and lately there had been a string of visits from European foreign ministers who were always talking about democracy. If this turned out to be the reason, she didn't know what she could do about it. What happened in the past couldn't be changed.

They sat in the passport office for two hours. John prepared notes for his class, though still he compulsively checked his watch, while Mariam had nothing to do but think. Thinking never made her optimistic. Finally, they were called into a tiny windowless office barely big enough for a desk and three chairs, and there they waited for a death-faced bureaucrat to finish looking over her file. According to the nameplate on the desk, this was Zafar Hussain, though he didn't introduce himself by name. Mariam wondered if he was from Sulat, but he had a more Eastern look to him. He examined official papers in her file. Mariam tried to see what they were but she couldn't recognize any of them. She gripped the cold metal arms of her chair. She wasn't aware of how tightly her fingers wrapped around them until John put his hand over hers.

"You don't have a birth certificate?" the man asked.

"A birth certificate?" Mariam couldn't believe it. "I was told birth certificates weren't standard until 1965. I have a residency card. I've never had a birth certificate."

"But we have no record of your citizenship."

"Why would she need that?" John asked. "She was born here. Her parents were born here."

"It doesn't matter. They left the country."

"During the war," Mariam said. "They had to leave. Then they came back."

This man, Mr. Hussain, looked at her as if she had no right to speak. He could not have come from Sulat, Mariam thought. Surely someone from her province would have shown more sympathy. He talked to her slowly as if she were a small child.

"People who leave outside of the proper channels relinquish their citizenship. When your parents returned in 1955, their citizenship was conditional. It would have been clearly explained to them upon reentry. They had to apply for restoration of citizenship, but we have no papers showing they completed the process. As far as the government is concerned, you and your parents are here illegally."

"That's absurd," John exclaimed. "Even if her parents aren't technically citizens, she was born here."

"But where is your proof?" cried Mr. Hussain. "I have no authority to issue a passport to a non-citizen. Bring us proof and we'll give her a passport."

"What kind of proof will you accept besides a birth certificate?" Mariam asked.

That question seemed to confound him. "Maybe an official letter from the hospital where you were delivered. It might work or it might prompt an investigation. Probably they would require an official interview with your parents."

"My father is invalid. He can't answer questions."

"You're lucky this is the only consequence. We could deport you."

"Deport me? To where?"

He didn't answer. Mariam wished they would deport her. Any place had to be better than this.

"All right," John said, leaning forward. "Forget about her parents for a minute. I *am* a citizen, unless that's also under dispute."

"If you have a passport, you are a citizen," Hussain said in all seriousness.

"Mariam is my wife. We have a marriage certificate. Why can't she apply for citizenship as my wife?"

The man looked impressed. "Yes, that's a solution."

"How long will that take?" Mariam asked. She wondered if that would also require her parents to make official statements.

"A year or two? I don't work for Immigration."

"A year? I can't get a temporary passport in the meantime?"

The man looked at John. "Please explain to her, we don't issue passports to people without citizenship. There isn't any country that does that." They both turned and watched her wipe tears from her cheeks, but Hussain was unmoved. "Bring proof. Or apply for citizenship as your husband suggested. Those are the simplest solutions."

John squeezed her hand. "Mariam, wait out in the lobby for a minute."

She sat in her chair frozen, staring at him. He tilted his chin toward the door. Slowly she stood up and said flatly to the man, "Thank you, you've been very helpful." She stormed out, walking all the way out of the building, and waited for him on the sidewalk. Tears kept falling down her cheeks. People stared at her as they passed. She wiped them away as fast as she could.

John came out a minute later. He hailed a taxi and got in after her. He told the driver where to go and watched him pull out. The driver was on his radio, having a conversation with the dispatcher. John leaned back in his seat.

"I asked if there was anything else that could be done," he told her.

"You mean like a bribe?" Mariam's heart was racing. All she needed was another paper in her file saying her husband had offered a bribe. Anyway, if it had worked, he would have looked more pleased with himself.

"What did he say?" she asked.

182 · CHAITALI SEN

"We danced around it for a little while. He pretended to be offended at first. Then he asked what I had in mind, I said five thousand . . . "

"Five thousand? That's insane."

"He said ten, and I said, what guarantee do I have that my wife will get her passport, and he said there are no guarantees, and I left."

"You gave him the money?"

"No, Mariam, I don't carry that kind of money with me."

She burst into tears again. This time she couldn't control the sound of her sobbing. John put his arms around her, trying to hush her. He said he didn't mean to snap at her. He was a little frustrated, that was all.

"I swear I didn't know anything about this," she said.

"Of course you didn't."

"My parents have ruined me."

"It's possible they just didn't understand, or they weren't well-informed."

She considered the possibility. "Maybe they're lying, John. What if none of this is true?"

"What do you mean?"

"This restoration of citizenship business. Who has ever heard of such a thing?"

John shook his head. "It sounds strange to me."

"I'm going to look into it. I'll get to the bottom of it."

"I know you will," he said, kissing her forehead.

"I don't want you to be troubled with this," she said. "While you're away, I'll take care of it. When you get back, you'll see, everything will be fixed."

"While I'm away?"

"It won't be fixed before Copenhagen. I can try but I doubt it."

His entire demeanor changed, his bravado falling away like a shattered porcelain mask. When they got back into their apartment, he poured a glass of whiskey down his throat before he went off to work.

Mariam called her mother. She told her as calmly as she could what had happened in the passport office. When she was finished with her story, there was silence on the other end of the line. "Mama, do you know anything about this?"

"Of course not, Mariam." She had never heard her mother sound so shrill. She had to believe that she was telling the truth.

"Are you sure? Did Daddy talk to Immigration alone when you came back into the country?"

"Immigration? There was nothing, Mariam. They stamped our passports and let us go. Do you think I would have left something like that alone?"

"But maybe Daddy knew. Maybe he was afraid to tell you because he knew you would be angry."

"How am I going to find out from him now? He can barely put two words together."

She could sense that her mother was getting too upset. Mariam felt she needed to calm her down. "All right, I'm sure there's a solution. Do you remember the name of the doctor who delivered me?"

"Of course, it was Doctor Shah. We used to run into him many times walking along the canal. He's long gone, Mariam. He was an old man when he delivered you."

"He's dead?" Marian asked, and somehow that made her laugh deliriously. She laughed so hard it alarmed her mother. "Stop, darling, you're frightening me."

Mariam put her hand up to her mouth, trying to stop herself, and at the same time, her fingers caught a flood of tears.

They consulted a lawyer. He told them Mr. Hussain had been correct, that there was such a statute that required returning

184 · CHAITALI SEN

refugees to restore their citizenship if their loyalty to the sovereignty of the country could not be established. He gave examples of scenarios in which the law was likely to be applied, for instance if a male bypassed his military service either before he left or upon his return, or if there were ties within the family to the secessionist movement. Mariam had to admit that both of those could have been true. Certainly her grandfather would have been considered a part of the secessionist movement, and if her father had ever done his military service, she never heard about it.

He advised them to take the least drastic route first, to try to get a statement from the hospital where she was born and resubmit her passport application. If the application was submitted through the lawyer, there was a chance they would take it more seriously and let the paperwork slide through. Mariam got a statement from the hospital, and they resubmitted the application through the lawyer. Even if that worked, she would be lucky to get a passport before the summer.

John was evasive about his trip to Copenhagen. Whenever she asked him questions about it, and tried to get him to show some urgency in getting ready for the trip, he told her he had it all under control. Mariam decided not to talk to him about it anymore. She wondered if he was angry with her, or her parents, for creating this situation. If he blamed her in any way, he didn't show it. He was working hard on his dissertation and the presentation for Copenhagen. He seemed tired, and he didn't want to talk about Copenhagen. Other than that, his behavior toward her had not changed at all.

In early March, when the trip was imminent, he came home and found her folding laundry on the bed. He came into the room talking. He told her he had canceled their plane tickets because he was not going to Copenhagen. He had already told Nehemia. It was already done. He was sorry that he had kept it a secret from her, but he had no desire to face another separation, even if it was for a short time. He rambled on, talking about lost years and regret.

As Mariam listened to him, all she could think was that they had made a mistake. She kept repeating it in her head, we've made a terrible mistake, a terrible mistake, until she blurted it out and John stared at her intently. "What do you mean by that?"

"You know what I mean. It's a mistake." She was crying again. Her nerves were so fragile.

He narrowed his eyes. "You mean us? We're the mistake?" She nodded and he grabbed her by the shoulders. When he saw that he had taken her too roughly, he laid his hands more gently on her cheeks. "Don't say that. Don't ever say that, Mariam. Are you unhappy here with me?"

"No," she said. Of course she wasn't unhappy with him. It was only his sacrifice that was intolerable.

"Then don't say that, Mariam."

She lowered her head, feeling ashamed and guilty. Her tears soaked his shirt. In a year, maybe even in a few months, she hoped she would look back on all this and realize how oblivious she had been to the temporary nature of their hardship. She imagined talking about it at a dinner party, describing her passport difficulties and saying, "It was such a nightmare," in the same way she had often heard people exaggerating situations that were stressful and even maddening, but nothing close to a nightmare.

NINE

When he came back from Copenhagen, Nehemia called John into his office. John expected a summary of the conference but Nehemia didn't want to talk about Copenhagen. He wanted to know when John would be turning in his dissertation. John said, "Any day now." Then Nehemia got to the point. He told John he would be announcing his resignation at the end of the week. John needed to defend his dissertation before the new director came in. "How soon is that?" John asked.

Nehemia said, "Any day now."

It wasn't that John didn't know something was going on. Nehemia had been under pressure for a while to run a more practical program. Every time he had a bad meeting with the college chancellor, he lectured his doctoral students about the importance of pure research, saying scientists were not in the business of nation building and the only way to judge the value of a research topic was by the scientist's engagement in the questions guiding that topic. John had heard his arguments countless times, and while he agreed with him in principle, he could see Nehemia becoming somewhat dogmatic about it. He called Malick's program kindergarten geology and Mount Belet a mining academy.

"Why do you think I wanted to take you to Copenhagen?" Nehemia asked. "I'm concerned about your future. I don't want to spend the rest of my life wondering what happened to John Merchant."

"I don't plan to stay," John assured him.

Nehemia didn't seem to hear him. "I remember the distraction of having a pretty new wife, John. But I had time. You don't. Everything here is about to change."

"There are some delays with Mariam's passport, that's all. As soon as she can travel, I'll put in my applications. If you know someone who can expedite things . . . "

"It's because you married a girl from Sulat," Nehemia interrupted. "Nothing against Mariam, but you've made things difficult for yourself."

John regretted telling him the truth. He'd made the same mistake with his own father, and got a similar response. His father had performed heart surgery on cabinet ministers, by all accounts adding years to their lives, yet he was afraid to ask them to do a small kindness for Mariam. It surprised John because he could see how quickly his parents had fallen in love with her, despite their resistance to his marriage. They embraced her with all kinds of loving gestures, especially his father, but they were equally eager to distance her from the family name as soon as a reason presented itself. He didn't understand how they could regard her with so much affection and shame all at once.

And still John was happy. Despite the attitudes of his parents and his trusted advisor, despite the crushing disappointment they'd already encountered in their young marriage, it was impossible for him to be unhappy. As long as he could protect her, as long as he could hold off his terror of her retreating, he knew happiness was his natural condition now.

For her part, Mariam was trying to control her nerves. He had underestimated her reaction to his decision not to go to Copenhagen. Though it was the right decision and he didn't regret it, he spent days undoing the damage it did to her confidence. She made him promise not to give up any more opportunities for her. If he had to go away, she would wait for him;

she would still be here when he got back. "You should know that about me by now," she said. It was meant to reassure him but she missed the landing. All of their conversations regarding Copenhagen were plagued with these tiny failures of intent and interpretation. In the end they agreed to move on from the subject. It helped to hand the problem over to a lawyer who seemed to understand the situation. All they had to do was follow his directions and wait. That was something they could endure together.

John told Nehemia he would take his advice to heart. Nehemia meant well, but there was nothing John could do right now to satisfy him, and no point in talking about it anymore. He left the office and went to look for Vic, who should have been dismissing his undergraduate seminar. John stood outside the classroom door, watching Vic through the glass panel. The class had gone over by at least five minutes, and Vic was still giving an animated lecture, talking fast and waving his huge hands around for emphasis. At one point Vic said something funny and his students burst into laughter. Vic waited for their laughter to subside before finishing his lecture. John shook his head, smiling at the spectacle. Vic had a gift for this. He was a fine scholar but this was his calling and his passion, and John felt a flood of pride and relief that he was doing so well. All of Vic's troubles seemed to be behind him.

He couldn't wait around for Vic anymore. It was four o'clock and Mariam's shift at the library was over. She was waiting for him on the steps of the science building and when she saw him, she smiled. It was a beautiful day.

Nehemia made sure John's dissertation defense went smoothly and secured him an appointment letter for the following year. He and his wife were giving their apartment to Mrs. Nehemia's niece and leaving in June for McGill University in Canada. At the end of May, John and Mariam went to their apartment for dinner. The women chatted like old friends while Nehemia tried to prepare him for the changes in the department. His replacement hadn't been chosen yet, but all of the candidates had backgrounds in ore mining or petroleum. Everyone loyal to Nehemia had been shut out of the selection process. "It will get ugly, John. Keep your head low and get out as soon as you can."

John found it difficult to say goodbye to Nehemia, who had influenced him more than his own father. The department gave him an emotional farewell party and even Malick came to town for it. As much as those two liked to insult each other, there was always an obvious affection between them.

John asked Malick if he was leaving the country too, and Malick laughed, hitting him hard on the back. He wanted Malick to stay in Alexandria for a few days and invited him to stay with him and Mariam. They had a narrow room that John used as an office, but Mariam had managed to fit a small bed across from John's desk.

"You shouldn't have gone through the trouble," Malick said when he saw the furniture so tightly fit into the room. "I could have slept on the floor."

"It's true Malick can sleep anywhere," John told her. "I've watched him fall asleep on a boulder."

Malick was happy to spend a few days in Alexandria. He was fond of the city. He asked if the parakeets and chipmunks still feasted together by the big cypress tree at the botanical gardens. When he looked around and realized neither John nor Mariam had any idea what he was talking about, he got excited and started packing a picnic with the lunch Mariam had made, insisting they go immediately to the gardens to witness an enchanting display of interspecies friendship. They took a taxi and in a while they were at the entrance of the gardens. They followed the main path until they came to the cypress grove and there they were, the striped chipmunks and green parakeets grazing on seeds children tossed on the ground. "Isn't it sweet?" Malick asked Mariam. Mariam agreed that it was sweet, and she passed the question onto John. John had to admit that he didn't understand all the excitement. "They're chipmunks and parakeets. They're the same size. They eat the same things. If they were lions and gazelles I'd be impressed." John could have gone on. These creatures weren't even interacting with each other.

"He's no fun," Mariam said. "Let's go and eat on the lawn." She led the way to a picnic spot and spread out a blanket. The lawn was full of children. A fleet of kites invaded the sky and they watched them fly as they ate their lunch. When she was finished, Mariam took out her book and said she wanted to read. She lay down on her stomach and opened her book. John was ready to lie down next to her and take a nap, but Malick jumped to his feet and said, "Let's go for a walk."

He didn't mind joining Malick. It would be a good opportunity to talk. They strolled past a children's exercise class that had begun on the lawn. A thin man with a high-pitched voice was shouting a rapid sequence of exercises into a bullhorn, eliminating children who could not keep up. Those children had to make a train behind him, each child wrapping his or her arms around the child in front. Sometimes the man turned to them with exaggerated gruffness, lowering his voice about half an octave, and scolded them in a way that made them quiver with laughter.

John asked Malick if he was going to pursue the research in the greenstone belt in Luling.

"I presented it to my graduate students," said Malick. "They weren't interested. It's such a small area. I don't think it will turn up much."

John had been thinking about this challenge. It was true there wasn't much to work with. The earth had sucked up most of what they needed. But in geology, there was this problem of scale and perspective. Every piece of surviving Archean rock that was scattered around the globe needed to be studied. It was the only way to get a full picture of the planet's evolution. There were studies on impact spherules already underway in Australia and South Africa that were run by scientists with more money and resources, but John was here, and he was interested in pursuing a study in Luling. Now that his dissertation was finished, he wanted a new focus. He wanted something that could put him on the map and he wanted Malick's help.

"Forget it, John. I don't have the money for it and Presidency won't fund it. It's a waste of time. Do something practical and get out of here. Go to America or Europe and you'll be able to do whatever you want."

"Don't talk to your students about it. At least if you're going to ignore it, give it to me."

"I'm not going to give it to you. If you do it, I do it with you."

"Then let's do it, Malick."

Malick made a strange sound and rubbed his sternum. "You're causing me a heartburn, John. I thought this research was only an excuse to come to English Canal and see your old sweetheart."

Suddenly John felt panicked. He'd been trying to take everything in stride but now he could see that his future was utterly bleak. He told Malick about Copenhagen and Mariam's passport, about Nehemia's warnings, and even if Mariam got a passport tomorrow, she would be reluctant to leave her parents behind and then there were visas and prolonged separations and why should he be forced to leave his own country in order to pursue significant research? He was bitter toward these old-timers like Nehemia and Malick telling him he had to leave. They hadn't been forced to make that choice when they were John's age, which was ironic to him because things were much worse then.

"Most people your age can't wait to leave," Malick remarked.

"My circumstances don't allow that."

"Let's see how things develop," Malick said. "I'll keep an open mind."

John wasn't satisfied. He dropped the subject for the moment, planning to take it up with Malick again the next day, and the day after that. They went back to Mariam. They spent another hour there, talking about nothing of importance.

Nehemia's replacement came at the end of the summer. He had spent the last ten years at the University of Vienna Center for Earth Sciences and evaluated his new department by coming upon people unannounced and asking them difficult questions in German, what he called the true language of science. No one's German was good enough. Most of the faculty was sacked within the first three weeks, including John, meaning they would finish the entire academic year and then look for jobs elsewhere. So there was time, at least, to come up with a plan, and also to spend the year working in a department they now hated. John was fired in German with a phrase that was difficult to translate: *Hier muessen wir wohl die grossen Jungs mit ganz anderen Waffen auffahren.* Here we probably have to mount up with the big boys all other weapons. He had no idea what it meant. He went looking for Vic, whose German was better than his. Vic didn't know what it meant either.

Vic had been put in a bad position too. He finished all of his coursework and was supposed to begin working on his dissertation topic, but he had no faculty advisor. He didn't do well with this kind of instability. In the past few weeks he'd lost an alarming amount of weight. He seemed wired in a way John hadn't seen since college. He tried to get Vic to come eat something with him, but Vic was pacing, working on something, he said.

A few days later, Mariam called John in his office. Vic had shown up at their apartment, shouting and making a scene. She was calling him now from the bedroom with the door locked, and Vic's voice, coming from another room, transmitted loudly over the receiver. He had to have been causing a disturbance with the neighbors. "How long has he been yelling like that?"

"About twenty minutes."

"What is he yelling about?"

"A lot of things. Food. Poison. John, I think I should go calm him down. What if someone calls the police?"

"Is he threatening you?"

"Not exactly."

"Mariam, I think you should stay in the room until I get home."

"Can't you call his parents?" Mariam asked. "How many Aroras can there be in the directory? I would do it myself but the book is in the kitchen. Do you know his father's name? I could call the operator."

"I'll call. Just stay where you are until I get home," he told Mariam. "Don't unlock the door."

He hung up the phone and went to the department secretary. First, he asked her if she happened to have a number on file for Vic's parents. "Why would I have something like that? We're not a primary school." Then she looked suspicious. "Has he lost his marbles? We've all been wondering."

"I need a phone book for Alexandria suburbs," he said.

"In which direction?"

He didn't exactly know. "Give me all of them."

She got out of her seat in very little of a hurry. "They're out of date. If they've moved in the past three years you're out of luck." She took three books off a low shelf and carried them over to him. He ran with them back to his desk. There were no Aroras in the first two but there were five in the third one. The first number didn't turn up Vic's father, but he knew the number and gave it to him. John couldn't believe the luck. He dialed it and a man who must have been Vic's father, sounding frail and ancient, answered with a slight accent John couldn't place. John told him who he was and explained the situation. His father sounded truly distressed, but there was a lack of urgency. "I have to wait for my friend. He'll bring me." Vic's father didn't have a car and wouldn't take a taxi, even when John offered to pay for it. He insisted on waiting for his friend who would give him a ride. "Vic won't hurt you. He loves you like a brother."

"It's just that he's home with my wife and someone might call the police."

"He won't hurt anyone."

"We may have to call an ambulance."

"But he never hurts anyone. I'll come right away."

John needed to get off the phone and go home. He repeated his address twice and still didn't feel confident Vic's father had gotten it.

He ran home as fast as he could. From the stairwell, he expected to hear Vic's voice, but right up to his door it was eerily quiet. He opened the door in a panic only to find Vic and Mariam sitting on the couch together, holding hands. John searched Mariam for signs of injury. She looked fine. Pained and uncomfortable, but not hurt. He didn't know how she'd managed to get Vic to stop yelling. He wasn't yelling now but he was still talking without stopping, and Mariam was nodding compulsively. John said, "Hi Vic," but Vic talked over him, taking little notice of him.

"Can I sit down?" John asked.

Vic still didn't stop. John was trying to track what he was saying but he was talking too fast. He sat down and Vic took his hand, gripping it tightly. He changed topics and once John's ears adjusted to the speed of Vic's speech, he was able to pick up some of it. Not all of it sounded crazy. His fractured mind still had some sense of scientific conceit. He talked about pesticides for a long time. Then he said during his military service he'd been recruited to develop a poisonous compound from the bonding of chlorine and neon. He was held in a high-security facility, forced to conduct experiments at gunpoint, and he only managed to escape by befriending a janitor from Ethiopia. Now John and Mariam were able to ask him some questions, which Vic seemed to enjoy. Mariam asked him the janitor's name. John asked him how he conducted the experiments. He was impressed with Vic's elaborate explanation.

John looked at his watch. It had been more than an hour since he'd called Vic's father.

"Why did you look at your watch?" Vic asked.

"I was checking the time."

"Why?"

"I like to know what time it is."

"That machine is controlling you." He tapped the watch face. "Take it off," he ordered, relentlessly tapping the watch like a crazed woodpecker. Finally John took it off and Vic snatched it from his hand. He stomped on it until it shattered. This was John's grandfather's watch under Vic's foot. It had been running more or less reliably for over half a century, the finest watch of its time.

Vic sat back down, took Mariam's hand and put his other hand out for John. He wasn't bothered by John's refusal. He tapped John's thigh like a drum and went on talking.

It was a long time before they heard someone on the landing, outside their door. John shot up and ran to let him in, ignoring Vic's howls for him to come back. The man in the doorway was tiny, hunched and wrinkled. John didn't understand how he could have spawned a giant like Vic. Stepping over the threshhold, the old man nodded a silent greeting and limped into the living room. There must have been something formidable about him. Vic stared at his father as if he'd returned from the dead. "Abbajaan," he said, awestruck.

Vic let go of Mariam and she stood up. She came to John's side and they watched as the old man spoke softly in a language John had never heard, and Vic, still staring, was soothed. His father looked back at them and made a gesture. He needed a glass of water.

Mariam hurried to get him a glass of water. Vic's father coaxed him to open his mouth. He placed a pill on his tongue, put the glass to Vic's lips and tilted it, gently holding the back of Vic's head with his other hand.

His father sat next to him while Vic's eyes went dull and his posture weakened. His father accepted a glass of water for himself, his eyes sadly skimming the splintered watch on the floor.

"It was an accident," John said.

He gave John a half-finished smile of gratitude, at last revealing some physicality that resembled his lumbering son. The old man took hold of Vic's hand and stood up. It was a good time to go, he said, and Vic followed him obediently in a quiet departure.

John and Mariam couldn't talk for a while. They stood over the shattered watch staring at it. She held his hand. His body felt waterlogged, swollen with loss and failure. He couldn't remember ever being gripped with such abject terror.

He would have recovered if things didn't continue to get worse. They met with their lawyer after Mariam's passport application was denied again. This time they said she needed to get her citizenship status changed separately from her passport application, so now they had to start her application for citizenship, which John had always thought they should have done in the first place. Mariam wanted to know everything about the process. What kind of questions would they ask in the interview? How thorough was the background check?

Would they interview her parents? Could her parents be punished? John listened to all her questions and the lawyer's answers and imagined them turning in one application after another for the rest of their lives.

Then in December a bomb went off on a train as it was pulling out of a station not far from Presidency College. Mariam couldn't stop staring at the television, where the news was unfolding around the clock. Besides the carnage, which was horrifying, there were a number of so-called experts blaming rebels in Sulat for the attack. The conflict in the north had been escalating in the past month and rebels might have been studying tactics from the IRA and other separatist groups around the world that concentrated their campaigns in the capitals. It turned out they got it all wrong. By the end of the day they knew who was responsible. It was a nineteen-year-old suicide bomber whose father had been taken to Menud Fort five years ago and was never seen again. Then the news was all about Menud Fort and everyone forgot about Northern Sulat, as if they hadn't just implicated without cause a group of people who turned out to be innocent. Mariam had been paralyzed with fear and worry and when they spoke about the boy who strapped a bomb to his chest, she fell across John's lap and wept, her whole body shaking with grief. He tried to soothe her even though his own spirit was breaking. He couldn't allow this to continue. He had been sitting around waiting for their troubles to simply disappear and he should have known that wasn't how the world worked.

He put Mariam to bed and stayed up all night, thinking. He must have needed something drastic to happen, something that could dislodge the obstruction in his imagination. A plan was taking shape. His cells fired up again, his vision righted itself. He would take Mariam to a place where they didn't have to beg for anything. He woke Mariam and described their new life to her. "It will work," he swore, and she didn't doubt him.

He called his father and told him he was going to sell the apartment because he needed the money. The fact was the apartment was given to him and it was only a courtesy for him to tell his parents.

"What's going on?" his father asked.

"We can't stay here. I've been fired from my job."

His father didn't sound concerned. He had news he had been meaning to tell John too. His sister Sonya's husband had been granted a work visa to America, and they would be moving there in a few months. His younger sister Theresa was unhappy at Mount Belet and wanted to apply to an American college. His parents wanted to go too. They were tired of everything, the traffic, the bureaucracy, the economy, and now being afraid to get on a train. They wanted to go but his father especially didn't want to leave his only son behind. "We'll go when you're ready. We'll wait for you but we want you to hurry."

"Don't wait for me," John said. He almost laughed. "Absolutely, don't wait for me."

PART THREE
Luling Province

TEN

I t took Arifah three days to write her instructions to the nurse and show her where everything was, with Omar shuffling along behind them. She had been preparing him for her departure, reminding him frequently that she was going to see Mariam. He asked more than once, "Where are you going?" with the exaggerated inquisitive intonation he had learned in his therapy. Arifah realized, later, that he had not meant to ask the same question again and again, but a different question, the why and how, words he couldn't recall at the time. As he watched her pack her suitcase, he labored to say the word "train."

"Yes, I'm taking the train," she said.

There was no train to Mariam. As a civil engineer, one thing Omar had known intimately was the country's transportation grid. She should have told him the truth, that she was getting a ride from Malick to Luling, where she would see Mariam.

"Mariam needs me," she said, her hand on her stomach for emphasis. "She needs me," she said, and Omar became still, his eyes intent on her belly. "Poor Mary," he said.

She hired a pretty nurse, sturdy, with an athletic build and easy smile. Arifah could see that he was pleased with her choice and another moment of understanding passed between them. She remembered the man he once was. She stroked his hair and gave him a light kiss on the lips, and she took her small suitcase and waited at the end of the path. She was never outside at this hour, before dawn, though she was always awake. She looked back at the house. Her husband was there at the window, looking for her, and she was surprised at the ache she felt in her bones at seeing him there. He watched her until the taxi came.

The taxi took her to Malick's house. Only when she saw him standing by his van did she realize the sun had come up. "Have I caused a delay?" she asked.

"Not at all. We've just finished loading."

He put her suitcase in the back and helped her up into the passenger seat, and they were off in a caravan, two cars full of students and camping gear in front of them. She had been looking forward to the drive, six hours to do nothing but relax. It started out pleasantly enough. For an hour they coasted southeast along the Sulat Highway, heading toward a green wall of forested hills. Omar, and Malick too, in fact, had been involved in the building of this highway twenty years ago, part of a gift from the central government to rebuild the infrastructure of the province after the war. It was supposed to stretch from the remote southern regions to the militarized zone in the far north. Omar's dream was to complete this highway, to sew one seam along the entire length of the province, but it was never finished and now it ended abruptly at a narrow road that wrapped around the pinewoods forest. Here the drive became more harrowing, as they had several near misses with large trucks racing around the bends. The constant jolting made Arifah dizzy, and involuntarily she began clenching her fists and squeezing her eyes shut. Frequently Malick looked at her instead of the road. "Would you like some soft music?" he asked. "Shall I stop?" She told him she was fine, but he kept trying to distract her.

"Is it like this the whole time?" she asked.

"Not the whole time," he said.

They pulled into a roadside stop to have lunch. It was nothing more than a covered patio with picnic tables and an assembly line of men skewering meat and cooking it on a number of charcoal grills, with the wide ancient trunks of forest pines in the background. Because she could not guess where these men used the bathroom or washed their hands, she did not dare eat anything though she was terribly hungry. She had to look away from Malick's students, who ate kabobs and chicken rolls as if their stomachs were meant for storing caches of food. There were three of them, boisterous young men who talked easily to each other, every now and then pulling Malick into their conversation. They took no notice of Arifah, except to comment on the absence of food in front of her. She wondered if these students had been to Luling before, if they paid as little attention to Mariam as they did now to her.

Back in the van, Arifah asked Malick if the students knew about Mariam's miscarriage.

"They know, but I've asked them to be discreet. I hope you didn't find them rude. When they get hungry they turn into wild animals."

Arifah laughed. "Yes, I noticed."

A part of her envied Malick. He had been a witness to Mariam's marriage in a way that Arifah could hardly imagine. She was ashamed to admit that even now, after five years, she did not know her daughter's husband well. She'd seen him a smattering of times. He was always distantly polite, and Mariam did not seem willing to ask more of him. Arifah had never gone to Alexandria to visit them—that was her fault—but later she couldn't help but feel his efforts had ceased after the Copenhagen disaster. The day Mariam told her she couldn't get a passport was the worst day of Arifah's life, worse than the day she discovered Omar mute and paralyzed in their bed, worse than years earlier when she saw his hand intimately brush the small of Elizabeth's back, and worse even than the day she realized her father had taken his own life, that she and her mother could not offer him enough solace to keep him alive. She spoke

204 · CHAITALI SEN

to Omar about it, trying to get the truth about what he knew, staring intently into his eyes for signs of comprehension. His eyebrows went up and down as they always did when he was struggling, like a dog whose ears twitch merely because he is being spoken to. Either he was still a masterful liar even as an invalid, or he truly knew nothing and they were all victims of their government's arbitrary punishment. To this day, Arifah wasn't certain about Omar's innocence.

She fell asleep. When she woke up the road had straight-ened, and she wondered if she had not fainted, her last memory being one of white-knuckled, stiff-backed tension. Malick assured her it wouldn't be much longer now. The landscape was gentler here, overlapping dome-shaped hills, startling in their uniformity, covered with green and purple shrubbery. Just when Arifah was getting impatient the road widened into a clearing, and John was standing there signaling the van to a halt. Arifah hardly recognized him. He was wearing a khaki jacket and cap like some kind of jungle guerilla. Malick stopped a short distance behind the students, but did not make a move to get out. They watched the students emerge from their vehi-cles, wobbly and stooped. John shook their hands and made a gesture to Malick, ushering him on toward the house.

Malick drove past the student cars and made a sharp turn up another rocky drive. She could see it at the crest of the hill, a small white bungalow much like their house in English Canal. The sight of it made Arifah smile. Mariam was there on the porch, a vision in a yellow dress, and before Malick had come to a full stop Arifah let herself out and hurried toward Mariam with her arms out. In a moment Arifah was holding her daughter, who was already crying onto her shoulder. "I'm here now," Arifah said.

When they heard the students approaching Mariam pulled away and wiped her eyes. "They're coming."

"Don't mind them," Arifah said. "They'll understand."

Mariam took her into the house and gave her a quick tour. The layout was as simple as a house could get. Two small bedrooms and a bathroom were in the back, behind the living room. The little guest room was bright, with a large window facing south, and it was impeccably clean, her bed dressed with a white embroidered bedcover she had given Mariam for a wedding present. A moment later John came in with Arifah's suitcase.

"I'll let you get comfortable," he said. "We'll be gone a few hours."

"Did they want something to eat?" Mariam asked.

"They said they had a big breakfast."

"They certainly did," Arifah said. This made Mariam laugh and even John could not help smiling, though it appeared as more of a grimace. Arifah could not believe how sun-worn his face looked. He came forward and gave her an awkward hug, which she ended with a hearty pat on his back. He looked at Mariam and tilted his head toward the door, and Mariam got up to follow him out. "I'll be back in a minute, Mama."

"Of course, take your time."

Arifah opened her suitcase and began to put her things into a small chest of drawers next to the window. She knew all of the furniture belonged to the owners of the house who were living abroad. It seemed a fine way to live, using someone else's possessions and owning next to nothing.

Arifah set aside the gifts she'd brought, a hat she knitted for Mariam and a scarf for John. She had done the scarf in a hurry. What she'd been working on, for two months whenever she had a spare moment, was a blanket for the baby, still looped to a knitting needle at home.

Mariam returned a few minutes later. "Are you hungry?" she asked.

"I could have some coffee," she said. Her hunger had passed hours ago.

Mariam sat on the bed and watched Arifah unpack her suitcase. "I know it was hard for you to leave Daddy. Is he all right?"

"He is improving more and more every day," Arifah said.

Arifah put her suitcase next to the bureau and went to Mariam. She stroked her hair and kissed the top of her head. "I'm so glad to see you, Mama," Mariam said.

"I am glad to see you, darling."

Mariam looked down and put her hand over her womb. "I felt the baby move," she whispered. "I felt her move for a few days before I felt the pain."

Mariam could not have been far enough along to feel the baby move, but Arifah knew women imagined all kinds of things to make the pregnancy feel real. "Do you know it was a girl?"

Mariam blushed. "No, I was hoping."

Arifah had also hoped for a girl, and her dream had come true, as she was sure it would for Mariam one day.

"You wanted some coffee!" Mariam remembered.

They moved to the kitchen, where Mariam had left many tasks unfinished. Every surface was covered with various preparations, flour, potatoes, onions, and even cuts of chicken, but nothing seemed close to completion. Mariam looked around, forlorn at the mess she'd made.

"What can I do?" Arifah asked. "Put me to work."

"No, sit here," Mariam said, pulling a chair out from the end of a long wooden table and moving bowls out of the way. In a few minutes Arifah had coffee and cream and toast with butter and marmalade, and she gobbled it all down while Mariam removed a tea towel from the top of a ceramic bowl and poured an expanded ball of dough onto a floured board. She pressed her fist into it and watched it deflate before kneading it gently. "When did you learn to do that?" Arifah asked her.

"I practiced in Alexandria. We'll have a simple meal, bread

and stew. I know that's a strange summer dish but it cools down here quite a bit at night."

"Is this homemade bread I'm eating?" Arifah asked.

"Yes, from yesterday."

"It's exquisite."

Mariam smiled and continued kneading. Her movements were rhythmic and hypnotic, and neither of them spoke until she was finished. After Mariam shaped the loaf and put it aside, she asked Arifah why she never had more children. Arifah was flustered, though she might have known the question would come up. She'd been thinking lately about how to discuss her own fertility with Mariam, but at the moment she couldn't think of a way to answer. While Mariam waited she poured more coffee into Arifah's cup.

"After I had you, I was satisfied," she said. The truth was that Mariam came along easily. The troubles began after Arifah wanted to try again, when Mariam was three years old. There were two miscarriages that she could remember and then Omar's infidelity. She didn't see any point in telling Mariam about this now. When Arifah suffered her miscarriages she already had a child, her daughter who seemed to come from another world. Her heartbreak couldn't compare to Mariam's, who was thirty-two and childless.

"I always thought I would be fertile," Mariam said. "I thought I would get pregnant easily."

"You are fertile. Of course you are."

Mariam frowned as she formed the dough into an oval loaf on a baker's stone. "I'll finish dinner," she said. "Do you want a warm bath? A nap?"

"Can't I help you?"

Mariam looked around at the chaos. "Do you want to do the chickpeas?"

Arifah was delighted. There was something so adorable about chickpeas, their round little wrinkled bodies.

They got everything baking and simmering. Before sundown John and Malick and the students pulled into the drive. They rattled to a halt and took their time getting into the house. "They're back already," Arifah said.

The house filled with voices, quiet at first, becoming more boisterous as the sunlight dimmed. Mariam and Arifah set the table right away, a large steaming pot of stew placed in the middle of the table with a warm loaf of bread resting on a wooden cutting board. Everyone piled into the kitchen and took seats around the table. Mariam put Arifah at one end and Malick at the other. John opened some bottles of wine and poured everyone a glass, and gave a quick toast.

"We're happy to have you all here. Especially you, Arifah," he said, and they raised their glasses to her.

The table was lively with conversation. Of the three students, the one named Adam talked the most. He was one of those overconfident young men who claimed to be an authority on everything just to provoke conflict. John seemed to find Adam tiresome. Every now and then he and Mariam exchanged looks of subtle annoyance.

She finished her first glass of wine and began to feel lightheaded. Somewhere in the fog of dining and drinking, the conversation had turned to the war. She only began to pay attention when she heard Mariam's voice, polite and sweetly demurring.

"It was not a holy war," she said.

Everyone was staring at her. Adam put his hand in the air, pointing his fingers toward the ceiling. "How can you say that? It began with the slaughter of Catholics."

"In one parish. There were no other Catholics killed anywhere in Sulat before the war started."

"Because they all fled."

Arifah wanted to suggest a change of subject. She'd seen Mariam become overly excited about this topic before. Her eyes were bright with confidence and she went on. "The churches used their ties to the central government to wield their own power. They could have anyone arrested for the slightest provocation. There was hatred for the Church but it wasn't about religion."

"Women and children were killed. Are you saying they deserved it?" Adam asked. Suddenly he caught John's silent admonishment and shoveled a spoonful of stew into his mouth.

"The bombs from Alexandria killed more Catholics than the rebels did, and that is well-documented," Mariam said.

Arifah took another sip of wine, allowing the warmth of it to wash over her. She was amazed by Mariam's confidence. In the midst of all these people she had not been afraid to state her opinion.

"I agree with Mariam," Malick interjected, certainly trying to diffuse the argument. "Sulat has always been a secular province. The religious element was a fringe."

"Ah, I can't believe it," Adam said cheerfully. "I'm surrounded by separatists."

Malick gently corrected him. "Sulat wouldn't have survived as an independent state," he said. "I think we would have splintered even further."

"You're saying the rebellion was a mistake?" the boy named Tarek asked. Arifah liked him best. He had a sweet face and was extremely polite.

Malick shrugged. "Not a mistake. It was no more a mistake than an earthquake. The tension builds up and has to find a release. But I think the outcome, in spite of how ruthlessly it was achieved, was the more practical one."

Arifah wondered how Mariam would react to Malick's statement. Mariam was listening to him as politely as the others. As much as she liked to criticize Alexandria's handling of the war, she didn't seem to disagree with Malick.

"What was it like for you during the war?" Tarek asked, still focused on Malick.

Malick chuckled. "We moved around a lot trying to avoid it, but it kept following us." He would not say any more and his students, looking uncomfortable, offered some deferential laughter.

"I remember the terror," Arifah said. Her voice surprised her as much as it did everyone else. "Even before the war started we were afraid of our own neighbors, people we had known for years. When we heard about the Catholics we knew there was going to be some terrible retribution. But we were very sorry for the children."

She did not even sound like herself. She was back in the schoolyard, having a hushed conversation with her girlfriends. Years before the war started, when Arifah was nine or ten years old, she regarded the Catholic children with a mixture of curiosity and envy. Their parents seemed to pamper them in a way that Arifah, in her simple undeveloped mind, must have thought to be a superior kind of love.

Suddenly Malick raised his glass. "To peace. May it come, and may it last," he said. Everyone echoed Malick. John turned to Mariam and kissed her cheek. She seemed to curl up a moment in its aftermath, like a little kitten.

The men wanted to go outside and smoke. Mariam cleared the table and washed the dishes while Arifah made coffee to serve with a brandied fruitcake she'd brought from a tea shop on College Street. After they had their dessert in the living room, Arifah said goodnight. It had been a long day, with a great distance traveled. The group said good night, but Arifah only looked at her daughter. Mariam said goodnight with the same inquisitive gaze she'd had as a child, always seeming to wonder if the people she loved were going to bed happily.

In the morning a clatter of activity woke her. The guests were still in the house, but obviously making moves to clear out. When the house was quiet again, Arifah got up, bathed, and dressed. She found Mariam outside in the garden. There were cabbages to be harvested and squash vines climbing up a trellis. Arifah never could have imagined her daughter living off food she'd grown herself. "Do you enjoy this?" she asked her.

"It isn't my favorite activity but it helps us get by."

After breakfast they went for a long walk in the hills, stopping in a small village where a woman showed them how to make wreaths with dried blueberry vines. They visited a chicken farmer to get some eggs, and they watched a rooster get slaughtered and cleaned. This would be another stew to last them all week.

John stayed with Malick and the students at the campsite for a few days. At night the house was a speaker amplifying the sounds of the wild, animals scampering in the brush, the nasal chorus of crickets, the short branches of bushes with their stiff tiny leaves pattering in the wind.

"Don't you get frightened here?" Arifah asked.

"Of what?"

"I don't know. Animals. Bandits." She laughed at her own paranoia.

"I don't stay alone at night. When Malick and the students come, either I go to the camp or John comes back. Right now you're here, so I feel safe." This made Arifah laugh, as if she could be of any help in an emergency. "But really, Mama, nothing happens here. It's the most peaceful place on earth."

That was a relief to Arifah. She wondered about the campsite and asked if they could go to it. She would have liked some idea of what they were all doing up there. Mariam discouraged her. She said it was a lot of walking and climbing over rough terrain, and what they did was look for things that were hidden under the surface of the rock, and their looking was quite tedious. And if Mariam and Arifah couldn't keep up with the climbing, they would be stuck hunched over the lit-

tle stove cooking unappetizing food. In all of Mariam's explanation, she had left out what Arifah had forgotten, that
Mariam had just gone through a terrible physical and emotional ordeal. It was why Arifah was here, to help her recover.
She pulled Mariam closer and listened to the nocturnal music
coming through the walls of the cabin. "It really is very peaceful," she said.

Every day was busy in a different way. In the evenings they
listened to a shortwave radio that broadcast from around the
world, sometimes tuning into the BBC or a German news
channel that Arifah was able to translate roughly. Though
Arifah loved spending this time with Mariam, she began to
grow restless. She missed the tall trees behind the canal. Here,
as far as the eye could see, there were squat shrubs with tiny
purple leaves. After the novelty wore off she found the landscape monotonous. The sky was always blue, with a thick dusty
heat that hung in the air. She missed her routine and she
missed Omar, his steady, predictable companionship.

One day Mariam said she wanted to straighten up John's
office. Mariam had much to say while she cleaned. John had
two papers coming out in the next month, and one recently
published, and there was a week's worth of international cor-
respondence, from Cambridge and Cape Town among others.
Mariam tried to explain the research John and Malick were
doing, that somehow that swath of earth, their ever-important
ancient rock, could help them unravel the evolution of continents.

"Things are going well for him, then," Arifah declared.

Mariam bit her lip, deliberating over something. "There's
something I've been dying to show you, Mama."

Mariam knelt down on the floor and put her hand lovingly
on a cardboard box. "He's writing a book. It's what we spend
most of our time on."

"We?"

"I help, Mother. I help him with everything."

"Of course you do," said Arifah. "What is it about?"

"It's hard to summarize," Mariam said, opening the box and showing Arifah the stacks of paper that filled it. "It's about land and history, and war, and geology . . . I can't explain it except there's a feeling I get after reading it—disoriented, like I've landed here from a place where time doesn't have the same function or quality. I notice the minutes ticking away and it feels like an aberration. I feel almost like I'll live forever and I have lived forever."

"My goodness, it sounds extraordinary." Like a hallucinogenic drug, Arifah thought.

"I haven't explained it well. No, it's about the value of this study, the study of the earth, and what we can gain from it. Not in the economic sense. More in the spiritual sense."

"Spiritual?"

"I don't know what else to call it. Inspirational, maybe. I mean having to do with ideas and aspirations, not God. Not religion. It's about how the study of the earth is affected by history, by war and politics, and religion. It's about our country, too, a kind of geological travelogue. I don't think there's another book like it. It leaves you wishing all of our self-imposed limitations would just fall away and humanity could be one, as it was meant to be."

Mariam spoke with a zealous rapture. She did not sound like she was talking about her husband so much as a prophet, and Arifah felt tears in her eyes. All these years she had tried to get Mariam to believe in something, in God, to let go of her doubt and feel the release and joy of knowing you were not alone in the universe, and now it had happened in a way that frightened her. Mariam was giving away this gift, her gift of worship, to her husband.

"You're very proud of him," Arifah said.

"It's something we've been involved in together."

"But it is his book? He will get the credit for it."

Mariam scowled. "I'm sure I'll get some credit. But not from you, apparently."

"I didn't mean it that way," Arifah said.

"Never mind, Mother. I'm sorry I said anything. I'm sorry I ever tell you anything important to me."

Arifah realized too late she'd said the wrong thing. When Mariam was young her father was often treated in a similar way, having to spend hours either defending himself against her stinging rebuttals or hiding from her, usually for something he'd said carelessly but in complete innocence. Omar learned to ignore her after a while. He seemed to realize these outbursts had nothing to do with immediate injuries but stemmed from long-standing resentments she could only forgive in her own time.

"I didn't mean to offend you, Mariam. I don't know anything about things like this. I only want you to be happy."

"I am happy."

"You are? You swear it?"

She could see Mariam was getting frustrated. "I swear it."

"But this place is so remote," Arifah argued. It wasn't enough for Mariam to say she was happy. Arifah wanted to understand her happiness. "No one can see you here. It's like the two of you have retreated from the world."

"Retreated?" Mariam cried. "The only other choice was for John to leave me and go abroad. Would you have preferred that?"

"No," Arifah said, chastened. "No, of course not." Here it was, Arifah thought, Mariam's secret blame. Perhaps Mariam never believed her after all.

Mariam sighed. "I'm sorry, Mama. I don't mean to be short with you. I've been going through so much lately."

"Of course you have, my love. I'm sorry. I misspoke. I didn't mean to upset you."

"It know it's hard to believe, Mama, but this was exactly what we needed, to get away from everything."

"I understand. If you say you're happy, I believe you. John seems to be doing well."

"He is."

Carefully, Arifah asked her if they'd done anything more about her citizenship status. Mariam used to give her regular updates, about how the lawyer was dragging his feet or John was distracted by his troubles with his department, when they were still back in Alexandria. But she had not spoken to her about it at all in over a year.

Mariam didn't seem troubled by her question. She explained the situation calmly. "It's difficult to do anything about it from here. The last time we were back in Alexandria, it was only to see his parents off. There was no time. I know we have to do something but I guess we lost track of what we were supposed to do."

This explanation made sense to Arifah. "I wonder if your father knew, and lost track, just in the way that you describe. He had no shortage of distractions."

Mariam frowned. "How could he have known?"

"I don't know. Maybe he knew, maybe not. I can't help doubting him, though."

"But he can't speak for himself," Mariam said, "So it's better not to doubt him. Don't you think, Mama?"

"It does make it hard for me to care for him sometimes."

Mariam looked worried. A pain rushed through Arifah's body, then. Her daughter had brought her the only happiness in her life, and she had failed her in return. Arifah didn't know what else to offer.

"I want some tea," Mariam announced. "How about you?"

"Yes. All right."

Mariam closed the box and they left John's office. Arifah was glad. She wasn't comfortable in that tiny room. She sat at the kitchen table and watched Mariam make tea with graceful precision.

When they were both sitting with cups of hot tea in front of them, Arifah said something that had been on her mind. "Mariam, I'm sorry for the way you grew up. I wish your father and I could have hidden our problems from you."

"That wasn't your fault, Mama."

Arifah kept going. There was so much she had wanted to say, ever since Mariam got married and left home. "I wish you didn't have to see him in love with another woman. It's true he loved her more," Arifah said, pausing there as the words caught in her throat. It wasn't her first time admitting it, but she never thought she would have to say it out loud, and it caused more heartache than she expected. "He loved her with a passion he never had for me, but I don't regret my life with him."

Mariam touched her hand. "It would be all right if you did, Mama."

Suddenly Arifah began to cry, losing control of her emotions. Mariam got up and brought her a napkin and sat back down with her hand on Arifah's shoulder.

"Oh, God, look at me. I'm supposed to be comforting you, and here I am feeling sorry for myself."

"This *is* a comfort to me," Mariam said. "We should be able to confide in each other."

Arifah nodded. They drank their tea, but Arifah's spirit continued to wither. She said she wanted to lie down and Mariam said, "Yes, go and have a rest, Mama." Arifah went to her bed and closed her eyes, and in a moment she was overcome with exhaustion.

When she woke up, she heard quiet voices in the bedroom. John was home. After a while, their bedroom door opened and there was a knock at her door. Mariam stepped inside to check on her.

"I'm awake," Arifah said. She sat up.

"John's home."

"Are the others here as well?"

"No, just John." Mariam looked very pleased. "He's had enough of camping. He said everyone is well-situated now."

Arifah smiled. "Let me freshen up. I'll come and help with dinner."

That night the three of them sat down and had a lovely meal. Mariam kept them entertained with her girlish chatter. John seemed to find everything she talked about amusing, from blueberry vine wreaths to German radio programs. Arifah felt he would want all of Mariam's attention now. Perhaps they needed to get working again on his book. And Arifah suddenly felt like she had not been of much use to Mariam. Seeing her behavior now, clearly it was John she wanted at home with her. How silly it would be for them both to be here, competing for Mariam's affection.

That night Arifah couldn't sleep at all. First she could hear John and Mariam talking without pause. Then they were quiet, but she heard the end of their lovemaking before everything in the house settled. Even after that Arifah remained maddeningly awake.

In the morning, at breakfast, they were all silent. Arifah's silence came from her night without sleep, but between Mariam and John there was an intimacy too sacred for words, an unspoken and unfinished desire that Arifah, in her own marriage, could never quite achieve. Mariam poured him some coffee, standing so close to him she was practically in his lap, and he looked up at his wife with his hand on her thigh, thanking her.

"I spoke to the nurse this morning," Arifah exclaimed. "Your father's becoming rather difficult. I think I ought to go home. There's a bus depot in town, am I right?"

Mariam frowned. "The bus isn't safe, Mama."

"I'm sure it will be fine," Arifah insisted.

"Malick can take you," John said. "He was talking about going home for a few days."

"You can't go yet," Mariam cried. "It's too soon."

"You'll be all right, darling." Arifah leaned forward and touched her arm. "Everything will be all right."

John looked too sheepish to bring up Malick's ride again. "Will you see Malick today?" Arifah asked him.

"I'm driving over there after breakfast."

"There. Fate has spoken," Arifah said. Mariam did not protest again, but she looked forlorn and Arifah already began to miss her. Mariam couldn't know how much Arifah missed her, always. The pain of her leaving had never eased.

She departed with Malick later that day and this time the drive didn't bother her at all. They made it back to English Canal by sundown. She gave her husband a firm kiss on his lips and slept close to him that night, with her hand resting on his bony chest.

In the morning Omar asked about their daughter.

"She's all grown up," Arifah said. She told him about the house and garden and this book John was writing. She told him how loved she was, their Mariam.

Eleven

Summer was wind and dust, all her summer memories dredged in beige. One morning after a new summer began, Mariam's whole body ached, as if the dust had seeped through her skin and found its way into her blood. John was on an international call, the volume of the conversation rising and falling with the howl of the wind. She couldn't keep her head up to listen. She went back to bed and shut her eyes and even her eyelids ached. Soon she would be out of this dust but it didn't matter. Knowing they were leaving made the dust less tolerable, not more. She wished they could move in October, when she could savor her final days in Luling more pleasurably. Here, autumn was her favorite season, but they had to leave in summer, and soon. At the end of August, John and Malick were going to the World Geological Congress in Washington. They had earned their place there and this time Mariam would not let him stay behind. After the conference, Malick wanted to retire to France, to be near his daughter and grandchildren. He offered his faculty position at the College of Sulat Province to John, and there was no question about his taking it. Without Malick, John would lack the funds and institutional affiliation to continue in Luling, and anyway, they had gleaned everything they could from their outcrop.

John finished his call and came into the room. A little rest had not revived Mariam much. He looked concerned as he helped her sit up, propping a few pillows up behind her. "Are you sick?" he asked.

220 · CHAITALI SEN

"I think my time of the month is coming," she said. Her torso felt tight and her breasts were sore. For a while, whenever her breasts were full and tender like this she would become convinced she was pregnant, until the first shock of blood made her feel foolish. "It's the dust," she added. "I'm sick of the dust."

"We'll be out of it soon enough," he said.

"I'm ready to leave," Mariam said, but she must have looked melancholy. John ran his calloused thumb along her eyebrow, something he did whenever he thought she needed consoling. He said, "It will be hard to leave. We've been happy here." She turned her head toward the smooth underside of his wrist, and set her lips there, thinking this was all there was, cycles of things ending and beginning. Even Vic was in English Canal now and eager for John and Mariam to join him.

They couldn't believe it when he appeared at their door in Luling three years earlier. He said he had come to give John a watch. The watch was expensive, not anything like his grandfather's watch but a very lovely watch all the same. John tried to refuse it. "I'm happier without a watch, really," he said, and Mariam said, "Yes, you were right, Vic. That watch was ruining his life." He stayed several days but didn't tell them until he was leaving that he was on his way to English Canal, that he had written to Malick asking if there was anything he could do to start teaching again. Malick offered him a chance to teach prerequisite classes and continue his doctorate. He had been embarrassed about telling John, thinking somehow he should have asked for his permission, but John was happy. He knew Malick would take care of Vic.

So it was that all roads converged on English Canal. They had been happy in Luling for four years, and could leave now knowing John's courage and instincts had not failed him back when his life in Alexandria fell apart and all he had was Mariam. Now, he was going to see some of this world that had spun on without him, and now she was going home to English Canal. She was going home with no passport, and no children, but she told herself she would again try to earn her rightful citizenship, once she was home, and she would have children, still young enough at thirty-three to have many children. She tried not to fall into despair, but once, John came home and found her soaking in the bathtub where she had stayed so long her fingertips formed ridges and valleys. He had asked her if she was all right. She said she was fine. She didn't tell him she had slipped under the water, imagining herself drowned, imagining his grief, but she couldn't get it right and came back up.

As much as they had loved their home in Luling, when it was time to go they drove away from their cottage without sentiment. They moved their few possessions into Mariam's parents' house and slept in the old master bedroom upstairs. The room was barren but comfortable, and John was given a little workspace in Mariam's old bedroom, which only had a desk now and functioned as an office for her mother to handle bills and other paperwork. Her mother was energetic and talkative and Mariam was happy to be with her again and have her meals cooked for her, and her father was also doing remarkably well. Every day he came up the stairs and limped up and down the hallway as part of his therapy. He could do it now without the aid of a walker or cane. The turning seemed to be the most difficult part, getting his feet and his torso and his head to work in unison. But he did it with more ease each time. Mariam could hardly remember what he was like before the stroke, and after three years since the last time she saw him he had become smaller and more lovable. His ears and nose looked massive next to his sunken cheeks, and he had little hair left on his head, yet he looked younger, freer and happier than he ever had when he was well.

Vic came over. He enjoyed an easy rapport with her parents

and Mariam felt a rush of affection for him every time he came by. He wanted John and Mariam to move into his building, a townhouse owned by the college. They put him off the first few times he mentioned it. To save money, it was most practical for them to stay with her parents until John's trip, and for her to remain there for the two weeks he would be gone, but Vic was persistent, saying the rent was subsidized and it was close to campus. He invited them over for coffee one afternoon and they decided to take a leisurely walk there, along the canal. The canal was lower but there were ducks and geese on the water, and the sky was thick with storm clouds. The air was clean and moist and Mariam's body no longer felt like it was clogged with dust.

It took them about twenty minutes to reach Vic's townhouse. From the outside it was starkly pleasing, orderly, made of light red brick accented with black shutters, its windows glowing with yellow incandescence, but the inside disappointed Mariam. It was dark in the vestibule and the lobby, and there was a smell that offended her, the smell of wet carpet, of pets and children, of cooking oil, the smell of everything caught inside that couldn't be aired out. She gripped the banister and John touched the small of her back, giving her a gentle nudge up the stairs. Vic was waiting for them on the landing. He said he wanted to show them the vacant apartment first, and went to the third floor to retrieve the keys from the building supervisor's wife. "I don't know about this," John said to Mariam, and she agreed, though she wanted to keep an open mind.

Vic came back, charging down the stairs. When he reached them he practically ran into the door as if he were going to break it down with sheer force. Hastily he put the key in the lock and rattled the doorknob. Eventually the lock yielded and the door opened, and Mariam was surprised by a flurry of cool air. The apartment was suffused with light and already furnished, and straight ahead a wall of mullioned windows framed a view of green trees and red rooftops. Some of the panels had been cranked open, which made Mariam think that they had already shown the apartment to someone that day. Vic showed them the two bedrooms, a master bedroom with a large window and a smaller bedroom with a smaller window, a nursery. The bedrooms were unfurnished, but the walls were freshly painted white. They looked at the kitchen, clean and functional. There was a dining room attached to it with a long table that looked valuable but difficult to move.

"What do you think?" Vic asked.

"It's not bad," John said.

"I want it," Mariam said. She wanted it as soon as possible. It would give her something to focus on while John was away.

John shrugged. "I guess we'll take it. You're sure we can afford it?" he asked Vic.

"The rent's so cheap, you'll laugh," Vic said. Mariam left it to John to go upstairs and talk to the building manager. She wanted to stay and look out the window of her new apartment.

Afterwards they went to Vic's apartment for coffee and biscuits. He had never had his own home before and Mariam could tell how much it pleased him to have them over. He had arranged it beautifully, all of the furniture configured exactingly. His living room was a perfectly ordered home library, and Mariam was content to browse through his books while John and Vic talked about the department meeting on Monday. The department had been reorganized. Instead of a department chair, a committee of faculty and doctoral students would run it collaboratively. Vic said John would fall in love with this model of collective leadership, but John was skeptical.

Mariam tuned out of their argument as she examined Vic's library, proceeding slowly along the wall of bookshelves. His collection fascinated her. In addition to the science texts, there was an entire case of books on history, politics, and economics, including the three volumes of Marx's *Capital* in the original

224 · CHAITALI SEN

German, and several works by Lenin, translated from Russian, and other books on similar themes. She knew some people collected a certain kind of book, almost out of an aesthetic sensibility rather than a genuine interest in its content. Mariam herself had never collected much of anything. She always got her books from the library and the ones she loved somehow stayed with her without becoming a weight to be carried from one place to another. She of course loved the French classics but had also developed a taste for reading expansive explorations of science and history. She would easily put John's manuscript in that category. Geology, being a descriptive science, seemed as poetic to Mariam as it was empirical, and John somehow had been gifted with a poetic mind. She envied him sometimes; his abilities were so varied and fluid.

"Have you read all these books, Vic?" Mariam asked, holding *The State and Revolution* in her hand. He was in the middle of an important point and she had interrupted. He looked up, disoriented, and said he had a lot of time to read the last time he was in the hospital, and before when he was in prison. "Did you know about that, Mariam?" he asked, meaning his prison term.

She had known. John told her many years ago, but she must have forgotten. Vic went back to his conversation with John, and Mariam went back to her silence, thinking everyone around her had come so far. John, her father, and now Vic, but unlike her father and her husband, Vic had done it alone, with no woman to take care of him, needing only his singular focus and determination. Lately, or perhaps always, these were the things she lacked, focus and determination. Her attention was unsteady and John could redirect it easily. She looked again at Vic's library and thought of her grandfather, whose story she abandoned. She wished she could have grown up in one of those multigenerational homes where stories were passed down, where no other effort was required to know exactly who you were.

Monday came. As John got ready for his meeting, he asked Mariam what she was going to do with her day. She told him she would spend time with her mother, and perhaps take her father for a walk along the canal. While she did do both those things after John left for his meeting, around midmorning she took the tram to the university. The tram ride made her feel ill, like she was falling backwards and never landing. She got off as soon as she could and walked the rest of the way to College Street. The old cafés were still there, and the book-sellers, but overall the street looked more glassy and modern. There was a new pharmacy, brightly lit and clean. She hurried into the feminine aisle and examined the pregnancy testing kits, which were all priced extravagantly, but she was afraid to choose any but the most expensive one. She hid her purchase at the bottom of her handbag and escaped the pharmacy.

Around the corner, on the sidewall of the building, Mariam stopped to read a message written in graffiti: *Governments should be afraid of their people.* The letters were a shocking red, with a patchwork of white paint in varying shades around them. Her first instinct was to agree, but she changed her mind. She wanted to say the relationship between a government and its people should not be fearful in either direction, though that was not very pithy and would not have fit on the wall.

She kept walking toward the campus, steering clear of the science building where John was in his meeting. She arrived at the library and stopped to admire its somber elegance, taking a deep breath before she stepped into the cool marble lobby. Once inside, she felt immediately at home. She settled on the things that had not changed, the brass sconces and old wooden study carrels, and tried to ignore the boxy gray computers littering the counter. She went to the reference floor and ran straight into Misha. Misha saw her, froze and blinked. "Mariam? What on earth are you doing here?"

Mariam smiled. As soon as Misha recognized her and spoke with her typical candor, it was as if no time had passed. Misha kissed both her cheeks and led her to an office with a window facing the lawn. "I'm head of research now. It's good that you left. It eliminated my competition." Misha pulled a chair out for Mariam and sat regally behind her wide desk. She showed Mariam a picture of her family, a husband whose marriage proposal she'd declined four times before she finally gave in and three children, twin girls and a boy. It was a studio portrait. They all wore the same shade of blue and looked happy enough.

"They're beautiful," Mariam said.

"What about you? Any children?"

"No," Mariam said.

"When you left I didn't think we'd ever see you again. I thought you'd be living somewhere exotic."

"John got an appointment here. I'll be close to my parents."

"Still, you must have been all over the world by now." Misha was smiling at her with an endearing, dreamy pride, and Mariam lifted her shoulders, a gesture for Misha to take in any way she liked. Misha was still smiling happily, and Mariam left it at that. She didn't want to talk about her passport. The subject bored her, and Mariam had come for a different purpose.

"Has the library been all right?" Mariam asked. "Has it been busy?"

"We're awfully busy, though I can't guess why. The students are always demonstrating. I don't know how they have time to study."

"Do you have enough people on the reference floor?"

Misha became suspicious, and leaned back in her chair. "Are you trying to get a job?"

"Yes. Why not?"

"On the floor, with the younger girls?"

"I don't mind. I'd be grateful, Misha. My husband is going

abroad for two weeks. I can't just sit at home waiting for him to come back."

Misha was amused. "Your husband. It sounds so funny to hear you say that. How is he? Are your lunches with him as exciting as they used to be?"

Mariam blushed.

"In that case," Misha said with her hand on her heart, "You must come and work here. There will be no waiting idly for husbands on my watch."

Misha made the call to the main floor right away, and sent Mariam to fill out the proper papers. On her way out, feeling a mad rush of optimism, she slipped into a restroom meant for the female employees and opened the box she bought at the pharmacy. The directions were simple; the answer came quickly. She was pregnant. Clearly, heavily, virulently pregnant.

She wouldn't tell anyone yet. Not her mother. Not John. For a little while she wanted to be alone with her happiness, and she wanted John to go to his conference unburdened. Later that day, as she told him about the job, she realized that was all the news he needed. He was relieved; she would have something to keep her busy while he was away. He seemed very much unburdened.

Mariam insisted on moving into the apartment that week. There wouldn't be time when he got back, with the fall term starting, and she wanted to settle in with him for a few days before he left. It occurred to her that she was acting strangely. John seemed confused by her demands. He kept asking if she'd be all right in the apartment by herself, since she'd never lived on her own before.

"I won't be *living* on my own," she teased. "You are coming back, aren't you?" He smiled weakly and she teased him more, thrilled by his minor suffering.

The night before he left, she shoved her bloated body into

the cheapest red lace lingerie she could find at the store. She examined herself in the mirror and decided she looked all right, just a little fleshy. He had been staring curiously at her breasts for days, but if he came to any conclusions about them he didn't say anything. She looked in the mirror and told herself she was ravishing. He would be waiting.

When she presented herself to him he looked at her body as if it were entirely new. "Oh my God," he said, in a tone more appropriate for a train wreck than a woman in lingerie, and she wriggled self-consciously until he pulled her toward the bed by her wrist and set his lips on her breasts. He pushed the lace of her bra away and sucked on her nipples before she pushed him off and stepped away, covering herself with the lace again. "Don't you want to just look for a minute?"

He smiled. "I'm looking."

She didn't know what to do next. She turned and tugged at the waistband of her panties and acted like she was going to touch herself. She stopped awkwardly when his expression shifted from amusement to pity.

"Turn around," he said. "Get on your hands and knees."

She turned around and lowered herself to her hands and knees, crawling a few inches and looking back. She took it as a good sign that his neck looked so taut. She slunk back to him, like a prowling cat, and when she reached him she put her tongue on his leg just below his knees. She grazed his thigh with her knuckles and slipped her hand through his boxer shorts and her tongue kept creeping and creeping up. Obediently he kept his hands to himself, waiting until his cock was in her mouth to grab hold of her head. He moaned and cried her name and after not much time at all he pushed her onto the bed and pulled her panties down just far enough to slip inside her and come.

All at once she began to sob. He lifted his head, alarmed, and gathered her up into his arms. "No, no, don't cry," he begged.

She turned away from him, but she guided his arm as she turned and held onto it like an iron bar. She cried into his wrist. "We'll have everything we want," he said. "Soon, Mariam. I promise."

It was before dawn when Malick came in a taxi to pick him up. John had mostly gotten ready while she slept. He woke her up only after he didn't need anything more than to say good-bye. She felt like a sleepwalker, following him down the stairs. He told her to wait in the vestibule because it was cold outside, too cold for her to be standing around in her dressing gown. The overhead light in the vestibule was dim and orange, dreamlike, and through the narrow window beside the door she watched John, Malick, and the driver load the trunk of the taxi. John ran back up the path. She opened the door for him and in the doorway he pressed his lips hard against her temple before he went back down the path.

She closed the door to keep out the chill. John disappeared inside the taxi and Malick stood outside it a moment longer, peering at the vestibule window, trying to make out Mariam's form, and when he saw she was still there he put his hand up in the air. He held it there until she answered his gesture with her own hand against the glass. Then, briskly, he got in the taxi and allowed it to pull away.

The women's clinic was white from ceiling to floor, with hard white formica chairs and nurses in white uniforms. The patients looked like globs of dark paint splattered onto a blank canvas. Mariam read a magazine, looking expectantly toward the reception desk at the end of every page. It was a half hour past her appointment time. A woman had called her up to the desk earlier, looking around the lobby for a man that might belong to Mariam. "Is your husband here?" she asked.

Mariam explained that he was away, on a business trip.

"Is no one here with you?"

"No."

"We like someone to be here with the mother. In case."

Mariam understood. The last time she'd had an ultrasound the news had been devastating, and John had been with her.

"Will they not do the scan then?" Mariam asked calmly. "No one told me when I made the appointment. Otherwise I would have brought someone."

The woman told Mariam to have a seat and she would be called up shortly, but ages went by before someone called her name. She was led into a room, another white room with a white machine that looked like a squat robot with a small gray screen for a face. She was left alone for a few minutes to take off her pants and lie down on the exam table. Staring at the plaster ceiling, she willed herself to breathe deeply and relax.

To her surprise, a man came in, a young man. He introduced himself as a doctor but he hardly looked old enough, and what doctor did an ultrasound himself? She breathed in and out, lifted her shirt and closed her eyes. He warned her that the paddle would feel cold at first. She flinched when it touched her skin. This was the excruciating part, the wordlessness. The punching of buttons that seemed to go on forever. As he slid the scanner and pressed it into her flesh, she wanted to ask him, "Do you see anything?" There had been no need to ask last time. She had already known her pregnancy was over.

Finally a sound filled her ears like she had been pulled underwater, a low-pitched rhythmic grinding, a swishing like sandy water being pumped furiously though a piston. Still the doctor was silent, listening. "It's a good, strong heartbeat," he said softly. She lifted her hands to her face and covered her eyes. She breathed, and breathed.

"Judging from the size of the fetus you are about fourteen weeks."

He was extremely professional, unmoved by the sound of

the heartbeat. "I have had a miscarriage at sixteen weeks," she confessed.

Still occupied by the machine, he asked, "Did you have a scan before that?"

"No," she answered.

"If the fetus is healthy at fourteen weeks, it's rare to have complications at sixteen weeks. Probably it was not a healthy fetus. Did they inspect the tissue afterwards?"

"No," she said. It was a little rural hospital in Luling. They did ultrasounds to determine the sex of the baby and the due date and had little interest in dead fetal tissue.

He moved away from the screen and wrote on her chart. "You have nothing to worry about. You can come back in six weeks." He left and sent the nurse in to tell her she was all done. They seemed to want her out of the room in a hurry.

She went to the tea shop and had a bowl of ice cream with a banana and melted chocolate. When the waitress slid it across the counter Mariam looked at her, beaming. "I'm celebrating," she said, and the girl smiled politely.

At the library she was given regular hours, Monday through Friday from eight to four. Misha found a desk in a storage room and tried to figure out where to put it. "Why don't we leave it here?" Mariam suggested. "Under this window." It was a high lunette, delivering sunlight in diagonal tubes toward the broken tile floor.

"You can't work in here," Misha argued. "It's horrible."

"I can work anywhere," Mariam said. She did not like all the trouble she had caused with her sudden hiring. "I'll hardly be in here anyway."

"I remember this about you," Misha said. "You were always so agreeable."

During the first week she mostly handled maps and microform and sat at her desk only to eat lunch. The work was easy

232 · CHAITALI SEN

but absorbing and the days went by quickly. If she spent a lot of time with microform she went outside afterwards, to clear the smell of acetate from her head. After a few days she asked Misha if she could avoid the microform room, saying it gave her a headache, and Misha was immediately suspicious.

"Are you pregnant?"

Mariam didn't want to deny it. Withholding was one thing but denying it, negating the existence of the fetus was another thing altogether and it made Mariam superstitious, and if she lied to Misha only to have to tell her the truth in a few weeks when her pregnancy became more apparent, she feared Misha would feel slighted. At any rate Mariam hesitated too long and Misha let out a little squeal of delight. "Don't tell anyone," Mariam whispered. "John doesn't even know yet."

Misha pressed her lips together and crossed them with her finger, but she still looked like she was going to burst.

On her first weekend alone Mariam decided to unpack the rest of the kitchen and bake cakes. A walnut cake for her parents, chocolate for Vic, and a lemon cake for the other neighbor who shared their floor, a woman named Dolly whom they had met briefly in the corridor before John left.

Whenever John called from America, their conversations were hurried and awkward. She couldn't hear him well and he never told her anything of consequence, except once after he had seen his family. His parents and sisters had all come down to Washington to spend a few days with him and reportedly sent her their love, which was one of those meaningless phrases she never believed or understood. They had loved her once, she knew, but what reason had they to love her now? She had kept him away from them for so long.

After his calls she always had trouble falling asleep, afraid of one thing after another. She was simultaneously afraid of losing her baby and having her baby. She was afraid of being childless, and afraid of spending the rest of her life in the service of a dream. At times she felt that's all children were, dream vessels holding the promise of something better. In their children, parents could cultivate all the strengths they'd given up in themselves. Their hearts would be kinder. Their minds would be steadier. They would know more, understand more, feel more deeply; they would be saviors.

She stayed awake formulating theories about procreation. She believed women and men had children for different reasons. Women with a boundless supply of love and deflated sense of importance needed outlets for their affection, a chance to nurture someone they perceived as more essential. Men had children to extend their own lives, to have their own efforts carried forth and their failures rectified. Yes, she had settled upon this before drifting off to sleep; a child was a man's legacy and a woman's eclipse.

All of her clothes began to feel tight. She spent her first paycheck on a new dress, one that was loose around her abdomen but didn't fall like a cloak around her either. It was green, with a pretty neckline and pearl buttons. The bodice fit perfectly around her swollen breasts. She loved the changes in her body and the closer the days came to John's homecoming the more acutely she craved him. When she closed her eyes she could almost feel his hands on her, peeling her dress away.

He was due home around midnight on Sunday. All weekend there had been a lot of noise coming through the walls, from Dolly and her teenage daughter, Zoya, from one family of rambunctious children running up and down the stairs, from visitors in and out the front door and from neighborly conversations in the hallway. All of it died down around ten o'clock and the building settled into a foreboding silence. It was past midnight when she heard the door clanging in the vestibule. She went to the top of the stairs and watched him put his suitcase down and hold onto the banister before he dared to look up.

He climbed the stairs, with some effort at first, then faster until he was at the landing and she jumped into his arms. He lifted her and held her tightly, trying to remember her, she thought. She told him her news then, and he kissed her so unsteadily she was afraid they would go tumbling down the stairs.

They didn't sleep at all that night. John washed the journey off of him and changed into his pajamas, then set himself to the task of unpacking his suitcase, destroying all evidence of his trip. He moved so frantically she couldn't find a way to help him, and he talked on and on about the conference, in particular about his conversations with a group of geologists who had also found other evidence of asteroid impacts in Archaean rock, similar to John and Malick's outcrop in Luling. Face to face they finally dared to discuss what had been on each of their minds, that bombardments of massive asteroids could have set off forces that accelerated the lifting of the earth's crust and the formation of continents. Mariam tried to follow along but she was distracted by his behavior, the movement of his hands, the pitch of his voice, the rise and fall of his eyebrows. There was something childlike about his insistent storytelling, and at the same time he looked tired. Not the kind that comes from an uncomfortable passage or lack of sleep but a weariness that comes from a disappointment so shattering there is no hope of an imminent recovery. He talked without stopping, without giving her a chance to ask a question or remind him that she wasn't able to grasp these notions of deflected plumes or shifting mantle convection patterns.

"Did you get to talk about your manuscript at all?"

"No. It didn't come up," he said.

She gave up then and stretched her arms above her head. "Are you hungry?"

He was frowning into his almost empty suitcase. She asked him again if he was hungry.

"I couldn't have talked about the book," he said. "It would have made me think about you."

"You didn't want to think about me?"

"I hated being away from you. I don't think you could understand. You were home, but I felt completely adrift."

Completely adrift. His voice was heavy with guilt and she imagined, not for the first time, what he might have done to moor himself when he was completely adrift. He was a man, after all, and weak sometimes, weaker than either of them liked to admit, and she knew how he liked to fuck.

"It was difficult for me, too, John. If I hadn't had this," she said, placing her hand on her belly, "I would have gone mad." He was perhaps on the edge of a confession. She had to stop him, because she wanted to put out of her mind the things she had imagined, without having them confirmed or denied.

She reached for him. He was beyond her at first until he crouched in front of her and kissed her hand. He was re-materializing, solidifying at her feet. She was surprised all over at how deeply and broadly his crow's feet fanned out from the corners of his eyes. He lowered his head onto her lap. His hair was still thick, but receding above his temples. One day he would be an old man, like her father, and she wondered if she would still know him then.

"Tell me about the heartbeat," he said.

"It sounded like a pump under water. It was so fast." She mimicked the sound for him, trying to get it right, and when she looked down again she saw that he had begun to cry. In all these years, she had never seen him with tears in his eyes, and had not thought him capable of weeping.

TWELVE

They found out they were having a girl. Mariam wanted to name her Sara. John heard the name in his head, Sara Merchant, and saw it written in a child's scrawl. "It's perfect," he said. Their daughter had a name, Sara, and he hoped she would have gold specks in her eyes.

Sara was active. When Mariam felt a kick she would stop everything and cause a sudden hush. She and John would lay their palms over her taut abdomen and feel their daughter's foot or fist moving like hard knots along that maddening barrier of skin and muscle. He would put his ear down to listen. Mariam liked to stroke his head when his ear was pressed against her, and after sinking, almost drowning in that silent intimacy, the world beyond them was monstrous.

One morning he watched Mariam get out of bed. They were both naked, for they had figured out how to make love around the intrusion of her ever-expanding womb. Mariam looked at herself in the full-length mirror. The light coming through the window was blue, and her body was shadowy in that blue light. He couldn't believe how close he had come to making an irreparable mistake. To leaving and never seeing her like this. His family, when he saw them in America, had tried to convince him to stay. He had taken a day off from the conference to see them at a nearby motel where they had all gathered, his parents looking aged but happy, Sonia and David doting on their two children, and Theresa not a teenager anymore but a confident young woman. All they could talk about was their desire for him to join them, about how deeply they felt his absence. He sat with his parents in their depressing beige room, looking out at an ugly parking lot, and listened as they begged him to abandon his wife for a green card, as if a green card were some kind of paradise destination. There were so many women there who wanted a good husband, they said. All he had to do was choose one and learn to love her. They said they loved Mariam and they were certain she would understand. They were certain she would let him go. And after a day with them, he couldn't quite get back to himself, and later he slept with a woman who was not Mariam, because there was nothing stopping him and he wanted to see if it would be easy.

Mariam was holding her nightgown in her arms. She unfurled it, ready to slip it on.

"Leave it," he said.

She looked over her shoulder and dropped the nightgown to the floor. It terrified him to know how close he'd come.

A few weeks after he returned he got a call from a university press in England. They offered to publish the manuscript he had worked on in Luling. Mariam couldn't contain her excitement when he told her the news. Only British geologists would read it, he told her. It wouldn't even be distributed in their own country. "It won't get you a passport," he joked. She didn't laugh at the joke but she wasn't offended either. He didn't understand, with her impending motherhood, how the book could still be important to her. To him, it felt like a relic from another lifetime.

They gave him a small load, one undergraduate class, Advanced Petrology, and a graduate seminar in research methodology. He had not been at the front of a classroom in four years, had forgotten that part of his life entirely until this new assignment forced him to remember, and when the vagueness of his memory gave him nightmares, he decided to forget again and act as if he'd never done this before. Both of the classes were small, twenty students in Petrology and eight in the seminar. The twenty in Petrology were unnaturally quiet and serious. At the same time as his Petrology class, other students conducted large and noisy protests on the common, often drowning out his lectures. His own students were already timid, and made more timid by the shouting outside their classroom window. John asked Vic if he should expect his classes to be disrupted every day, or was this a passing phase? Vic, visibly impatient with John's irritation, explained the situation slowly and simply. Earlier in the year students in the technical colleges and high schools north of the militarized zone had gone on a hunger strike, and a solidarity movement had spread rapidly among the students throughout the province. The demonstrators called for an opening of the militarized zone, to end what they called the occupation of the north. Vic had taught a number of students who participated in the movement and had held study groups for them outside of the regular curriculum. "Sometimes these movements begin spontaneously," he said, "but without ideological leadership, they die out."

John was stunned. "Don't tell me you've taken it upon yourself to provide ideological leadership?"

Vic laughed, slapping John on the back. It made John feel better to know Vic wasn't taking himself too seriously in all this. He seemed all right, in full control of his faculties.

He had trouble reconciling the image of Vic's students with his own undergraduates, who never spoke unless they were asked a direct question, and even then never without consulting their textbooks. Whenever he tried to begin a discussion, all that came back to him was a symphony of shuffling pages. Eventually he told them to leave their books at home. He made them cut their own thin sections of rock specimens and analyze them. After a while the students found they knew more than they thought. By the time they had their first field class, they were far more lively and confident.

His graduate students in Research Methodology were older and more animated. John often lost control of the class because they were prone to argue and sometimes their arguments were more interesting than anything he had planned, but he learned how to redirect their considerable energy. Besides his two classes there were torturous department meetings run by consensus. Much of what they discussed had nothing to do with earth science. They talked about petitions, student politics, faculty politics, what to have for lunch, what to have for dinner if their meetings ran long. There were eight of them, John and Vic, two doctoral students who both looked sickly in different ways, three other unmarried or soon to be married men, and Cyrus, who was married and had a son, but his wife and son were not in the country. John was curious about Cyrus. He was a tall, bony man with narrow shoulders and a thick black mustache that overwhelmed his gaunt face. There was something haunted about him.

One day, during a break in one of their department meetings, Cyrus asked him if he wanted to go up to the roof for a cigarette. John was eager to join him, needing a cigarette badly. "For some reason," Cyrus said, "when there are long meetings I prefer to go up instead of down."

"Maybe it feels like more of an escape," he said. Cyrus laughed. It was a short flight of stairs up to the roof. The breeze up there was nice, and they could see the whole lawn and all of the college buildings around it. John could see the library. "My wife works over there," he said.

"I've seen her," Cyrus said. "She's expecting?"

"Yes," John said, smiling. "We're having a girl."

Cyrus congratulated him. "I have a son. He's in Hungary, with my wife. In Budapest."

He lit John's cigarette and they smoked in silence for a minute. John thought his silence was somewhat inquisitive but Cyrus did not read into it. "You must miss him," John said at last. He didn't mention the wife because of the varied nature of marriages, but any father would miss his child.

"Yes," Cyrus said, "but I'll join them soon."

"Is it easy to get a visa to Hungary?" John asked.

Cyrus didn't immediately answer and John stumbled. "Why Budapest, if you don't mind my asking?"

"We know people there. Budapest was recommended."

Their conversation halted as they finished smoking. When Cyrus looked at his watch and turned toward the door, something made John grab his wrist and stop him.

"How soon will you join them?"

"I'm waiting for some papers," he answered.

"Papers?"

Cyrus gave a wincing smile. Clearly he didn't want to be rude, but he was not planning to answer any more of John's questions.

"My wife," John said cautiously. "She can't get a passport." He wanted to ask Cyrus if he already knew his situation. Vic or Malick had likely told the department about it, as a way of explaining some things about his academic career and his four years in Luling. Vic certainly would not have seen a reason to keep it a secret. From his passive expression, John couldn't tell if Cyrus knew or not. He didn't know him well enough to read any meaning into his restrained reactions.

Cyrus nodded. "Later," he said, and opened the door to the stairwell.

Back in their meeting, Vic made a proposal. Some students wanted to send a group of people, a delegation of sorts, into the militarized zone to meet with youth leaders on the other side. For this delegation to have maximum impact, they wanted endorsements from all of the academic departments at the college. John couldn't believe how readily the group had taken on the proposal. Without blinking they discussed the level of support they were comfortable giving. There were two issues, whether to endorse and whether to take an active role in the campaign. It wasn't that John didn't see value in it, but these weren't the discussions he'd been expecting to have at an academic institution. They would have been unheard of at Presidency, but he'd been outside the academic structure for so long, he didn't know if times had simply changed, if this was the world now.

"You've been quiet," Cyrus said. "Are you uncomfortable with the discussion?"

"No," John lied. He remembered Malick's mapping expedition in the north, and the story of his unfortunate friend who lost his life in the minefield. "There is a safety concern, isn't there, in sending a delegation?"

"I would imagine," Vic said. "That's something they'll have to work out in the planning."

"I have nothing against students wanting to make a statement, but what does that have to do with our work as an academic department?"

The others seemed bored by his question. Cyrus attempted an answer. "Demilitarizing the north is essential to our discipline. We haven't been able to gain any access to the area in decades. We can't get a full geological picture of our own province. And we have colleagues there working under dangerous conditions. We can't get any information to them and they can't get it to us."

It was a surprisingly thorough answer and John appreciated it. "What if we endorse something that causes a confrontation, and people get killed?" he asked.

"That would be terrible," Vic agreed. "But they're less likely to be harmed if more eyes are on them."

In the end, the group decided to endorse the proposal but abstain from taking an active role until Vic could get more information.

John left feeling disoriented. He picked Mariam up from the library and they began to walk home. Lately Mariam preferred to walk because she found their small car too uncomfortable, and after being indoors all day she wanted fresh air and exercise. As often as he could, he tried to walk with her and continue the rest of his work from home. These walks were his only chance to relax. Once he was home he was always busy until late in the evening.

He had a lot on his mind, the talk with Cyrus and Vic's proposal during the meeting. He only told her about the meeting, admitting to her that he had felt stupid and out of place.

"Do you think you'll get used to the way they do things here?" Mariam asked.

"I hope so," he said.

"It's temporary," Mariam said. "It is temporary, isn't it?"

He didn't know why she was asking in that way. "Of course it's temporary," he said. They had discussed it back in Luling. They had set a deadline of two years. Within two years, there needed to be a resolution to her passport issue and he needed to apply for positions abroad, but with the pregnancy and Mariam working and John trying to adjust to his new position, they had not figured out exactly what needed to be done. And now, two years seemed a very long time to wait. He was certain Cyrus had found some way to circumnavigate the system. He needed to find out more from him.

Mariam took his hand. She wanted to stop for a minute by the canal and rest. He looked around for a place for them to sit, but there were no benches and they were almost home. She leaned against the canal wall.

"Something occurred to me the other day," Mariam said in a hushed tone. "Our daughter will have a birth certificate. Her status can't possibly be questioned. It will be easy to get her a passport."

"Sure," John said, looking uncertain. He wanted to hear

what she'd been thinking, but the way she began made him apprehensive.

"Maybe you and Sara could go ahead of me," she continued. "Do you think you could get a visa for yourself and for Sara? Your parents could take care of her for a while. They must have some mercy on a mother and child who are separated. We can get a lawyer here, who might understand the situation better."

John stopped her. "What are you talking about? That could take years."

It was obvious Mariam hadn't thought through her idea. He didn't want to upset her when all she was trying to do was have a rational discussion about their options, something they had been putting off for too long. But he felt she was on the wrong track and he had to disrupt her pattern of thought. While it was true they had not exhausted all of their legal options, there were a million things that could go wrong waiting for the government to change her status. They could make an example out of her parents. They could punish her for being the granddaughter of a political agitator. They could simply string her along without any intention of granting her citizenship. And now that they lived here, he could see how this place was constantly on the brink of turmoil. The situation was unstable at best. It was another reason he was alarmed by the rampant political discussion in their department meetings. If he and Mariam were going to be under scrutiny, he couldn't afford to have a reputation as a troublemaker.

He brushed a wisp of hair away from her face. "Mariam, there may not be a solution inside the system. Have you considered that?"

She hesitated. "I've considered it," she whispered.

"Good," he said. "That's good." A window had been opened, at least. For now he didn't want her to worry. He would find out more. They had lived with this long enough and he was determined to find the fastest way out of it.

*

Later, as promised, Cyrus followed up on their rooftop conversation. He didn't reveal more than he had to. He said his wife had been sponsored by relatives in Hungary and had emigrated legitimately. It was Cyrus who had no chance of leaving the country without a forged passport and visa. He didn't say why but John had a suspicion it had to do with some political activities in his student days. John had overheard veiled references to some troubles he'd had in the past, and he'd begun to notice how many of the department's unconventional attitudes were led by Cyrus. In contrast, John didn't hold back anything about Mariam's history. He told him all the reasons they needed to have an alternative plan.

Then Cyrus told him about a father and son who forged documents, but he cautioned John not to go to them unless he was sure. Once he was sure, things could proceed quickly, but they were the best and they weren't cheap, and they didn't like their time to be wasted. John said he wouldn't be ready for a while. First, he needed to talk it out with Mariam, and he wanted to wait until their daughter was born and able to handle the journey. He imagined it would be six months at least before he could reasonably commit.

But in his mind, he'd already made his decision. This was the way forward. And he would not do it Cyrus's way, enduring a long separation from his wife and child. John had his own plan. He and Mariam and Sara would all travel with forged documents. It was important to stay together, and it was even more important for them to travel as equals. The importance of equal status had been fixed in his mind for some time. He was beginning to realize how much it wore on them, the inequality, the immobility of one person juxtaposed against the mobility of the other. They either all needed legal documents or they all needed false ones.

He told Mariam about the father and son, asking her to

keep her mind open. She had questions, many questions he couldn't answer yet. She said they would know how good the papers were only after Cyrus made it safely to Budapest. John had to admit that was true. He had no idea when Cyrus was planning to leave.

She didn't quite understand the part about equal status. He was having trouble explaining why he wanted forged documents for all of them. How would he work without legal papers? How would he get an academic position? Her questions were making him tired. "One thing at a time," he begged.

Mariam became distracted and stopped interrogating him. "She's kicking like crazy."

"She can't wait to come out," he said. "All we have to do now is get ready for her." Their baby would be here soon, and after, whatever had to be done would be done together.

THIRTEEN

Mariam's water broke in her mother's kitchen, a few days earlier than expected. Arifah called John in a panic, just as he was leaving his office to teach his research seminar, and asked if they should wait for him to arrive. "Can you take her to the hospital? Can you get a taxi?" he asked, in a panic himself. Arifah assured him she could, and after he told his students his baby was coming and received their congratulations, he went to the hospital. He got there before them and waited anxiously, wondering if it would have been better to have picked her up in the car, but in a few minutes he saw them pull in. He helped Mariam out of the taxi and into the hospital. Under her wool coat she still wore her nightgown. Her feet were in fuzzy pink slippers.

If she was in a lot of pain she bore it stoically. She stared and nodded at the doctor in utter obedience as she held on tightly to John's hand. The doctor and nurses came in and out, checking her dilation, taking her pulse, offering water, making small talk. Arifah stayed as long as she could. Before she left she kissed Mariam's forehead and said her labor took only three hours. The nurses were impressed, and Mariam was happy, taking Arifah's final pronouncement as an edict.

But the labor was long and brutal, and loud, and at the end of it, hours later, was a silence that wouldn't cease. The doctor held their baby awkwardly. She was a good size, well proportioned, with all the expected wrinkles and folds, exquisite in every way except that she was inanimate, and not the right color, and not a sound came out of her. Mariam couldn't see her and waited, smiling, and John had to look away. He had never seen anything as heartbreakingly beautiful as that, Mariam slick and weary from her labor with her fading smile and stubborn hope.

The nurse carried their baby out and the doctor gestured for John to follow him into the hallway. Thinking back on it he couldn't imagine what Mariam must have thought, left suddenly alone. "Something went wrong," the doctor said. "Sometimes these things happen. Will you tell her or would you like me to do it?"

John heard himself say, in reaction to the doctor's clipped tone, that he would tell her. He went back into the room and walked slowly to her side. She was staring at the ceiling, the first signs of despair in her unflinching eyes.

"Where is she?"

He took her hand weakly. Her fingers were cold. "Mariam," he said, and stopped. He had no language to continue and his mind was a black void.

Two nurses came back in. One of them, the delivery nurse, held a bundle as stiff as a loaf of bread, which was supposed to be their daughter. The other nurse prepared an injection, a sedative for Mariam. The one with the bundle nudged him out of the way and tried to get Mariam to take her, to hold her baby and say goodbye, but Mariam, giving her an imperceptible glance, said that wasn't her baby. She was quiet, polite, but her terror pounded the walls, and when the nurse tried again Mariam cried out and pushed her away. The woman reeled back, clutching the baby close to her chest as if dropping her would matter.

Mariam turned to John, her mouth twisted and scowling. "They took our baby. Go find her."

He looked pleadingly at the nurse with the needle in her

248 · CHAITALI SEN

hand. "For God's sake, what are you waiting for?" Mariam followed his gaze and saw the needle and pulled her arms in close to her body. She looked at John like he was some kind of demon, and screamed.

"Hold her down," the nurse ordered. He put his hand on her forehead, pressing her head against the pillow. He put his hand over her mouth to stop her screaming, and after a while, overpowered, he felt Mariam's neck relax and her head sink back into the pillow, all the tension under his palms withering. The nurse quickly plunged the needle into a blue vein and said, "There's a good girl."

He was left alone with her for a while. They brought him a chair, in which he sat staring at the wall, occasionally glancing at Mariam to make sure she was really sleeping. At least in her dreams, he hoped, there was a chance she could do all the things she imagined, holding, nursing, cooing, kissing her baby. It would be better if she stayed there, he thought. It would be better if she never woke up.

The nurse with the bundle came back. "One of you has to hold her." He put his arms out and let her hand him his baby. He moved the blanket away and saw her face, her wrinkled eyes that had perhaps never opened, and short and straight black lashes. He felt her silky hair and kissed her cold blue cheek. Her hands were little balled fists. Her name was Sara and she was a corpse. He wept over her for a few minutes until the nurse took her away.

Mariam needed to be washed up and he remembered they'd left Arifah in the waiting room hours ago. He found her there, sitting with her head in her hands, her shoulders heaving violently. Someone, perhaps the doctor, had given her the news. One of the nurses saw him standing against the wall and gestured toward Arifah, a gesture that said he ought to do something, to get her out of here. She was upsetting the others who were waiting, now captives to her grief. Everyone was staring at Arifah, no one daring to speak, until a woman went over and put an arm around her. Arifah lifted her head and cried, "The water is poisoned. I told my husband we should never go back."

The woman was kind, holding Arifah and listening. He watched them for a while before he approached, nodding gratefully to the woman, who looked at him with great pity and went back to her seat.

Arifah straightened up when she saw him. "I want to see her," she whispered.

"They're cleaning her up," he said, and it sounded terribly harsh, as if he had thought Mariam to be filthy. Polluted. Arifah wiped her face with a handkerchief and after a few minutes he took her back to the room. They sat there silently, waiting for Mariam to wake up.

He didn't know how long her eyes were open before he noticed them. She was perfectly still. John touched her cheek but she kept her eyes on the wall and asked for her mother. "I'm here," Arifah said, and he left them alone. In a half-hour the man who handled the burial arrangements would come and John waited outside his office, wanting it to be done.

For the next two months they moved around the apartment like chess pieces. They did speak to each other, even about their baby, what had happened to her, what the doctor said, why Mariam never held her, but they weren't communicating so much as delivering lines from a script. *She couldn't breathe. Her lungs didn't work. She was asphyxiated.* He could almost see the words written out for him. They slept next to each other without touching.

It went on like this until a day Mariam sat on the edge of the bed watching him get dressed. He felt self-conscious, his movements being followed too closely, and he imagined himself saying something she might have wanted to hear, that everything would be all right. They were walking blindly through a fog of grief but surely one day soon the fog would lift.

"I've decided to go back to work," she said.

"That's wonderful," John said with undisguised relief. The hardest part for him had been watching her give in to this relentless indolence. For the first few weeks he had to carry her into the bathtub to bathe her. He wondered guiltily how she would manage to get herself dressed and ready for work, but he hoped necessity would force her back into a proper routine.

She looked like she wanted to say something else, but her lips remained parted and unmoving. He stood in front of her and waited.

"I think it's time for you to start over somewhere else," she said.

"In what sense?" he asked. It was a reflexive question, something he asked his students or colleagues when he needed some time.

"I think you know."

"Are you kicking me out of the country, Mariam?" He laughed, but she didn't react. "And what am I supposed to do? Forget that I have a wife here?"

She stared at him impassively. "Why not? You've done it before."

It took him some time to understand her intent. It wasn't an accusation. An accusation would have implied a measure of uncertainty. Mariam had already collected the evidence and was handing down her sentence, and he stood in front of her exposed, shamed and utterly despised. This woman couldn't be Mariam. There was no forgiveness, no warmth. He thought he had gotten away with something and her sole desire now was to show him that he hadn't. She was someone who had been pretending to love him, but she must have stopped loving him many months ago.

"You've been waiting a long time to say that," he said.

"No. It just came to me now."

That was a lie and it enraged him. "If there's something you want to know, Mariam, just ask me."

"If there's something you want to tell me, just say it."

He stopped himself from saying something he would regret. "We have to talk about this later. We can't possibly make any decisions now. Not after what we've been through."

"But you did do something," she cried. In an instant, all of her steely composure fell away. She was herself again, vulnerable. "You forgot me."

Surely this was not what she needed to talk about. They had other things they needed to talk about, not this. He shook his head. "I didn't forget you. I tried to forget you, and I made a mistake. That's all."

She pretended to find this amusing. He didn't blame her. It was a ridiculous defense. "Did you try every night? Was she someone you can try again next time?" He could see now what had happened. Mariam had spent her pregnancy imagining the details he had not provided himself. Now she was a breaking dam. She held her stomach and cried, and he couldn't help but think how their baby had been in that body full of pain. He couldn't move closer to her, he couldn't touch her. There was a barrier between them he couldn't cross. He stayed where he was and waited until she could speak again. "I don't have anything else to give you, John. Everything I wanted to give you is dead. I don't have anything else."

When she put it that way, with such weary defeatism, he realized his will to go on was not as strong as her will to give up. There was no fight left in him after all. "Maybe you're right, Mariam. Maybe it's time."

Suddenly she relaxed. Her head fell forward, her shoulders slouched, her spine curved. She closed her eyes and inhaled. Her apparent relief was more revealing than anything she'd said that morning. "It isn't a failure, John. It's just time."

He knew everything was lost now. He had always kept his gaze on something ahead, something they could run for, but now the road was at its end. In front of them was something impenetrable, and neither of them had the strength to climb it.

After that morning they settled into a strange, new domesticity. Their future had been decided in that brief exchange. She offered to go back to her parents' house but he asked her to stay. He didn't want anyone to know they were separating until it was already done and he was out of the country. They continued to share the same space inside their apartment, but it was like sharing an office, or sharing a room as siblings. If he was ever tempted to touch her he held back, knowing how awkward it would make their new arrangement. She continued to organize his life, which he continued to appreciate. She did everything she could to help him figure out a plan, and sometimes she described his future to him so enthusiastically he could hardly wait to leave her behind and get started.

They were prepared for it to take some time, a year or more, but there was a wealth of opportunity and everything happened faster than he expected. Before long he got a call from a department in Michigan. They conducted their interview over the telephone and made an offer. As long as he got his visa in time, he could begin in the fall semester.

Mariam said she was impressed and happy for him. She asked about this place, Michigan, if it was beautiful there, and he said no, it didn't seem to be particularly beautiful. He thought it would be all right, just then, to brush a wisp of hair away from her eyes. She seemed surprised by his hand. She turned her head to let his thumb reach her lips. Nothing could have felt more illicit than that turn of her head. She must have realized at the same time he did that their restraint had been a kind of grief-driven madness. But there was also madness in this, in the way she wanted to be broken. She brought him to the floor and turned her back to him. She wanted to be penetrated but not inseminated. Her body was pressed against the floor. She used his forearm to protect her face from the tile. She bit his wrist and dug her nails into his palm.

When it was over, they cleaned themselves up and went on as if nothing had happened, but after the sun went down, when they were in bed and shrouded in darkness, he stroked and kissed her. He said this time he wanted her to face him. She obliged him, but she was trembling, terrified. He understood her terror. He was also afraid, entering the place where she'd birthed their daughter. She cried the whole time, even as she pulled him in. At the end she turned her head, his lips settling on her wet cheek. He felt the rise and fall of her chest against his own and he wanted to know what it all meant.

In the morning he found her making an omelet in the kitchen. "I think it's all right," she said. "As long as we don't lose our focus, I don't see why we shouldn't say goodbye properly."

They spent the next few weeks saying goodbye constantly, not losing their focus but gathering momentum toward his departure. He made plans to travel to Alexandria to apply for his visa, she found out how to get a divorce, and they proceeded as if they knew exactly what needed to be done and why. He had to wonder when they had started on this path. They had come to this decision after they lost their child, but they came to it too easily. It had to have rooted itself earlier, though he couldn't find an exact moment. Was it back in Alexandria, in the passport office? In Luling, which he thought of now as a long delusion? Here in English Canal, after he returned from his conference? He had come back from the conference changed. It was impossible not to. There he had allowed himself to acknowledge, for the first time, what he had missed in Copenhagen.

One night, he was holding Mariam, holding her tightly, listening to her heart thrumming against his ear. "You know I can't go unless you forgive me," he said. He was prepared to confess everything, the details of his betrayal in America, the things his parents had said, but without asking for any of those things she said she did, she forgave him and she would love him until the day she died.

Slowly he realized the college was no longer functional. His students were often absent, the crowds on the common were more unruly, and some days everything simply came to a halt. The students called for a full strike and gathered on the lawn one day for a march to the Governor's Palace. He and Mariam listened to some of the speeches, still about the demilitarization of the north, before they decided to come home. In the car he had asked her if she thought all these students making speeches really cared, or did they just like the attention? Mariam said some of the students seemed a little pompous and disingenuous, but not all of them. No, not all of them, he agreed. He was relieved that she'd seen some of that too, that he wasn't just being old and cantankerous.

At home it was a normal evening. She made dinner while he sat in the dining room reading a rather discouraging set of exam papers, but later a rising commotion brought them out to the hall. Their neighbors from the floors above them had gathered on the stairs and in the vestibule. When Dolly saw Mariam she began talking excitedly.

"The police attacked the march on College Street. Two students have been killed."

"Killed?" Mariam asked.

"Yes, two students," Dolly cried. "Zoya is marching with them. I told her she was too young."

Mariam nodded then and took Dolly's hand. "Zoya will be all right," she said. "She knows how to take care of herself."

John looked around for Vic. "I'll be right back," he said, starting down the stairs, but he stopped when he realized

Mariam had followed him, and Dolly too was close behind. "Wait here," he said.

Mariam stiffened and glared. He'd never seen her look so defiant. Behind her, Dolly picked up on his communication and touched Mariam's elbow. "Stay with me, Mariam," she said, making herself sound helpless. She kept her hand on Mariam's elbow until at last Mariam surrendered and turned up the stairs. She looked back at John and he waited until she was on the landing before he continued down the stairs and went outside. The sun was still up, casting an even light over the street. A few people had gathered on the street viewing the disturbance on the other side of the canal, where demonstrators and riot police were in a confrontation. The police had formed a barrier and the crowd was shouting to be let through. The two sides churned back and forth, swaying like treetops in a storm. These streets never looked so narrow before. They couldn't accommodate a crowd this size and people were flush with the canal wall. He was afraid they would start falling into the water.

Their side of the canal wasn't quiet for long. There was a surge of demonstrators coming toward them, and the people who had been standing with him had to either step out of the way or join the surge. John couldn't decide what to do. By the time he thought he should go back inside, the marchers were upon him. They were elbow to elbow and there was no room for them to step around bystanders. He had to go with them or risk being trampled. Someone pulled him in and held onto him until he seemed to have the rhythm of the march. People in the front and behind him held bullhorns and led chants. The chants coming from the front were different than the ones from the back, and mostly around him people were shouting out their own slogans. John looked for gaps where he could move toward the townhouses. Even if he was pushed a long way down the street, if he could get to the sidewalk he could cut through the narrow front yards to get back home. He didn't want to be out all night in this. If he was gone long enough, he was sure Mariam would come out, and she too would be swept up.

At the end of the street they had to stop. John couldn't see what was going on at the front of the march, but there were warnings over a loudspeaker for the marchers to disperse. The crowd still tried to surge forward and was pushed back, causing the swaying he had seen earlier across the canal. He was starting to feel panicked, claustrophobic and he wove his way further toward the sidewalk hoping no one would prevent him from leaving the march. He made it to one of the iron fences in front of the townhouses. Behind the gate, residents of the townhouse were passing out water. He asked to come through the gate, explaining that he needed to get back home. He had lost all sense of distance. Everything looked different with all these people and he didn't quite know where he was. They heard glass shattering at the front of the march and someone opened the gate for him just as the crowd surged forward.

His progress along this route was painfully slow. He couldn't cut through the front gardens without having conversations with the people standing in them. Most of them were from the college. He recognized them and they recognized him, even if they didn't know each other by name, and he kept explaining how he'd been pulled along with the marchers for a while but he'd left his wife at home and wanted to get back. All the while the clashes on the street seemed to be intensifying. There were sirens now, and helicopters overhead. People had brought out their radios and were listening to news reports. From windows and rooftops, cameras were flashing, leaving bursts of white light lingering in the darkening sky. Even the trees and lampposts had been invaded by people trying to get a panoramic view. John had never experienced anything so overwhelming to all of his senses. By the time he made it back home, the sky was dark and marked with clouds of white smoke. His legs ached; he must have hurdled twenty fences. Some of his neighbors were in the yard. He looked for Dolly and Mariam. He didn't see them and went inside. From the bottom of the stairs he could hear Dolly's television blaring.

He sat down on the stairs for a moment, feeling strangely exhilarated by the chaos outside and unsettled being away from it. Even the people who were frightened didn't want to miss any of it. He should have been worried about Vic and Zoya and his students, but he found it impossible to worry and felt something close to what he remembered as happiness. Then, just as soon as he remembered that feeling of happiness, it faded and was lost. He got up, suddenly weary, and lumbered up the stairs. Dolly's door was ajar and he slipped into her apartment, looking for Mariam. Dolly and two women from upstairs, both nervous types, were huddled on the sofa watching the news on a national channel. John squinted at the screen, struggling to recognize College Street, now a scene of great violence. Dolly leaned forward. She thought she saw Zoya, but the camera moved away and she couldn't confirm it. The other two said it wasn't her, but Dolly didn't seem convinced. They showed the police dispersing students with water cannons. The riots were spreading far beyond College Street now. There was a report that more shots had been fired, and the number injured was growing. They didn't say if anyone else had been killed.

John tapped Dolly's shoulder. She turned and grabbed his hand.

"Is it bad, John? Did you seee Zoya?"

He shook his head. He wanted to tell Dolly not to worry. If there was a time for reckless fellowship, it was now. Zoya would be crazy to miss this.

"Where's Mariam?" he asked.

"She said she wanted to lie down. I tried to make her wait until you came back."

He left Dolly's apartment, annoyed with her for letting Mariam out of her sight. They had both seen her entranced gaze toward the outside, her pull toward the street. He hurried down the hall, calling Mariam's name out as soon as he opened the door to their apartment. She didn't answer. He was about to go back down the stairs, convinced she had gone outside, but Dolly had said she wanted to lie down and he decided to check the bedroom. He found her there, not sleeping but sitting up on the edge of the bed. The room was dark, and the light coming in through the window had a different quality. It was harsher and flickering, and carried with it the sounds of the riots.

He was alarmed by her stillness and stepped forward carefully. She didn't look at him, or give any sign that she knew he was there. He stood in front of her and knelt down. Her hands were cold. He held them, trying to warm them, and suddenly she inhaled and her eyes filled with tears. She said, "I'm tired." It was all she said. She slipped off the bed into his arms and he cradled her, kissing her face softly, kissing her wet eyes and cold forehead. There was no strength left in her body. She was as slack as a wet towel and he held her until her eyes fluttered closed. He lifted her onto the bed and pulled the covers over her. She seemed to be asleep.

He wanted to seal off the noise from the outside. He closed the curtains and left the bedroom to lock the front door and disconnect the telephone in the kitchen. When he came back in the room, he placed a towel in the gap beneath the bedroom door. The window still filtered in some light and noise, but it was muted. He got into bed beside Mariam. She was still for a while, apparently asleep, but after a few minutes she turned to him and put her hand up to his face, her fingers lightly touching his jaw. "What did you see out there?" she asked. Her eyes were a little clearer.

He didn't know what to describe. From the way he talked about it, what was going on outside was not much more than a rowdy parade, but still she seemed moved and on the verge of tears again. She bit her bottom lip, as if all of her emotions could be halted there. "I was watching it on the television, and then . . ."

"What, Mariam? What happened?"

"I realized there wasn't anyone else to blame this time. Not the war, not the government, not my parents. There was no one."

He put his thumb on her lips, knowing what she was going to say next and trying to stop her from saying it, but she went on. She said their daughter had died in her body and she was the only one to blame. She would have continued but he took hold of her chin, forcing her to look at him and not look away. The shock of it stopped her. She was frightened and though he regretted startling her, it was important that she listen to him. "It wasn't your fault," he said. If he ever made her feel as if it was her fault, he should be shot dead. "I know whose fault it is. I know who took her." She frowned, looking at him as if he'd gone mad, and he did feel gripped by a certain madness. He'd been thinking about this for a long time. He told her it was Rohana Bul's father, haunting him, cursing him until all of his children were replaced. He knew now, had known for a long time that he had killed that man. This was his first time saying it out loud, thinking it might put the dead to rest. For killing him, and going on as if nothing had happened, there had to be consequences. It was his fault. Mariam and their daughter were innocent, but they had to suffer the consequences with him.

Mariam didn't look away. Her gaze softened and he could see that her fear had turned to pity, and at the same time he had not convinced her. She was as committed to her own guilt now as she was before.

He put his head back down and they were quiet for a while, recovering from his outburst. She was strangely calm. Something about his revelation had not surprised her. She must have known all along that he had beaten Rohana Bul's father to death, but she would not have forced him to face it. He had to come to it on his own.

"I'm sorry, Mariam."

"I'm sorry too, John."

With that, there wasn't anything more to say about the matter. Arguing about who was to blame would not bring their daughter back. It was time to stop talking. It was time to rest. There was only one more thing Mariam wanted to know.

"What did she look like, John? Did you hold her?"

It wasn't hard for him to remember their daughter's face, her black hair smoothed over her forehead, her little dumpling cheeks, tiny eyelids and thick eyelashes. It wasn't hard at all to go back to that time and describe her carefully, so that Mariam could see her too. "We should have held her together. I should have helped you," he said. As much as it felt now as if their daughter had never existed, he had felt her solid form in the crook of his arm. He at least knew that she hadn't been something they'd dreamt up. She was real. She had grown for a while.

"I couldn't have, John."

She came closer to him, fitting herself against his body, pressing her forehead to his lips. He put his arm around her waist. All he could hear were the helicopters whirring overhead, and after a while the monotony of it lulled them to sleep.

An insistent tapping settled in his ear and woke him. Mariam was still sleeping. He rolled to the edge of the bed and grabbed his watch from the bedside table. He had no idea how long they'd been sealed up in the bedroom. He recalled getting up a handful of times, examining the light and cocking his ears to the tumult outside, drinking water and stumbling to the bathroom and tumbling back into bed. He tried to read the time on his watch. It was around six o'clock in the morning or evening. He couldn't narrow it down.

The tapping started again and he realized someone was knocking at the front door. He got up and put on his pants and slipped out of the bedroom, running to the door so the knocking would stop. He didn't want Mariam to wake up. He saw Vic through the peephole and opened the door.

"Where the hell have you been?" Vic asked, coming inside. "Why aren't you answering your phone?"

John shook his head. The whole apartment stank of something. He turned and started for the kitchen and stopped short. Mariam had been cooking when the riots started. They had left the food out and now it let off a sour, fermented smell.

"Let's go in the hall. Mariam's sleeping," John said. They went back out the way they just came, and John explained that he had turned the phone off because Mariam was trying to sleep. In this light Vic didn't look that great himself. His clothes smelled musty, like they had been wet and dried against his skin, his hair was unwashed, his eyes red and his eyelids drooping, and there was something that looked like a bloodstain on his jacket.

"What happened to you?" John asked.

"The police couldn't handle the uprising. They sent in the army and the militia. We're under martial law."

"But what happened to you?" John asked again. He hated when Vic answered specific questions with a broad overview.

"I fought, John, with the rest of them. The whole province is in a state of rebellion. What happened to you?"

"What do you mean?"

He pointed to the door. "Is Mariam all right?"

"We needed some time," John said.

Vic looked uncomfortable. They had never exchanged

words about his daughter who never came home, but he knew that Vic was pained by it. In a way John appreciated his refusal to lapse into meaningless sentiment.

"We needed some time," John repeated.

"I know," Vic said, "but now you have to come out. There are other people who need you."

John doubted that, and besides that, he didn't care. All that mattered to him was inside his apartment, and Vic who had no domestic life would never understand how that could happen. A marriage was not populous enough for Vic.

John opened the door. "I'll see you later. You should get some sleep. You look like shit."

"Call Arifah," Vic said. "She's been calling everyone in the building. Dolly had to convince her not to call the police."

He felt a little guilty, mostly because now Arifah had burdened everyone else with her hysteria. He promised Vic he would call and waved him off. He went to the kitchen to connect the phone again, but he decided to clean up the kitchen first. Then he made coffee and took a cup to the bedroom to wake Mariam. She was already sitting up, looking beautifully disheveled and alert.

"Was that Vic?" she asked.

He nodded, handing her the coffee. "They've sent in the militia. The whole province is in a state of rebellion," he said, repeating Vic's phrase. "We need to call your mother." She sprung out of bed, taking the coffee and walking out to the kitchen. He opened the curtains. The sun was up. He was surprised by the silence outside.

He went into the kitchen and watched as Mariam dialed the phone. She sipped her coffee while she waited for Arifah to pick up. He could hear the frantic hello. Mariam kept the conversation brief, saying she'd had a difficult night. "I'm sorry, Mama, I'm sorry," she said as Arifah carried on.

John shook his head and signaled to her to hang up.

"I have to go now. I'll call you later."

Mariam said she was starving. She made some toast, and after breakfast they showered and dressed. They could hear the television turning on next door in Dolly's apartment. They listened for voices, wondering if Zoya had made it home. In a while they heard Zoya and Dolly arguing.

"Sounds like things are back to normal," John said.

Mariam opened the window to let some air in. The air coming in was smoky, carrying a bitter, chemical smell. "Should we go outside and see?" Mariam asked. It was still early in the morning and it seemed safe enough to go out. There were no helicopters. Everything sounded quiet. Peaceful.

They crept down the stairs and went outside, turning their faces away from the wind. Their eyes burned and watered. When they managed to squint into the sky they saw bits of ash floating in the air. Along Canal Street whole sections of the canal wall had collapsed. The broken bricks were strewn everywhere, along with other debris, shards of glass and metal, papers and plastic cups, and strangely an incredible number of cloth rags. Across the canal they saw the burned-out frame of a police car.

They only made it to the end of their walkway. A military jeep came out of nowhere and stopped beside them. An officer of the army, not a militia reserve, came out and told them to get off the street. John pointed to their townhouse, saying they lived right there. He wanted to argue that they were still on their own property, not on the street at all. "Go on inside then," the man said. He wouldn't get back in the jeep until John and Mariam were inside. They went back, shutting the door and watching him surreptitiously through the glass panel. The officer got back in the jeep and sped away.

John looked at Mariam. "You're crazy if you think I'm leaving you here." All of this had to have resolved something for her, their time locked away in the bedroom, and this scene outside their door, as it had for him. He was certain they would never be free of each other. She would be a prison for him no matter how far apart they were.

She took his hand and started up the stairs. Then she turned and faced him, her head tilted and eyebrows furrowed. "Will you forgive me for this life, John?"

He smiled. One day she would understand. He wanted nothing but this life.

PART FOUR
Sulat Province

FOURTEEN

T he night he came home without Mariam, he drank half a bottle of whiskey and passed out on the couch. When he woke up his ear was throbbing. Slowly he remembered the nightmare of his waking life, Mariam being taken away, the baton swinging at his head, Vic picking him up from the courthouse and bringing him back before they could find her. He got up and wandered around the apartment, hoping irrationally that Mariam had simply returned while he slept, or better, that he'd imagined the whole thing.

Then he looked for Mariam's things, expecting them to have vanished as well, but everything was where it should have been—her clothes, her shoes, a few books and jewelry, even the scrapbook about her grandfather, which she compulsively kept in her bedside drawer wherever she went. He hadn't seen her with it since she'd placed it in this drawer, when they first moved into this apartment back in August. He pulled out the notebook and studied it. The front of it bubbled from papers that were slipped inside it, but more than half of its pages were compressed, flat and pristine. In the front, there were the newspaper articles. After that, some letters from Marseilles written illegibly in French, and then there was only one more item, an address scribbled on a sheet of notepaper, in the same handwriting as the letters from Marseilles, but in German. *Flüchtlingszentrum*, refugee center, Stuttgart.

Reluctantly he put the notebook back in the drawer. He

had hoped to find something in it that could help him, but there was nothing.

He went to the bathroom to look for medicine that could kill the pain in his ear and was shocked by his deformed face in the mirror. His cheekbone was swollen and bruised, his earlobe bright red, and when he turned his head and painfully moved his bloodied hair, he saw a cut that was still bleeding.

He found a bottle of aspirin and slammed the door of the medicine cabinet shut. He opened it and slammed it shut again. One, two, three times it hardly made a sound over the simultaneous ringing and pounding in his ear. He pressed a wet towel over the cut on his scalp and continued to pace around the apartment. After a long time, with great dread, he went into the nursery, where he had found Mariam the previous morning.

This room had been empty since February. Mariam had not been home from the hospital a week before she said she wanted the room cleared, exorcised of baby things. It was Dolly who had taken everything out and donated it to an orphanage. Dolly had asked him secretly if he didn't want her to simply hide some of it away, store it in her own apartment. It was her way of encouraging them to try again. He had told her he was sure they didn't want any of it. At the time he didn't want to imagine enduring another failed pregnancy, and even if they were to try again, he wouldn't have wanted to pass on the things meant for another child. That was what went through his own mind but in Mariam's mind, he had no idea if she hadn't already decided they should separate, that any future children would be his children alone, bred by some other wife. And what she was thinking in the nursery yesterday morning, lying on the hard floor, was even more of a mystery.

He couldn't remember if anything had been left stored in the closet, anything unrelated to the nursery. Mariam had been shedding all kinds of things, first because he was going to leave the country and she was going to go elsewhere, back to her parents presumably, and then because they were going to leave together. She had made him believe they were going to leave together. There was one strange thing she had said about suitcases. Their suitcases were so old, she remarked. The one he dragged to America, a massively awkward piece of baggage, especially was tearing at the seams and would not withstand a long journey. He thought it was strange because they were not to the point yet of worrying about suitcases. He said, "We'll make do with what we have," and she had not mentioned it again.

He opened the closet door. It was empty, except for the suitcase she had wanted to retire. When he tugged at the handle it should have teetered, full of air, but it fought him with its heft. He pulled it out of the closet and dropped it in the middle of the room, staring at it for a moment before he opened it and stepped back. It was full, perfectly stacked from edge to edge, with an unknown number of velo-bound booklets. He knew without looking that it was the war archives, the work that had consumed her during his military service. He pulled one out and flipped through its pages of small text. A window was cut into the plastic cover, just big enough for the title. *Archived Documents of the War Crimes Commission, Volume 7.* At the bottom of the title page there was a stamp. REFERENCE MATERIAL: DO NOT REMOVE: PROPERTY OF CSP LIBRARY.

He opened it and started reading. He had never asked Mariam for details about these archives, and she had never explained how truly horrendous their contents were. He read for a while but he had to stop. His head was full enough of darkness.

He threw the booklet back into the suitcase, pushed the suitcase back into the closet, and left the nursery, closing the door behind him. Then he took a shower and dressed as if it were an ordinary workday, and went out before the sun came up.

The campus was empty, the front doors of the science building chained shut, but he was able to get in through a side door with his master key. Once he was in the building he rushed up the stairs to the Geology wing and unlocked the door. The offices were dark but he didn't turn on any lights except for his own desk lamp. On his desk there was a framed photograph he'd lost the habit of noticing. It was Mariam in Luling in front of a hill covered with yellow wildflowers. They had gone for a walk and she looked so vibrant and beautiful, her hair blowing softly in the breeze, her collared dress buttoned almost to her neckline. He had wanted to preserve their time in Luling, to preserve that morning in early spring. After he took the picture he pulled her into the grass. The sun was bright, the sky cloudless, and they had never made love in such perfect brightness before. Tiny beads of musky sweat erupted all over her skin and soaked him. They should have stayed there, in Luling, and let the world fall apart without them.

He sat at his computer and typed a letter accounting for everything that had happened the last morning he was here, when he had stood at his office window thinking about Mariam on the nursery floor and feeling sorry for himself. When he was finished he didn't bother reading it. He sent it to the printer in the main office, which sputtered awake disastrously before it spit his paper out.

Back at his desk, he unframed the photograph of Mariam and took it to the copy machine, where he struggled for too long trying to get a decent reproduction. He tried various settings until he found one that gave him the essence of the picture, rather than a mere map of her face and its regions of light and dark. When he found the right setting he made several copies. To one he attached the letter he typed. He put the letter and the picture into the fax machine and laboriously programmed the numbers of his most important contacts abroad. With his hands shaking he made a lot of mistakes before he finally finished, and then the machine started up, louder and shriller than the printer or the copier. There was no way to silence it as it dialed number after number.

Some of the recipients would not understand it, but some would be alarmed. At the very least it would mean something to Malick and Nehemia. He imagined expatriates had some kind of clout, and Nehemia's wife was very fond of Mariam. She would do something, call someone of influence.

He took a black pen and held it above another photocopy of Mariam's picture. He was going to write her name and the details of her disappearance, and a way to reach him with information. He didn't know which phone number to write. His own? Arifah's? The pen hovered over the paper for a long while but he couldn't manage to make a single mark. He wondered if the picture could speak for itself. People would see her and wonder who she was. They would ask questions. It would be an embarrassment to the government. He made more copies of the photograph, as many as he could before he ran out of paper. He found a field bag in one of the other offices. It had tools in it, rock hammers, chisels, folding hand lenses and maps. He dumped them all out and went around his office grabbing things, current projects, notebooks, an address book, and a pile of unopened mail. He looked out the window and didn't see any military vehicles. He needed to hurry and get his car out of the courthouse lot. After that, he didn't know what to do.

He hoisted the heavy field bag onto his shoulder and went cautiously out into the corridor. The corridor was clear and quiet, so he opened the door to the stairwell. He ran down the stairs and got all the way outside before he fell upon a trio of militia guards. They pushed him against the stone exterior of the science building and tore the bag from his shoulder. "How did you get in there?"

"My key," John said. "I have a master key."

They searched his pockets for the keys and pulled out his key ring. He was ordered to turn around and identify the master. One of the guards pointed a rifle at John's chest, the other held up the key ring, and the last one opened the field bag and shuffled through its contents.

"What is all this?" the field bag guard asked.

"My research."

"You can't take anything out," the one with the rifle said. "The campus is closed."

"Since when?" John asked. "It was open yesterday."

"It's shut today," he said glibly.

"That's my work," John said.

The one with the field bag held up Mariam's picture. "What kind of work is this?"

For the first time, John took a long look at them and recognized one of the guards from the elevator, the one with the key ring now.

"You were at the library yesterday," John said. "You remember my wife. Do you know where they took her?"

The one with the key ring didn't answer. He walked away and tested the master in the lock. The door opened. He pocketed the key and handed the rest of them back to John.

The rifle was lowered. The field bag was zipped.

"You're free to go," one of them said, but they flanked his bag when they noticed him staring at it. John had no choice but to leave it and walk away, which he did timidly. When he was able to turn a corner and they were out of sight, he ran.

He went to College Street and waited for a tram to take him to Courthouse Square so he could retrieve his car. He waited for twenty minutes before he realized the trams weren't running and started walking. By the time he got there, the scene outside the courthouse was chaotic, with people trying to get in and held back at the gates by the police. The police looked tense, as if they were waiting for something to pop, something to allow them to surge forward and break up the crowd. People held up pictures of their loved ones, wanting to know what had happened to them. In the past day, it seemed many had been taken into custody. Why now, John wondered, and why all at once? He knew martial law had brought a false calm, that the unrest it was trying to contain would bubble under the surface, but he had not expected things to erupt again so soon. He thought that would happen months, maybe even years later, long after he and Mariam were gone.

He walked around the block to find the lot where he had been told his car was parked. He saw his car through the chain-link fence, but there was a lock on the gate and no atten-dant. He rattled the gate and shouted until an officer came up behind him. The officer asked John for his arrest record. At first John panicked because he would not have thought of bringing it with him. But he remembered folding the paper into a tight wad and placing it in the inside pocket of his jacket. He took it out and handed it to the officer without unfolding it.

"Unfold it," the officer said.

John unfolded it. He held it up to be examined.

"License?"

John pinned the long document between his arm and rib cage and pulled out his wallet. The officer, satisfied that John hadn't stolen someone else's arrest record just to get his hands on that battered old Fiat, unlocked the gate and let him through.

John got into his car and sped out of the lot. He rushed to get home but when he got to his street and parked, he sat in the car for a while thinking about the lost contents of his field bag. They were probably in a trashcan somewhere near the sci-ence building and he was tempted to go back and look. It was true he hadn't thought through what to do with the copies of Mariam's photograph, but not having them was a terrible loss, and he realized he'd left the original photograph in the copy machine. He had nothing now but Mariam's name pounding in his head. He could have stayed in the car, consuming nothing but air until it all ran out, but he had to find Mariam and he forced himself out of the car.

He didn't hear the commotion on the staircase until it was too late to turn back. From halfway up the stairs he heard their voices and saw their severely anguished faces; Dolly, Zoya, and Arifah had formed a brigade, looking down on him and firing questions. Dolly came down to meet him and help him up the stairs. She said his head was bleeding. He put his hand up and felt the blood above his ear. "I was hit with a baton," he said. He had forgotten the pain for a few hours, but now it was back.

He should have stayed in the car.

Examining his injury in the kitchen, Dolly said he should have gone to the hospital but it was a good sign that he was still alive. She used words like hematoma and contusion and told Zoya to run next door and get her medical kit. The few times John had seen Dolly in her nurse's uniform, it always surprised him that she had a job at all, but now her professionalism was a good distraction. Arifah placed a glass of water in front of him and he thanked her without looking her in the eye.

"There's a ringing in my ear," he told Dolly. "My ear feels blocked."

"You've probably ruptured your eardrum. It will take a few months but it should heal on its own."

Arifah finally spoke, impatient with the medical proceedings. "Where's my daughter, John?"

He swallowed. All he could do was go over it again, what he saw from the moment he got to the library to just now when they'd found him on the stairs. He didn't tell them that at some point in the past few weeks, Mariam had brought home a suitcase full of documents and hidden them in the closet, or that he'd found her on the floor of the nursery yesterday morning, and he had questions for Arifah as well. He would have liked to know what she knew. Did Arifah know their plans had changed, that he wasn't going to? There were so many shameful things Mariam could have told her mother. His parents urging him to abandon her, the book and his feeble dedication, her suspicions about his infidelity, his coldness toward her after the stillbirth, which he could only now acknowledge. If Arifah hated him for all this, she didn't show it now.

"The question is what to do," Dolly said. "What about a lawyer?"

Neither John nor Arifah said anything. A lawyer meant a particular thing, that Mariam had to be proven innocent of a crime they couldn't name, assuming there was some rule of law at work. As it was, John knew what happened was lawless, it was illegitimate, and at the courthouse where one would think lawyers abounded, all of those people looking for their lost ones waited unassisted. For an entire year in Alexandria he and Mariam had worked with a lawyer, who took their money and delivered nothing.

"I'm sorry," he said to Arifah. "I left her alone."

"It wasn't your fault," she said unexpectedly. She must have known something about Mariam's state of mind lately. Arifah seemed frightened, but not completely surprised by Mariam's absence.

Dolly set to work cleaning his wound. She began by cutting away at the blood-soaked hair surrounding the gash and he flinched, startled by her fingers tugging at his hair.

"I need to talk to Misha," he said. He'd never had a reason to know Misha's last name and didn't know how to contact her at home. "Do you have a college directory?" he asked Dolly, hoping he could find Misha in it.

"We might have one somewhere," Dolly said. "Zoya will look for it."

"Where is the Inspector's Office?" he asked. Arifah and Dolly said they'd never heard of an Inspector's Office until today.

Here Zoya spoke up. "The Inspector's Office isn't part of the provincial government. They're 'advisors,'" Zoya said with a particular emphasis that showed them what she thought of their advisory role. "To the police, militia, and army during domestic disturbances."

"How do you know that?" Dolly asked.

"They're always at the demonstrations. They have a certain look. Dark suits and sunglasses."

John realized Zoya could have plastered the city with the pictures of Mariam. He was beginning to wonder if Zoya wasn't the most important person here.

"How do we find them?" Arifah asked. "There must be a way to contact them."

Zoya didn't know. "I can recognize them easily. What if I follow one of them, track him for a day?" It was hard to tell if she was being serious.

"You'll do no such thing," Dolly shrieked, but John didn't say anything to discourage her.

The phone rang and they all jumped. Arifah answered it. "It's Malick," she said. She listened to him silently for a minute, and then handed the phone to John.

"You don't need to say anything," Malick said. He told John he would make some calls himself, but there was a list of people who might be able to help him if he went to them in person, contacts from the Governor's Office, the provincial interior secretary being the most important. Malick had already spoken with him and told him John would go talk to him today. John wrote down all the names, as well as home and office numbers, and handed the receiver back to Arifah.

As Dolly disinfected the kitchen table, they made a plan. Dolly would call the people on Malick's list from her apartment,

John and Arifah would head to the Governor's Office, and Zoya would stay here by the phone; but before they dispersed, Vic showed up. John was anxious to speak to him alone and lagged behind, telling Arifah he would come find her next door when he was ready. Both the women took the hint and Zoya left too, saying she would look for the college directory. Finally John and Vic were alone in the kitchen. They started talking at the same time, but John stopped and Vic kept going.

"I came here to tell you they're using the abandoned power station off the old highway as a detention center. Maybe Mariam is there."

"Can we go there?" John asked. "Can we go now?"

"There are people there, trying to get the names of everyone inside. We should wait and see what they find out."

"Which people? How do you know them?"

Vic didn't answer him. He said no one should try to deal with the authorities alone. "Where were you this morning? I came to get you early and you were already gone."

John told him about the office, the letter and Mariam's photograph, the fax, and the guards who caught him. Vic was annoyed. He made John promise he wouldn't go out alone again.

"I found something," John said.

He took Vic to the nursery. The last time Vic was in here, he had halfheartedly helped John build a crib. Now the crib was gone, the room bare, and John opened the closet to show him the single suitcase. He didn't want to pull it out and unzip it again. He told Vic what was inside it.

"Do you think it's what they were after?"

John pushed the thought away, trying not to panic. It was bad enough believing Mariam had been taken away for no reason at all. This was much worse.

"Have you ever looked at these documents?" John asked. "Do you know what's inside?" It didn't seem impossible that

Vic might have studied them at some point, but Vic confessed he'd not even known they existed. John couldn't tell him about the little bit he'd read that morning. He couldn't repeat it. "If I were trying to stop an uprising, I wouldn't want these unaccounted for."

Vic stared at the suitcase. "But no one has come here looking for them," he said. "Which could mean no one knows they're here."

"Or they're not important?" John asked. It would be all right with him if they were important to no one but Mariam. Even while it hurt him to find something she had kept hidden from him, it would be all right if they meant something to her alone.

"All the same, I think we should get it out of here," Vic said. John didn't argue with him. He allowed Vic to take the whole suitcase to his apartment.

John went to Dolly's and rearranged everything. Now that Vic was here, he would take John to the Governor's Office, Arifah would stay by John's phone, and Dolly and Zoya would go to the hospital and find out who was being brought in.

By the time John found the right office, the interior secretary had been called into a meeting. He waited a half hour and then had an unproductive talk with his assistant, who asked him if he or Mariam had any affiliations that might have caught the attention of the Inspector's Office. It was not an unfair question, and all John had to say was no, that there were no affiliations, but he found it difficult to continue the interview. Government types were especially good at twisting events and finding culpability. He tried to emphasize these facts: that Mariam was a librarian, and she was mourning the loss of their baby. Politics were the furthest thing from her mind.

The assistant invited him to come back in the morning, adding that the interior secretary usually got in around ten, never before ten, sometimes after.

Vic didn't need to ask how it went. He offered John a cigarette and they sat in the car blowing smoke out the windows.
John kept catching his own reflection in the side mirror and
looking away, trying to keep his eyes on the dashboard.
Occasionally he glanced at Vic, who was cocking his head out
the window, trying to hear what was going on in front of the
courthouse.

"People are never as afraid as their rulers think they should
be," Vic said. "Every regime finds this out the hard way."

John flicked his cigarette away. He rubbed his eyes, feeling
exhausted, and unlike the people Vic spoke of so admiringly,
he was gripped by a terror so powerful, he felt he would do
anything to be free of it.

Vic started the engine and pulled away from the curb. They
were silent during the drive home, and remained silent all the
way into their building and up the stairs, until Vic told him
again, before they parted, not to go out alone. John watched for
a moment as Vic walked down the hall and disappeared into his
own apartment. He was grateful Vic was here to help him.
Without Vic, John would not have had any direction at all.

He unlocked his door, remembering Arifah as he entered.
She was still sitting in the kitchen, by the phone, and failed to
notice him until he was standing in front of her. He said he had
nothing to report. Neither did she. "Do you want something to
eat?" she asked.

"I'm going to lie down," he said.

She stood up. Since the stillbirth Arifah was always
hunched, always bent over as if she was about to fall to her
knees. For a long time she had seemed to defy her age, but now
she looked older than her years, her skin like weathered paper
wrapped around a lamppost.

"I'll be at Dolly's if you need me," she said.

He didn't move out of the doorway. "Did Mariam tell you
I'm not going to Michigan?"

"Of course," she said. Although she answered him readily, she didn't seem eager to extend the conversation.

"Did she tell you we were leaving, the two of us?"

"Yes, she told me."

"And was she happy about it?" He tried to remember her expression when they discussed their exit plans. When she saw her passport photos laid out on the kitchen table. When he asked her where she wanted to go. He tried, but all he could see were objects, the photos, an atlas, the imagined passports.

Arifah seemed to consider her answer carefully. "Happy? She felt you had given up so much for her. But she wanted to go with you."

John had to accept her answer. He was desperate for a shred of relief. "I'll find her, Arifah."

She touched his arm. "I don't doubt that, John."

After she left, he couldn't bring himself to go into the bedroom. He poured himself a drink and sat on the sofa and watched the light fade as he thought about another day passing. Another night. The apartment was dark but he didn't switch on the lamp. He held onto his glass even after it was empty. He didn't know how long he'd been sitting there when he was startled by heavy footsteps up the stairs. He heard Zoya shouting and Dolly's door squeal open. Dolly's and Arifah's voices joined Zoya's in the hall and someone started banging on the door. John switched on the lamp and stumbled across the living room.

When he opened the door, Zoya was still on the stairs, yelling for him to come down. She said, "I see her," and somehow John managed to follow her without believing her. He could hear Dolly and Arifah on the stairs behind him and ran faster, as if this were some kind of footrace to the street.

Zoya ran to the middle of the street and pointed west. There was a figure, a woman, but he couldn't tell if she was moving forward or standing still, if she was Mariam or not. He ran and called her name. She was limping, and stopped. It was Mariam, waiting for him. When he reached her, she fell into his arms. He could smell the blood on her.

Hardly feeling the weight of her in his arms, he pushed past Dolly and Arifah and went up the stairs. Vic was in the apartment, turning lights on like a madman, and Mariam's face was pale in the bright light, with a red scrape on her cheek. He took her into the bathroom and Dolly and Arifah came in behind him, turning on the water and gathering towels. He laid her carefully on the floor. She had no shoes and her dress was bloodied and torn, and as he lifted his hands from her body to stroke her hair they were smeared with blood. He cried out. He may have screamed, and Mariam stirred for a moment. In that moment, when he had stopped to stare at his hands and Mariam opened her eyes, Vic pulled him off of her, out into the hall, and the door in front of him was shut. Vic kept pulling him back, clamping his thick hand over John's mouth. John's arms were pinned and he had no idea how to fight this force surrounding him. He had no choice but to settle into the compression. He heard water pour into the bathtub and Mariam's cries.

Zoya knelt down next to him with a wet rag and wiped Mariam's blood off his hands.

"Let me go," he said to Vic. He tried to sit up but Vic tightened his hold. "Please," John said. He had been helpless all this time. All he wanted now was to stand up.

Vic loosened his grip slowly, waiting until he was sure John wouldn't go lurching into the bathroom. He let go and helped John up. John stumbled, forgetting how to balance, and Vic walked him to the living room, sitting him down on the sofa. Zoya brought him glasses of water, which he drank obediently. After a while he was able to stand up, and pace around the room. The voices in the bathroom quieted. Sometimes he couldn't discern any talking at all.

Soon the door opened and Dolly came out. She came into the living room but looked only at Vic. "Can you drive me to the clinic?"

"I'll get the car," Vic said.

"Shouldn't we take her to the hospital?" John asked. He had stood in front of Dolly but she hadn't noticed until he spoke. She seemed impressed with his ability to stand and form words.

"She's dehydrated. I can bring an IV drip home sooner than she'll get a bed at the hospital." She told Zoya to get her purse and wait for her downstairs.

She waited, looking past him until Vic and Zoya left. When they were alone, Dolly turned to him. "I'm sure the blood is from her period. I don't think she's been raped."

He wished Dolly sounded more certain. "Did she say anything?"

"Not much. It will help you to have an official doctor's report," she said. "I'll get you one. It may take a few days."

"We'll never forget what you've done for us, Dolly."

She tilted her head. She was only a few years older than him but her smile was achingly maternal. He couldn't even imagine his own mother in a situation like this. His own mother was fading from his consciousness altogether.

Arifah opened the door and called to her.

"Wait here, John."

She went away again. He could hear them all come out of the bathroom. Mariam was talking quite a lot, her voice melodic, somewhat trilling and birdlike. They were getting her into bed.

In a few minutes, Dolly reappeared. "She's asking for you. Go and see her," she said, and hurried past him to meet Vic outside. It was strange to be left there, so suddenly alone. He was eager to see Mariam, but he walked slowly toward the bedroom, afraid of finding it empty again, unsure of what was real anymore. Even as he approached the door and heard the whispers coming from the room, even as he saw Arifah sitting by the bed, he was afraid of it all disappearing.

Arifah kissed Mariam's forehead and stood up, passing him with a brief glance. When she was gone he walked over to Mariam and knelt beside her. She was looking at him amazedly with a strange, drug-induced smile. She had been cleaned up. Her hair was wet and he worried about her getting cold in the night. He pulled the covers up to her chin. She frowned and moved her hand to his injured ear. "What happened to you?" she asked.

"I was looking for you," he said.

"And they hurt you?"

"No, not very badly. Not like they hurt you."

She smiled again. "Dolly gave me something to make me forget."

"Did she save any for me?" John asked. This made her laugh. One cheek was badly scraped and slick with ointment. He kissed it softly.

"I'm ready to go now," she said.

He hoped he understood what she meant. He said, "Soon," and watched her fall asleep.

FIFTEEN

M isha could not have known what she was doing when she told Mariam the archives would be transferred to the War Office in Alexandria. She had talked about the burden of the transfer, of organizing them into boxes with all of the appropriate documentation. Mariam had listened impassively, while on the inside her anger was spreading like a bruise. She was certain the transfer of the archives was a punishment, because of the rebellion, because of the disobedience of the province, and Mariam harbored some unfair bitterness toward Misha as well. She thought Misha was trying to get her off the reference floor. She had made people uncomfortable by coming back to work, and all of the younger women looked terrified whenever she came near, as if her presence was poisoning their wombs.

"I'd be glad to handle the transfer," Mariam said.

"I'm so relieved," Misha said, smiling weakly. "You're the only person I can trust with this." Mariam began to pilfer the documents immediately, removing a few at a time and taking them home during her lunch hour.

Naturally, after all that, she wasn't surprised the Inspector's Office had come for her. They didn't announce their reason for taking over the library, but they swept through expediently and Misha only had a few seconds to tell her she knew the archives were missing. "If they ask, tell them you don't know anything more than that." But the inspector had not asked her about them. His questions were about secret meeting rooms and the layout of the stacks and certain students whose names he called out, of which Mariam genuinely knew nothing. She could have answered him in complete innocence, but she was mute and her silence made him increasingly suspicious. When he stepped out of the room again, shortly after John had come to see her, Mariam ran through the storage room into a back stair-case. She had planned to run out to the car. She had imagined John starting it as she ran, and driving before she even slammed the door shut, but the guards caught her on the stairs. They pinned her legs together and shackled her ankles and wrists. In the car they put a sack over her head and she was not allowed to see anything again until they dumped her in a ditch by the highway.

Mariam woke up and realized she was home now. Her skin was covered in scratches that were scabbing over and made her itch. She wanted to scrub them away and stumbled on her bandaged feet to the bathroom. Her mother came when she heard the water falling into the tub, rushing to the floor to undo the bandages, to unveil her feet. Mariam leaned back against the tub, half awake, and thought how lovely her mother still looked. Her dark gray hair was always tied now in a small bun. Her cheeks were more sunken and her eyelids sagged, but her eyes were as bright as ever.

"I woke up on a bed of pine needles," Mariam said. Her mother looked as if she already knew. Perhaps Mariam had already told her, but did she tell her the first thing she had felt was not pine needles but the constricting pain of her womb? Her uterus was convulsing, expelling something as pointless as her blank menses or as significant as a pea-sized embryo. She had started bleeding in front of them, and there seemed to be no end to it. It was heavy, thick, a year leaking out of her. There were two of them with distinctly alternating voices. She never saw them, with her head in a sack, but they performed for each other, prodding her and joking about the things they would put inside her to stop the bleeding. She felt their hands on her ankles and cold metal on her thigh. She didn't scream but bled and bled and bled. Her blood had saved her. She woke up in the ditch off the highway and walked inside it until it tapered and deposited her onto a lonelier road girding the pine forest. She didn't want to be seen by passing cars. Somehow she thought being seen would be the death of her.

"I heard Daddy's highway and followed it home."

"What a miracle you are," her mother said. She inspected the bottoms of Mariam's feet and pressed her thumbs into them. "Are they hurting?"

"Only a little. Where's John?"

"He had to go out. He'll be back soon."

"Is he all right?" she asked.

"He'll be happy to see you up."

Her mother threw the bandages away. The tub was full of water and she turned off the taps. Mariam stood up, gathering the bottom of her nightgown in her hands, and Mama left her alone. She stepped into the tub. She sank into the warm water and scrubbed herself with a washcloth. Her jutting collarbone, the hard points of her shoulders, the narrowness of her thighs surprised her, but the truth was that her body had always surprised her, and after the labor she had stopped looking at herself altogether. After the labor she hated her failure of a body, but now she rose from the water and glanced at her reflection and saw that it was simply her body in the mirror, not a failure or empty casing.

She put her nightgown back on, combed her hair and brushed her teeth and opened the bathroom door when she was ready. Across the hall, the door to the nursery was closed. Certainly John would have gone in there since that morning he found her on the floor. She had suffered there all night thinking about the past, her thoughts laid upon her like stone blocks—her grandfather in exile, her father and his soulmate, the question of her citizenship and even Nina, even Nina was a heavy stone on her chest. Then there was her baby, a loss she still couldn't believe. In the morning when she opened her eyes and saw John looking down on her, she knew that he was hurt. She had obviously changed her mind. She would stay and he would go. She had to look after the archives, and he didn't need her anymore. He was only afraid of being without her.

She had to gather her courage to go into the nursery again. She did it all in a few steps, entering the room, opening the closet door, seeing that the suitcase had been removed and leaving the empty closet and empty nursery with all the doors swung open. She left the bedroom door ajar as well and put on a yellow dress. Then she sat on the bed, waiting for John.

She heard him come home and ask a question to her mother, who answered back in a lilting tone. He walked down the corridor, his footsteps urgent until he reached the open door of the nursery. He must have imagined Mariam in there, looking in the closet. After that his steps were slower and faint. He appeared timidly in the doorway, looking thin and clean with his hair carefully parted and combed like a schoolboy's. It was a relief to see him in this daylight, to sit up with her head clear and be able to examine him. He looked back toward the door, toward the hallway and the nursery, distracted by the secret she had kept from him. She wanted him to understand why she had taken the archives. She had to take them. It wasn't a choice, but she didn't know where to begin.

He said, "Vic has the suitcase."

Mariam had not been at all worried about the whereabouts of the suitcase. She knew John had moved it, and that Vic had helped him. "Misha said the archives were going back to Alexandria," she explained, "but they belong here. They'll be destroyed in Alexandria."

John said he knew, he understood, trying to keep her calm.

He assured her they would not go back to Alexandria. Vic would take care of them. He would know what to do with them. And Mariam tried to show him she was satisfied. She could see that John was anxious, lacking confidence in himself. It must have been such a shock to him, preparing for one thing and finding out she had been preparing for another.

She reached out, needing him to come closer. She had always hidden her need, thinking it was a yoke he would want to cast off. It had made him insecure, unsure of what he had given her, but now he would know. She needed him to take care of her. He came forward, knelt and bowed his head. He brushed his fingers gently along the edge of her foot that had been bandaged. He was hurt too. His ear was red and his cheek bruised. She didn't know what had happened to him, but one day there would be the time and desire to tell each other what they had suffered. "I was going to stay with them," she confessed. "I was going to give you up and stay with them. I thought, that's all I can do. I can keep the archives here."

He looked wounded, and at the same time relieved. This was what he'd wanted to know. "Were you afraid to go with me, Mariam?"

"Yes, I was afraid," she said truthfully.

"Why? Have I hurt you too much? Are you angry with me?"

"I wasn't angry with you, John. I was afraid everything that had happened to us would happen again somewhere else. That thought kept coming into my head and I couldn't stop it." Her fear was of the past constantly repeating itself, but it was gone now. She was able to remember it without it conjuring any of the same sensations, the same terror. She was stronger, maybe because she now knew what it meant to truly be afraid, to fear for her life and body, making all of her old fears that were not rational seem childish. The inspector had frightened her. The militia had frightened her. She had run from them because she didn't want them to take her, but they had caught her and frightened her more. She was trying to get back to John, where she knew she would be safe. "We survived them, John. They have no authority over us anymore." Did he know what she meant? There was a force that was always taking things from them, always fighting them, and they were always losing. They had given up enough. She wanted some things for herself now.

He took her into his arms and held her, cautiously at first and then more tightly. He said, "I'll die before I let them take you again." His body was shaking, pulsing with adrenaline and heavy with exhaustion. "When can we go?" she whispered.

He said they could go as soon as she wanted. Their passports would be ready the next day. John was confident they'd be done well. Cyrus was already in Budapest. He had reported to Vic that it was an easy passage.

Her mother called them for breakfast. They went to her, and ate only a little, and after breakfast, they spent the whole day preparing, cleaning their apartment, emptying cupboards and closets. They couldn't rest until nightfall, when they forced their aching bodies to bed. "Tomorrow you'll have a passport," he said, and she could almost feel the weight of it in her hand.

The next morning was a vigil. The phone rang three times and stopped. John picked up the receiver and hung it up without saying hello.

"They're ready," he announced.

Mariam, Arifah, Dolly and Zoya saw him off and then waited, drinking cups of tea and eating biscuits. Dolly and Zoya argued lightly about everything under the sun. Arifah made more tea and Mariam watched the hands of the clock. They moved, but time was not passing. "What's taking so long?" she asked. She didn't even find out where he'd gone, how far away it was.

Two hours went by. Her mother was exceptionally quiet.

After hardly saying a word, she asked quietly, "Will it be easy to leave us, Mariam?"

Mariam held her hand. She didn't want to think about the pain of that separation. "Of course not, Mama."

Her mother dabbed her eyes with a napkin. "Look at me. I'm being ridiculous."

No, they all protested. It wasn't ridiculous at all.

"I think I'll go and get Omar. Bring him here for lunch."

"That's a wonderful idea," Dolly said. "We'll all have lunch at our place, all together. Maybe Vic can join us. Zoya, you'll see if Vic is home and invite him to lunch."

"He isn't home. I saw him go out this morning and he hasn't been back," Zoya said wistfully. Zoya, Mariam had observed lately, was a little bit girlishly in love with Vic. Poor Vic and poor Zoya.

"I would like to see Daddy here," Mariam said.

They were discussing it when they heard John's key in the door. He came in beaming, not looking at all surprised that everyone had stayed, waiting for this passport. Mariam shot out of her seat but her legs shook too much to walk. Dolly and Zoya flanked him. "Do you have it? Can we see it?" they asked.

John paid no attention to them. He kept his eyes on Mariam and told her to sit down. When she was back in her seat, he came forward, took the passport out of his breast pocket and presented it to her like a single rose.

It was a beautiful object, thicker than she had imagined, with a burgundy cover that was plastic, but leathery, embossed in golden lettering and the emblematic seal of their country, a cypress tree. Inside she saw her black and white photograph and a name. Marie Chaboud. She flipped through it and found a form stamped in purple ink, their French visa ostensibly issued from the French Consulate in Alexandria. The blanks were filled in heavily with a fountain pen. She tried to imagine a real bureaucrat at the real consulate stamping and writing with practiced efficiency. Names. Dates. *Genre de visa. Long séjour.*

"It looks so real," she said.

"It is real," he reminded her. "We have to believe it's real."

"Enfin je deviendrai à l'aise en français," she said. The French rolled off her tongue so easily she could barely catch the words before they fluttered away. Everyone looked at her, amazed by her foreign speech. Only John was likely to have understood her. He knew a little French, though he was always shy to use it around her. She didn't want to let go of the passport but her hands were trembling and she was afraid of tearing the pages. She handed it to her mother, and while the rest of them looked at it, John and Mariam sat across from each other, missing all the activity around them. Arifah left, Dolly and Zoya left, and suddenly they looked around and found themselves alone, having missed everyone's departure. But everyone was back for Dolly's lunch, even Vic, who came home just in time.

SIXTEEN

The passports were forged in a large concrete block apartment building, its long, institutional corridors stretching and bending like sewer pipes. John found the right apartment and knocked on the door several times. A groundswell of chaos erupted, children shouting and a dog barking, before the door opened and John was ushered into a back room. From the kitchen he could smell something being fried in oil, an aroma that aroused a wild physical hunger for the first time in days. When he first came here he was doubtful about Cyrus's recommendation, but both father and son seemed competent and sufficiently cautious. Yesterday, when he called on them unexpectedly to explain his new situation, with the mystery of Mariam's disappearance and reappearance, they listened with great sympathy. They had questions about Mariam, about why she was taken and released so quickly. They wanted to know if she'd been compromised, if she was possibly being followed, and if she knew exactly where John was at this moment, and John said no emphatically to all of their questions. Overall, it was a relief to tell these strangers what he'd been through. They must have felt his sense of urgency since it was less than twenty-four hours later and he was back to pick up the passports. The son discussed with him their new names and why they were chosen. His surname was French because of a newly imagined French grandfather. John had schoolmates in Alexandria with French surnames so this didn't seem at all inconceivable. He was also given a new driver's license so that he would have a secondary identification, and with this, John was convinced his documenters had thought of everything.

The father showed him the route on a map, driving northwest through mountainous backroads to the Kulna Fort station where it was easy to cross the border by train. They would switch to an express train to Istanbul, take another train to Bucharest, and fly from Bucharest to Paris. The train crossing was the hardest part of the journey but safer than taking a flight out of Alexandria these days. John had questions about how to behave if certain situations came up, which they answered if they could, and finally, anxious about getting home to Mariam, he shook their hands and left. He said he would never forget what they'd done for him.

The women had arranged a lunch at Dolly's. Afterwards, he and Mariam sequestered themselves inside their apartment and talked about their exit. They looked at a map of Alexandria, hoping the capital had not changed much in the years they'd been away. They had to recreate a life there. They had to write a new story over the last six years of their lives and convince themselves they had lived in Alexandria exclusively, that their passports were issued on Park Street and their visa at the French consulate in Parliament Square, that they were both teachers in Cypress Gardens, childless, and using a small inheritance to travel and work abroad for a few years. They went over what they would say if they were interrogated, but there was a limit to how much they could imagine things going wrong. He found there was an inverse relationship between imagination and confidence and they decided, not explicitly but by omission, by the way their voices became weak when they spoke about being stopped or separated, that confidence was paramount.

He told Mariam they could pack nothing that contradicted their made-up history, nothing that could reveal their true identities if they were to be interrogated. It might have been preferable to have something to offer as evidence, papers, photographs, small gifts from Alexandria to give out to people they expected to meet on their journey, but there was not time for that. Mariam said an imaginary world that was too elaborately constructed could easily become a trap, and they could always use the length of their sojourn abroad to justify their light packing. Who wanted to drag a heavy suitcase around Europe?

Choosing the right suitcase and filling it was the last thing they did. Before that they had to make sure whatever they left behind could be cleared out easily. Dolly had volunteered but Mariam didn't want her to be burdened with decisions. She had their few possessions organized into stacks and boxes with instructions placed on top. In the dining room, she was preparing packages for Dolly to mail to Malick. John came up behind her as she wrapped her notebook about her grandfather in newspaper and slipped it into a manila envelope. Her treatment of it was careful but unceremonious.

"We could put that in the suitcase," he said. He was afraid of what would happen if it was lost.

"I'd know it was there," she said. "It's safer this way."

She sealed the envelope and looked around, surveying the table. Her eyes settled on the book, which had remained on the dining table since their celebration. It had been moved to the edge and sat by itself, unpackaged and lacking instruction. "I thought we could give this to Vic. He'll want to read it."

John agreed, though he didn't care if Vic read it or not. The book was too many things at once, and he didn't know how to let go of those things and simply let it exist as an object separate from the circumstances that created it. For him, he realized, it had mainly been a way to keep Mariam occupied in Luling, to distract her from the fact that they were trapped there. Luling was a cage within a cage, a courtyard of a prison.

If he had not found something to engage her, she would have died of boredom and despair. She would have left him, thinking it would improve his life to be without her. Now there was a book with his name on it, a theft of her time and intellect, and there was nothing in it to show what it really meant to him, that he loved her, he loved her more than it should have been possible to love someone, and he needed her.

"Do you think the book will help us?" he asked. If it helped him get a job, if it helped them in their immigration applications, if it helped them find a country that would welcome them, then at least it would be useful.

"I'm sure it will help," she said. "And it will help us remember our home. We may never see it again."

He felt a rush of emotion, understanding something now that he couldn't understand before. Perhaps Mariam had always known they would leave like this. He wanted to imagine a time when they would long for this place, their hearts overflowing with nostalgia. They would be old, with all of their struggles behind them. Missing a place they left long ago would be a minor heartache, a twinge, something that came in waves.

Together they packed one suitcase. This was their final task, and strangely ritualistic, as if this undertaking replaced the other important things they should have done together. They had not held or dressed or buried their child, but they could do this. They could put their life in a suitcase. Once they had done that, and their apartment was nearly empty, it was unsettling to linger in it. He went down the hall and told Vic they were ready. They had already said goodbye to Dolly and Zoya, but Vic would walk them to their car. Vic carried their suitcase for them. He heaved it into the trunk. He held onto Mariam for a long time, whispering something into her ear. He gave John a hearty embrace, slapping him on the back, but before they let go, Vic kissed him gently on his cheek.

That night, they stayed with Omar and Arifah, turning in at a reasonable hour after an evening meal and a few hours of conversation. In the old master bedroom upstairs John tried to soothe Mariam's restlessness. She worried about the morning's goodbye. "We should leave quickly," she said. "There's no point in dragging it out."

"We'll leave early," he agreed. "It's a long drive."

"She'll try to feed us."

"We'll have coffee and go."

He had no idea if she slept at all. In the morning, he found her sitting with her parents in the kitchen. It was just past dawn and still dark out. Arifah said they would be stopped if they left now.

John didn't argue. Unlike Mariam, he wasn't even dressed yet. He had a cup of coffee before he went back upstairs to get ready. He tried to be quick, but as swiftly as Mariam had wanted this to pass, the moment of their departure couldn't be hurried. Arifah stroked Mariam's hair, and kissed the bridge of her nose like she must have done when Mariam was a little girl. Mariam balled up her hands as she clung to her mother, and wept quietly against her shoulder.

Then, Omar, who seemed willfully confused. Mariam wrapped her arms around his neck, but he could barely lift his own to return her embrace. John wondered if anyone had explained this parting to him. Mariam pulled away and held both of his hands, looking intently into his eyes for some sign of comprehension. She said she loved him, and asked him to take care of her mother, and he spoke, finally. He said, "Mariam," in a soft, high-pitched voice, and John realized he did understand. He understood this was the last time he would see his daughter. Whatever their relationship had been, there were no more chances to improve it.

His own goodbye took no time at all. He kissed the top of Omar's head, and Arifah's. She patted his cheek and gave him a stern look that he had no trouble interpreting.

Once they were in the car, Mariam's body heaved for a minute. John was afraid to start the engine, but then she breathed in, and composed herself almost unnaturally, as if she'd been smoothed by a sculptor's hand.

When John told Mariam they would be traveling through Kulna Fort, she didn't believe him. In Luling, she had told him of her desire to visit it, and he said they would go one day. That day, remarkably, had come. For the book, they had written about the construction of Kulna Fort from red sandstone without ever seeing it, studying pictures in order to describe the walled city, the five gates, the villages in its shadow and their crumbling economy. All of their research could not have prepared them for their first glimpse of the red wall, and its gradual unfurling along the road that wrapped around its base like a ribbon. The sun was setting behind the looming central mosque, darkening the sandstone to an ashy maroon. Mariam opened her window and craned her neck to look up at the high octagonal towers.

They found a charming inn just inside the wall, not as expensive as he'd feared, and they spent the evening walking around the old city. They were surprised to see quite a few tourists, some of them foreign. There were a lot of stalls selling the same souvenirs, and beggars of all ages who followed Mariam faithfully, seeing how often she stopped to hand out coins. The atmosphere was a bit depressing but the fort itself was grander, sturdier, redder, more ornate and more complex than they could have imagined. Mariam was elated. This was their only chance. Soon they would be gone and they would not be able to come back, not for many years at least.

They ate at the inn, where they were served generous helpings of lukewarm stew and stale bread. There was cheap wine and they drank it. They watched a sad man play his violin and to make him happy they danced, lazily and sleepily, John's arm around Mariam's waist, her cheek holding him up, until the man stopped playing his violin and collected his tips in a hat.

Their room was rustic and romantic. It had a shuttered window with no glass and no screen, and they could leave it open to let in the breeze. Mariam opened the shutters, her arms stretched out wide across the window. Over her head he saw a section of wall and the outlines of turrets, and a nearly full moon.

He kissed her in front of the window. Her body looked thin and fragile, much like it did when they first met, and she was worried about his head. They were delicate with each other at first, but they discovered they wanted more, and neither was as ailing as the other thought. He lay on his back, looking up at her, at her hair grazing the tips of her eyebrows. Her hands pressed hard into his chest and then he was shuddering, and cold. He lifted one hand, weakly, and pulled at her hair. He pulled her down to cover him.

At dawn a low-pitched song reverberated across the city stones. Mariam lifted her head toward the window. "The *fajr* prayer," she said. They had talked about it once, on a cold grassy slope at Mount Belet.

Now Mariam told him what it meant, as she had heard it from her mother. *Wake up, wake up, prayer is better than sleep.*

He had to agree. This was better than sleep. They listened to the melodious call, and the hush that followed.

Their train was scheduled to leave at ten o'clock but reportedly it was often late, so they moved slowly. He called the front desk for some coffee and rolls. They bathed thoroughly and changed their minds about what to wear. When they were ready they took a taxi to the station, leaving the car empty and abandoned outside the city wall. He bought a first-class private compartment, as he had been advised to do. Having the tickets in his hand stirred up a wave of nausea. He told himself to stay calm, to look confident, to give off an air of entitlement. The platform was crowded and it reassured him that many of these people, statistically, were crossing the border with fake documents. It would be an easy passage. They bought snacks and several newspapers and magazines, enough to keep them occupied, because they both were certain they would not sleep.

He put the suitcase in the storage rack above their bunk. As the train pulled out of the station, an hour late, the conductor came and checked their tickets. John and Mariam watched him. He took no more than a cursory glance before he handed them back and left, but John remained standing by the door of the compartment as if he were guarding it. Mariam sat and looked out the window, getting her last view of the fortress wall and its main arched gate. The train creaked along the tracks for a few miles, but after that they descended steeply into a valley, where the land leveled off and the train could gather some speed. When the surrounding hills became monotonous Mariam pulled away from the window and stood up.

"It will be a little while until we get to the border," he told her. "We should try to keep busy."

They tried to read, but they were restless and took turns pacing the cabin. In his mind, John kept stumbling over the story they were supposed to tell. He had to remind himself again and again, who were they, where were they going and why?

In three more hours they were at the border. When he looked outside there was nothing—a low horizon splitting a sea of grass from a broad sky and nothing more. He couldn't see it yet, but soon they pulled into a stop with a short platform, a checkpoint station and a tower in the near distance. It was identical to the desert station where he was posted during the first part of his military service and he remembered Sherod and Flaco and Gordo. He came away from the window smiling, remembering how lax they were about their jobs.

The conductor slid their door open and told them to get out their tickets and passports. He asked them to leave the door open until the border patrol had gone through.

They didn't have to wait long. An officer not in military uniform came in to check their passports. He asked them about their journey and their destination. He had a round amiable face with a clownish, bulbous nose. "You're taking the long way to France," he remarked.

"We decided to take our time," John said. "We don't know when we'll be back this way."

The officer looked at Mariam's passport and at Mariam. He winked at her. "Did you see Kulna Fort?" he asked her.

"Yes. It was very impressive."

He closed Mariam's passport but didn't hand it back to her. He opened John's again and leafed through it.

"Do you have other identification?" he asked.

John reached into his pocket for his wallet, which he had emptied of everything except the cash and his new driver's license. He thought now the wallet looked suspiciously empty. He tried not to fumble as he took out the license and handed it to the officer.

The officer didn't look at it. With the two passports and the license in his hand he said he would be right back. He walked out with their documents, and Mariam sat down on the edge of the bunk, her chest heaving.

"We're doing fine," he whispered. "This is the hardest part."

He looked out the window but he couldn't see anything happening at the checkpoint. After a minute he saw there were militia guards out on the platform, coming off the train and waiting for something. One of them turned and walked past the window. He was talking to someone on the train. It must have been the border officer. Then he stepped out of view, and in a minute the officer was back, joined by the same militia guard he had just seen on the platform. The guard stayed in the doorway, blocking it. The officer came in still holding the documents in his hand. "Mr. Chaboud?" he asked, watching John carefully for his response.

"Yes," John said.

"Have I pronounced your name correctly?"

Mariam corrected his pronunciation. The "ch" was soft. The officer apologized for his mispronunciation.

"Is there a problem?" John asked. He felt it would have been suspicious not to ask.

The officer opened the passports again. "These were issued in Alexandria?"

"Yes."

"Is that where you live?"

"Yes, in Cypress Gardens."

"Why did you not fly out of Alexandria?"

"We've planned to take this journey by train for a long time. My father died recently. He left us some money. We decided this was the only chance we would have."

"You have no children?"

"No children," John answered.

"How long have you been married?"

"Ten years," he said, rounding up.

"What was your father's name?"

They had not drawn out a family tree. He said the first name that came to his head, Cyrus, but there was a delay, which the officer certainly noticed. The officer pressed him for more details about his father, and John provided them, no longer making things up but telling his own father's life story. He was a doctor, a cardiologist. He was seventy years old. When asked how he died, John invented a heart attack.

"How tragic for a cardiologist to die of a heart attack," the officer said, sounding amused.

Mariam exhaled suddenly, a loud exhalation as if she had been holding her breath underwater. The officer looked at her, alarmed. "Are you all right?"

"Yes. Sorry."

"Are you from Alexandria as well?" he asked her.

She nodded. "I grew up in Alexandria, but my family comes from Belarive in the south." She had adjusted her accent to sound like she was from Alexandria. John never knew she had that ability and he was amazed by it, amazed at her capacity to surprise him, still.

"Belarive," the officer mused. "It used to be a beautiful place. Have you been there?"

"Only once when I was small."

"Well," he said, cheerfully slapping the passports together, "if one of you could step outside with this gentleman, I'm sure we'll have this resolved quickly."

"Have what resolved?" John asked.

The guard stepped forward. He stood in front of Mariam, waiting for her to stand up and accompany him. Mariam was about to stand up but John put his hand out in front of her, and she sat back down. "What is this about?"

"We have to verify the authenticity of your documents."

"The documents are authentic. Surely you can tell a fake passport from a real one."

The officer chuckled. "You would think this is true, but you'd be shocked at how many people pass through here with false documents. It's causing problems for our neighbors. You understand."

John couldn't think of anything to say. This seemed to be standard procedure and there didn't seem to be a way out of it. "I'll go," John said. "I'll go with him."

The officer looked at Mariam again. "You're not afraid of him, are you?" he asked, pointing to the guard incredulously. "This baby face? He won't hurt you."

Mariam played along. "I've never faced a military interrogation before."

The officer looked back at the guard and they both laughed. He turned back to Mariam.

"You have nothing to hide, do you?"

"I have nothing to hide, but it isn't every day one is accused of forgery." She stood up now, but she wasn't looking at either of the men standing in front of her. Her eyes were on the window. John followed her gaze and saw what she saw, a silent gathering of militia guards a few cars down the platform, five or six of them. Passengers were coming off the train, perhaps to be questioned in the same way John or Mariam were about to be taken off the train and questioned. Soon the passengers outnumbered the guards on the platform. Three men were put immediately to their knees, with their hands on their heads, barrels of rifles pointed at their backs. The commotion grew as the other people taken off the train began to plead with the guards. The voices had reached the window of their compartment now, finally capturing the border officer's attention. He turned and looked out the window and frowned. He waved over his guard, who took a brief look before rushing out to the platform.

Then John peered out further into the grass and saw a figure, perhaps a boy of twelve or thirteen, or else a small man, running fast. Mariam squeezed his hand. He glanced at her and saw her staring in the same direction.

The officer took out his radio. There was a stretch of static before someone from the tower answered his signal.

"Someone's running in the field," he said. "Don't you see him?" There was a garbled response which somehow the officer seemed to understand. "Take a damn shot. What are you waiting for?"

John couldn't hear any shots fired. He only saw the boy run a little longer before he stumbled and fell into the grass. Two guards ran out after him. It didn't take them long to reach him. He had not gotten as far as John had thought.

He felt Mariam lean on his shoulder. He turned his chin toward her, trying to assure her he wouldn't let go of her now. They had come close to being separated, which would have been a terrible mistake, but for now they were forgotten, with the trouble on the platform and the boy shot down in the grass, and whatever happened next he wouldn't let go.

As the officer stepped away from the window, Mariam lifted her head from John's shoulder. He tightened his grip on her hand, bracing for a confrontation. Everything outside was settling and John had not yet thought of another way out.

"What a mess," the officer said, shaking his head.

A voice came on the radio again and the officer answered it. A guard was reporting to him but the message kept breaking up. He looked like he wanted to throw his radio out the window and began walking out of the compartment, then turned back, absently handing the passports back to John. The license fell to the floor and he bent halfway down to pick it up, but changed his mind, probably remembering he had more important things to do, and continued walking out of the compartment with the radio to his ear.

John clutched the passports, expecting the officer to come back any minute. Maybe there was a place on the train they could hide, or they could get off the train and run in the other direction while everyone was distracted. A woman, likely the boy's mother, was screaming. If there was a time to get off the train, it was now. But then what? Then what?

The border officer appeared on the platform. He made a gesture, his hand waving high in the air. The train lurched and sighed.

Mariam called John's name. He turned to her and watched her lips.

"We're moving," she said.

Even as he felt the grinding under his feet he thought she had gotten it wrong. He looked out the window again. The platform and the people it held like a stage slid past, slowly, until it was gone.

MORNING

O mar made breakfast every morning. He let Arifah sit with a cup of tea by the kitchen window while he buttered the bread and sliced a banana. His grip on the knife improved daily. In the beginning it constantly slipped out of his hand. If it fell to the floor instead of onto the table, he would simply leave it there and get another one out of the drawer, and after breakfast, when Omar had left the kitchen, Arifah bent over picking knives up off the floor.

When he brought her the plate she would try to be gracious, smiling at him while he patted her head. Often when they sat on the sofa watching television they held hands. At night, lying next to each other, they would stay awake for a long time and have a conversation.

Arifah tolerated all of his kindness, but she had no more use for human company. Somewhere inside this harmless old man was the man she married, the man who had done her much harm. She had not wanted to come back here. They all would have been happier if she had let him come alone and made her way without him, but she had wanted a family, and she had not been raised to leave her husband. Even when he abandoned her she was loyal, and she hated herself for it. She blamed him entirely for her loss. She couldn't spare him.

Dolly told her not to be so morose. Mariam and John were in France. Wasn't it something joyous that they had made it across a continent?

"I'll never see my daughter again," Arifah said.

THE PATHLESS SKY · 307

"How can you know that?" Dolly asked, but Arifah did know, and Dolly knew it too, and they did not discuss it again.

Then Dolly and Zoya came to say goodbye. They were leaving for Switzerland. The university was closed and there was nothing here for them anymore, though Zoya disagreed. She wanted to stay and find out what new world would come from this chaos. She was sullen and listless and had not said a word during the entire visit. When she got up to go the restroom, Dolly confessed that she and Zoya fought constantly now. She feared there was no affection left between them. "It's difficult to have an only daughter," Arifah said, perhaps unkindly. Dolly would likely see Mariam, perhaps not soon but sometime, and the thought of it made Arifah's body ache.

One morning she and Omar were sitting by the window, watching a rainstorm, listening to the low rumbling thunder and the rain coming down like silver arrows. Omar squinted and brought his head closer to the glass, and she followed his gaze to the street. A car had pulled up in front of their house, and after a minute a door on the passenger side opened and a long bud of an umbrella suddenly bloomed like a giant black flower. Arifah went to the front door and saw Vic running up the path, holding the umbrella with one hand and gripping a brown bag to his chest with the other. He got to the porch and put his umbrella down without collapsing it. "Come inside," she said. "You're drenched already."

She closed his umbrella and brought it inside, and took his coat. "Can I make you some tea?"

"I can't stay long. There's a car waiting for me."

"We'll go to the kitchen, regardless, where it's warm."

In the kitchen Vic urged Omar to sit down. He sat down himself, placing the paper bag, splattered with rain, on the kitchen table. He accepted a cup of tea from Arifah.

"I've been meaning to pay you a visit. I wanted to know how you are," he said.

"On a day like this? Are you mad?"

He smiled. "It had to be today. I'm leaving tonight and won't be back for a while."

Arifah's heart clenched. She didn't know why she hadn't been more prepared for this news.

"Are you going back to Alexandria?" she asked.

"Not back to Alexandria."

"Germany?" Omar asked. It was not a question so much as a command. He once told Vic to go to Germany, which was funny to Arifah given how quickly Omar had abandoned Germany.

"I'm afraid not," Vic told him.

Arifah could see he didn't want to reveal any more. It was none of their business, anyway.

Vic picked up the paper bag and pulled out a book. It was the book John had written, the one Mariam had shown her when it was a bunch of loose papers in a box. She remembered the argument it started. "They left this in the apartment and I'd been meaning to give it to you. Do you already have a copy?"

"No," Arifah said. She had seen it in Mariam's apartment, but it hardly took up any space in her mind with everything going on.

"I apologize for holding it so long. I was reading it."

"Any good?" Arifah asked jokingly.

Vic smiled. "It's very good." Vic looked at Omar and slid the book across the table to him. "You will like it, Omar. For people who love our country, it's an important book. I never knew John had so much love for his homeland."

Omar frowned at the cover. Arifah had never told him anything about John and Mariam working on a book, so this object was a mystery to him in more ways than one. Every time she thought about telling him, it made her irritable.

"Mariam helped him with the book," she informed Vic.

"Yes, obviously. Her voice is everywhere in it."

Yet she only saw John's name on the cover. She didn't know what she expected, really. It was John's book, mostly, but that love Vic talked about, that love, she was certain, came from Mariam.

Omar opened the book, leafing through the pages carefully. He still couldn't read any of the words himself but he found the pages of photographs and peered at them. She supposed she could read it to him. Mariam would want her to read it to him.

"Have you spoken to John?" she asked Vic.

"I received a letter from him. He sounded hopeful."

"Yes. Mariam is hopeful too. Malick is taking care of them."

"Malick is a good man."

Omar interrupted, asking for his glasses.

"They're on the coffee table," she said, and he got up himself to look for them. While he was out of the room, Arifah made a confession.

"I tried to convince Mariam to stay, after the riots when she told me she had changed her mind. You know they were going to separate?"

"I knew a little about it," Vic said.

"I told her what a hardship exile is. I reminded her about my father's suicide." She didn't know why she was confessing this now to Vic, but she was ashamed of herself and wanted to lighten her conscience.

Vic patted her hand. "Exile *is* hard, Arifah, you're right about that. And what mother would want that distance from her daughter?"

"Yes," she cried. "You understand, don't you?"

"I do."

"Will John survive it? Will he take care of my daughter?"

She had finally overwhelmed him. He stared at her help-lessly.

310 · CHAITALI SEN

"Oh, never mind me, Vic. I'm an old lady. All I can do these days is feel loss. I think when we get old, we become like children again, only thinking of ourselves. All I see is that she left me. She was my life and I'm alone now."

"You'll join them one day."

"No," Arifah said adamantly. She refused to entertain that dream.

Omar came back with his reading glasses. It seemed so cruel to call them reading glasses. He sat back down and busied himself with the pictures again. He pointed to the words, trying to make sense of them, or just pretending to read in front of Vic, to save face. She looked at him with pity. This man, her husband, had tormented her for thirty years with his damaged heart. He was never capable of loving her properly. Mariam had been right about their farce of a marriage. She had been right to run away from that, but had she learned from it? Had she found something better?

Vic pushed his chair back, getting ready to depart, but he did not get out of his seat. He started to tell a story, and Omar looked up from the book, wanting to hear it.

"Mount Belet was an experiment for me," he began. "I don't think my parents or I had any faith that I would last there. I didn't know how to behave around other people."

"That must have been difficult," Arifah said.

"John and I were thrown together in our first week. I got to know him a little and I realized he would be a good model for me, that if I tried to emulate him I might get through my four years there. I watched him, copied him. I learned everything I needed from him. I wouldn't have survived without him."

Arifah could see that. John moved easily in the world, probably even more easily in his youth, and that must have captivated Vic as much as it had captivated Mariam.

"One day," Vic continued, "he and I were sitting in the student union arguing about something. I liked to provoke him into debate because that was my idea of conversing. He was in the middle of a sentence when he stopped suddenly to look out the window. I couldn't understand it, how he could have been there in front of me, engaging with me, and be gone in an instant without even moving his body. I looked out the window to figure out what could have distracted him so completely, and saw a girl standing by a tree. She was looking up at our window, smiling and waving. This beautiful girl. I looked back at him, curious to see how he would respond. He lifted his hand like this."

Vic demonstrated, lifting his hand ever so slightly, laughing as he showed Omar and Arifah. "She must have thought he was ignoring her, or that he hadn't seen her after all, but it was obvious to me, Vic Arora, to whom all other subtleties of human behavior were indecipherable. He was in love with that girl. He was so in love he could hardly move. I knew it before either of them did."

Vic was still laughing. He took a handkerchief out of his pocket and wiped his nose. Then he settled into a profound silence. He was that boy again, watching, afraid of making a mistake.

"And I envied her," he said. "Very much."

Arifah understood that he had not misspoken. Vic had fallen in love once too, and no one had witnessed it. She didn't know what to say. He was pensive, but not ashamed of his candor, and she was full of admiration for him.

He rose and said his goodbye. Omar stood and shook his hand.

She walked him to the porch. "Will you be going far, Vic?"

"Not far," he said. "You'll hear from me again."

"I do hope so, Vic. I do hope you'll come back one day."

He squeezed her hand and kissed her cheek, and ran out under his umbrella into the dark rain, out to the car that was waiting for him.

Arifah went back to the kitchen and poured more tea for herself and Omar. She sat next to him with the book between them, and started reading out loud.

Chapter One. Alexandria.

The land I think of as home came from another continent. It was pushed to the summit of a high mountain and crumbled into the hills of my childhood.

"It's quite lovely, isn't it?" she asked Omar, wondering why there was a sadness to everything that was beautiful.

ACKNOWLEDGMENTS

There are no words to express my gratitude to Betsy Lerner and Michael Reynolds for believing in the potential of this book before it was fully realized on the page.

Several works helped me absorb the language of geology. John McPhee's *Annals of the Former World* and Richard Fortey's *Earth* captured the poetry and passion of a geologist's work, and F.J. Pettijohn's *Memoirs of an Unrepentant Field Geologist* gave an endearingly enthusiastic history of American academic geology during its formative years. There were many more, and I hope that in my fictional treatment I have done justice to a discipline I admire very much.

To Sharbari Ahmed, Sue Benham, Rob Benham, Elisabeth Cohen Browning, Shari Getz, Jon Greene, Jo Ann Heydron, Donna Johnson, Swati Khurana, Ed Latson, Seela Misra, Rose Smith, and Kirk Wilson, thank you for all your support and encouragement. You helped me see this through. I am grateful also to Jo Ann Heydron and Bharti Kirchner for reading early drafts, and to my teachers at Hunter, Peter Carey and Jenny Shute, for everything you taught me. Big thanks to Amin Ahmad for your generous feedback, your sharp eye and analytical mind.

To the first generation of SAWCC women in New York City, and all my NYC people, thank you for dreaming with me.

I am forever grateful to Soyinka Rahim and Rinku Sen for repeatedly talking me off the ledge, to Jude and Scott Benham for giving me so much space and time, and to my mother, Bharati Sen, who inspires me every day. I love you all dearly.

This book is for my father. I wish you were here.

ABOUT THE AUTHOR

Chaitali Sen was born in India and moved to the U.S. at the age of two. She received an MFA from Hunter College. Her short stories have been published in *The Colorado Review*, *New England Review* and *Juked*, among others. She lives in Austin, Texas.

She was awarded a Tennessee Williams Scholarship to attend the Sewanee Writers' Conference.